Philanthropist

A NOVEL

Larry Hill

TEXT COPYRIGHT LARRY HILL 2014

Copyright © 2014 Larry Hill

All rights reserved.

ISBN: 1502448092

ISBN 13: 9781502448095

Library of Congress Control Number: 2014917118

CreateSpace Independent Publishing Platform

North Charleston, South Carolina

COVER PHOTOGRAPH BY THE AUTHOR, CIRCA 1969

Dedicated to my teachers, my students and, most importantly, my patients.

"The afternoon knows what the morning never suspected."
Robert Frost

Table of Contents

JAMESON · 1
A SCOTCH AND TWO SAUVIGNON BLANCS · 9
JAIL · 24
THE NEW WIDOWER · 29
HOUDINI · 36
HENNESSEY VSOP · 49
ERNESTO · 57
GENERAL HOSPITAL · 66
ON THE MEND · 81
GOING HOME · 86
TONIC WATER AND A SLICE OF LIME · 90
MEGAN TURNS THREE · 101
BRUNELLO DI MONTALCINO · 111
THE PHILANTHROPIST · 129
JASON MOVES NORTH · 136
MORE TWINS · 143
THE PYRAMID · 166
WE DON'T WANT TO BE MORMONS · 176
STEPMOM · 186
THE TRIAL IS SET · 192
GLEN FIDDICH ON THE ROCKS · 198
THE JUDGE · 201
DOM PERIGNON · 207
CHATEAU D'YQUEM, 1921 · 216
A FUNERAL · 225
A VENEZUELAN · 230
A CAN OF 7 UP · 236
ABOUT THE AUTHOR · 257

Jameson

Ten hours before Fred Klein killed a rich young woman and two days before he appeared on the front page of the *San Francisco Chronicle*, he learned that he had high cholesterol.

Klein, noted Bay Area philanthropist, rarely went to doctors. In fact, he had not seen his primary care physician, Allison Jameson, in five years. It wasn't that nothing was ever bugging him; if anything he was a bit of a hypochondriac. On his seventy-second birthday, he consulted a urologist because he had to get out of bed to urinate three or four times a night. The doctor ruled out cancer and told him that he could make the problem go away. Klein refused all treatment. He, by no means, felt great, what with pain in his thumbs, age spots on his face and slowly deteriorating vision, but he figured that those were a result of having turned 75. His poker buddies suggested an orthopedist, a dermatologist and an ophthalmologist but he opted against any and all. Each specialist had his office downtown and parking was too goddam expensive; he refused to take a bus, claimed he couldn't afford a taxi and refused his young wife's offer to drive him and sit with him, either in the waiting room or the examining room. Plus he was convinced that nothing good would come of seeing doctors for such minor ailments – in spite of his wealth, he was sure that they would run up big bills on blood tests and X-rays, and come up with nothing that would make him feel any better. Sure, he had Medicare and a supplement but there was always more to it – he invariably had to write a check. "Screw it – I'm going to live to 90 and any more than that won't do me or anybody else any good."

A couple of weeks before Fred's black-letter day, his wife, Jennifer, more than 30 years his junior, came home after a breast ultrasound with a red-letter report – there was nothing to worry about. All is well. Her sister had a breast removed for cancer at 40 so Jennifer was rightfully frightened that she was a victim-to-be. Jen's annual mammogram suggested that maybe something sinister was growing in her ample left mammary gland; the ultrasound, the following day, proved it to be a simple cyst.

"Damn, I feel good! I don't have cancer!" she exclaimed. "You know, Fred, you should go find out how you are. You haven't had a physical since we were married."

Not pointing out to his wife that she was no better off than she would be had she not had the breast test, he countered, "Maybe after the Super Bowl?" A fan of the new national pastime was he, but she had no sense whatever of the timing of the pro football season; he figured he could sell that as a reason to put off a trip to the internist.

She persisted. "Come on Hon. Do it for me. I didn't marry you for the short term; I want you around for a while."

"All right, but this is a one-time thing – don't expect me to go next year."

"You gotta deal."

The next afternoon, she interrupted his Netflix. "Did you call Dr. Jameson's office?"

"Forgot all about it. I'll call tomorrow."

"Huh-uh," Jennifer growled. "I'll call today."

Half an hour later, as the sci-fi film neared its destructive climax, she returned to the TV room. "You're on for next Tuesday, 9 AM." I made sure to get you her first appointment so you won't go nuts waiting." Klein was not a patient patient – once he'd walked out of an ENT office fifteen minutes after his scheduled appointment, even after being told the doctor was in the midst of a tonsillectomy gone bad and would be just a bit late.

"And, you've got to go to the lab Monday morning to get blood and urine tests. You can't eat or drink anything after midnight on Sunday."

"That's a load of crap," he snorted. "I can't do a thing until I've had my coffee and bagel."

The lab was on Sutter, across the street from the old Jewish hospital, now an annex of the University. For reasons beyond Klein's understanding, all of the others waiting for their blood draws were Russian. He waited hungrily, surrounded by Slavs and their guttural tones, until his turn came. He had nearly left, but knew that Jennifer was waiting in the car out front and would not allow him at her side without a bandaid in the crook of his arm. The pretty blond Russian phlebotomist-in-training, younger than Jen, tried three times to get blood from Fred's deep veins, failing with each effort. Only after her weight-lifter of a boss tried once without luck and then succeeded on attempt #2, were the three test tubes filled with his hemoglobin and serum. He filled half of the plastic cup with urine and was embarrassed as he left the lavatory and walked through the waiting room, sample in hand. Five minutes later, Fred and Jen seated themselves at the last table at House of Bagels.

Fred drove his year-old Lexus into the parking lot underneath the medical office building well before his 9 o'clock appointment. He noticed the posted price list as he took his ticket from the machine - two dollars for every twenty minutes - and berated himself for having come early. By 9:05 AM, he was called by the medical assistant, a Lois Lane look-alike. He reluctantly put down the People magazine, having read part of its feature Tiger Woods article and was marched back to one of the two examination rooms. "Please take off your shirt, Mr. Klein," said the assistant.

"No," he responded gruffly. "I'm not going to freeze my ass off here waiting for the doctor. I'll take it off when she comes through that door."

"I'm so sorry, sir. I just wanted to do an EKG before Doctor sees you."

"Why do I need an EKG? I don't have any chest pain. And, do you know how much those goddamn things cost? I'd bet its $300. No EKG for me."

"Yes, sir." She left the room, closing the door with a muted slam.

The doctor entered the room seconds after the departure of her assistant. Allison Jameson, MD, was distantly related, without a fiduciary connection, to the Irish Whiskey Jamesons. Fred had only seen her twice in the five years since he switched from his 83-year-old GP. Once was for advice about stopping the antidepressants that he had taken since the death of his first wife, the other for blood tests before he married Jennifer. "Good morning, Mr. Klein. Mind if I call you Fred?"

In spite of the physician's 68 years, Klein looked at her as very much his junior and was taken aback by the request. But he, after some hesitation, nodded in the affirmative. He assumed that she knew of his refusal to have the cardiogram.

"What brings you in today, Fred?"

"My wife. She demanded it. I'm just wasting your time, Doctor. I'm fine."

"That's great news, especially for someone who's been around as long as you. Are you sure there aren't any symptoms that are bothering you? You'd be a rare 75-year-old if there weren't."

"My thumbs hurt and I can't pee as well as I used to and I have a few itchy spots on my face and arms."

They spoke about the symptoms and the doctor did the usual physical exam finding the blood pressure to be just a few points higher than normal for adults younger than he, a regular pulse, normal sounding lungs and heart, and normal feeling liver and lymph nodes. The rash was nothing that a little over-the-counter cortisone cream couldn't cure, the thumb joints were arthritic like those of so many seniors, and his weight of 215, coupled with a height of six feet, suggested that he probably needed to eat less or exercise more.

Klein balked when Jameson started putting on the latex glove suggesting a prostate exam was to be done. He was not pleased by the idea that this...woman... was going to put a finger in his anus. "I don't think I need that. I recently saw Dr. McAlpin."

"The urologist?"

"Yeah.

"When?"

"Three years ago."

"Not exactly yesterday, Fred. If you are still having symptoms, we ought to check it out."

"So you think I have cancer?"

"I doubt it. I'm sure Bill McAlpin told you that most urine flow issues in your age group are due to enlargement of the prostate, not cancer, but you have to be sure, and the best way to do that is a rectal exam and a PSA blood test."

"What's my PSA? Was it high?"

"I didn't order it. I didn't know you had any problems down there."

"OK – go ahead, goddamit." She did. He held back a yelp.

"Yeah, enlarged but I don't feel any nodules to suggest cancer. We'll make sure with the PSA."

"No. No more blood tests for me. They had to stick me five times to get blood for this visit – that's it for a while."

"OK. If that's what you want."

"Plus, I read in the Times about prostate cancer. They say that treatment in old men like me isn't worth doing. Why try to diagnose something if treatment doesn't help?"

"You know, I can't argue with that approach. Let's watch and wait. By the way, I did get the blood and urine test results. Good news, bad news. You're not anemic, your liver and kidneys are fine but your cholesterol is too high; it's 260 and we want to see it below 200."

"And, doctor, if it isn't below 200, what's going to happen to me?"

"You're a well-read man, Fred. You know that high cholesterols are associated with heart attacks, and maybe with strokes."

"So what do I have to do not to have one of those?"

"You have to change what you eat. Take this brochure, follow it as best as you can, and let's repeat the test in a couple of months."

"A friend of mine says that he takes some pill and never worries about what he eats. Can't you just give me a prescription?"

"I'd prefer we did this without pills if possible. Those drugs, statins, do have side effects, so let's try diet and use the pills only if that's not enough."

"OK," Fred grumped.

On his way out of the office, he found no patients waiting and the opaque window separating the waiting room from the receptionist's desk closed. He stealthily slipped the People magazine, with the unfinished Tiger article, into his deep pocket, promising himself he would return it at his next visit.

"How'd it go, Honey?" Jennifer inquired as her husband exited the Lexus.

"I don't know why the fuck I let you make me an appointment. I was feeling fine when I went in and now you'd think I need to be in a rest home."

"Huh – what did the doctor say?" she asked nervously as they went into the house. Does he have Alzheimer's? Cancer?

He slammed down the brochure on the dining room table. "Look at this!" The document, if followed to the letter, was going to more than alter his diet; it would take away one his two great pleasures in life. If given the choice of eliminating his occasional Viagra-facilitated roll in the sack with his trophy wife, or cutting out saturated fats and cholesterol, i.e., most of the good tasting items of his regimen, like butter, bacon, eggs, whole milk, white bread, marbled beef and kosher dogs, he wasn't sure that he'd be able to decide.

"Son of a bitch. I'm 75 and feel fine. I may have another ten, maybe twenty years left and then again, I might not. But I sure as hell don't want to have to take up an all-plant diet. I'm not going to give up chocolate cream pie for yoghurt or steak for tofu. Screw that doctor! I want to find an old fat guy to take care of me."

"Honey, honey, honey. Take it easy. It won't be so bad. There are some great cookbooks for cholesterol-free cooking. I'll buy one tonight while you play cards."

Fred called his closest buddy, in fact, his only close friend, Art Schofield. Art and he spoke almost every day. They didn't email; neither was comfortable on line. Fred relayed the events of the medical encounter, getting more than a bit worked up over the dietary instructions.

"Come on Freddy. It's no big deal. Eat a couple of fruits and vegetables and maybe skip the bacon and eggs and the corn beef from time to time. They'll check your cholesterol in a few months and it'll be OK or not OK. If not OK, she'll give you Lipitor. I've been on that stuff for years and my counts are real good. And, you know as well as I do that I don't suffer when it comes to eating what I want. I gotta run. See you tonight at Kreutzer's."

Every other Friday was poker night. All the players brought snacks. As he was leaving the house, to stop at the 7-Eleven, Klein's wife showed up with a platter full of celery, broccoli and baby carrots. "Take these – I'm sure the other guys will appreciate the change." Fred always brought Doritos and dip. It was all he could do to not hurl the platter at the wall.

His poker games were post-dinner affairs. As usual, Klein had a scotch-on-the-rocks before dinner and a glass of sauvignon blanc with the meal. A second glass of wine was downed to punish Dr. Jameson. Fred was not worried about his driving capacity; he handled this little bit of alcohol just fine, thank you. Jennifer served grilled chicken, no sauce, steamed broccoli and a green salad with a hint of oil and vinegar. Klein ate it, knowing that there would be snacks at the game.

It was Bill Kreutzer's turn to host the game; he lived less than two miles from the Kleins. The 7-Eleven, depository of the widest nearby selection of chips and dip, was about midway, on California Street. Fred drove the Lexus. The celery, broccoli, and carrots sat covered in Saran on the passenger seat. Obsessed by the new restrictions which he knew were going to be strictly adhered to by Jennifer the Enforcer, Fred was two blocks beyond the convenience store before he recognized that he had passed it. "I can't just bring vegetables! He made a U turn.

Meagan Spencer, 2, was wet. Her mother, Teresa had run out of Pampers. Dad Mark, a venture capitalist successful beyond even his fondest dreams, was on a seven day excursion to West Africa looking for opportunities in cocoa.

"We've got to go to the store to buy diapers," Theresa said to Meagan, as if she were a lot older than 2. She buckled the child into the rear baby seat and had the beagle Bob jump in the front passenger seat of the Nissan SUV. The 7-Eleven was only five blocks away. As she turned on to California Street, three blocks from her destination, Bob leaped onto her lap as he had spotted a large dog being walked on the other side of the street. "Damn it, Bob," she said pulling over to the curb so she could get out and put him in a harness set-up in the seat behind her own.

Fred Klein peripherally noted a person walking to the right of his passenger door but chose not to react to the minor bump and drove on to Kreutzer's house, not stopping for chips and dip.

The police report described a "late model silver luxury car, probably either a Lexus or Infinity, traveling about 45 miles an hour in the 30 MPH zone…which left the scene without stopping or slowing down." A young couple who had been walking their German shepherd across the street recognized the car as a luxury vehicle but were unable to describe the driver, except to say that he wore a beret. The man made note of the three numbers on the license plate, but failed to remember the letters. They said that the victim was knocked several feet to the right and her head collided with the concrete curb. When the woman dog walker, a one-time nurse's aide, came to the side of the victim, Teresa was breathing but unresponsive. They called 911 on her cell and quickly looked back into the car where a baby and a small dog were both asleep.

A Scotch and Two Sauvignon Blancs

"How'd you do, hon?" Jennifer asked sleepily when Klein returned to their bedroom about 1 AM. On poker nights, she battled against falling asleep. Fred always relayed the win/loss outcome to her, even if it required her being awakened for the news.

"Not so good – lost about fifty bucks. I didn't play good – too wired about this diet shit." In spite of their high six figure income and nine figure net worth, he played poker for a pittance and felt that fifty dollars was a meaningful loss.

"Sorry to hear it, my love. Better luck next time. Oh, by the way, how did the guys like the veggies?"

"Nobody ate 'em. They're still in Bill's fridge."

Jennifer rolled over and turned off the light. Sex was not in the cards after a card game. Jen knew that her mate would not sleep well. He never did after a poker game, either reveling in his victory or replaying the hands that he lost. He'd toss, turn, and blurt out comments like "I shoulda folded the hand." She swallowed half an Ambien and offered the same to Fred knowing that he wouldn't accept.

At 7, Jen awoke and found her bed otherwise empty. She encountered Fred in the kitchen bent over the *Chronicle* and coffee. She noticed a difference – he was reading Bay Area, not the sports. Bay Area is where one reads about politicians, potholes, and crime. She said nothing about it. They chatted about the day; she was scheduled for volunteer work at Traveler's Aid at the airport and his calendar was blank, as usual. "I'm gonna take the Lexus in – it's been shaking, might need wheel balancing."

Fred hadn't checked out the car, either before or after poker. He feared that there was a dent but didn't want to know.

There was nothing in the *Chronicle*, either Bay Area or the front section. But he knew that his possible little problem had occurred late enough that it likely wouldn't be in the morning paper. Radio, TV maybe, but he turned nothing on. Probably was right that it was only a minor thing – nobody hurt. He had gotten to his poker game on time, but without the Doritos and dip. He had purposefully not looked at the front of his car, feeling certain that he barely grazed the person. He didn't even know if it was a man or woman. He hadn't stopped because he was afraid that the scotch and two sauvignon blancs could have given him a blood level higher than the magical 0.8. He was certain that his driving was unimpaired and that the person, who probably thinks he was the victim, was at fault. Why the hell had he or she gotten out of the car on the driver's side without looking to see what was coming? I know I should have stopped and helped whoever it was get back into the car, but at my age I can't risk the DUI. It'd probably kill me. For sure, I'd get raped in jail.

Klein had told his wife that he'd take the car in – how could he not do it? She'd lambast him as she always did when he failed to do as advertised.

He went out to the free-standing garage, walking purposely around the back to the driver's seat; something told him not to look at the front. But he had seen more than a few TV shows in which the cops tracked down criminals by canvassing the body shops. He hesitatingly got out of the front seat to look at the right front fender. The dent was unmistakable – broad and deep – too deep to be explained by a glancing blow. He was reassured by the fact there were no spots of blood or bits of cloth.

What now, goddamit? Were there options? Sure. Go to the police and fess up. No way would they get him for DUI now – it had been 14 hours. But that would be an admission of hit and run, even if the injuries weren't anything of consequence. Or, he could talk to Art Schofield, not only his best friend but also his lawyer. Or he could wait until Jen came home and ask for her help. Or, he could hope for the best.

He chose to do nothing. Surely this would all blow over. The cops in San Francisco were over-worked. They couldn't spend any meaningful time traveling down a minor hit and run. I'm sure that idiot is walking around just fine. No injury – no investigation.

Leaving the damaged car in his garage, Klein returned to the house, pulled out the pile of photos from the past half-century that he was in the midst of digitizing; he turned on both the photo scanner and the local talk radio station. Twenty minutes into the photo work, as he was tossing out most of his pictures of cathedrals, waterfalls, and unknown women dressed in black, the hourly news came on. A few seconds about the G-7, a little more about the budget crunch in Sacramento and then the San Francisco bulletin. "A Cow Hollow mother of one is near death in the ICU at San Francisco General Hospital. Twenty-seven-year-old Teresa Spencer was struck by a hit and run driver on California Street at about 7 PM last night. Police are seeking a late model Lexus or Infinity, probably with damage to its right front fender. If you have information regarding this case, call 415… Klein pushed the off button.

Art Schofield had known Fred Klein for most of both of their lives. They had bonded in school through a mutual love of poker, a lack of athletic skill, and a shared failure to score with girls. Traveling different routes, they ended up in San Francisco around the same time, after the death of Barbara Klein and during the period between Schofield's third and fourth wife. Each became the primary confidant of the other.

Klein rarely visited Counselor Schofield in his office. He had had little need for an attorney; he hadn't bought a house in 31 years and had never run up against the law. He never took a tax write-off that he wasn't absolutely certain would be OK with the IRS. He had made out a will, no easy matter in view of his three sons' discomfort with their stepmother who was younger than any of them.

"Hey, Fred," Art said, picking up the phone, "What's up? Still pissed off about losing with the full house?"

"Art, did you hear about that young woman who got hit by a car on California last night." Schofield had heard it on NPR on his drive to work.

"Yeah, why?"

"I'm afraid that I'm the guy who hit her." Neither lawyer nor client said anything for what felt like minutes.

"You gotta come over to the office right now, Fred."

"I can't take the car out of the garage – the cops are looking for a dented Lexus."

"Forget that. Just get your ass over here, now."

Klein arrived at Schofield's 8th floor office in half an hour. He was upset enough not to care when he found that storing his car was even more expensive than it had been at the doctor's office.

A lawyer's waiting room bears no resemblance to a doctor's. There are hardly ever any other clients waiting and the reading material tends to be The Economist or a recent Wall Street Journal. Plus, you hardly ever are in the waiting room long enough to read anything, especially if you are well known to your attorney as a close friend, a high-roller, and an alleged felon. Klein was barely able to fall into the five thousand dollar waiting room sofa when the strikingly gorgeous Asian secretary asked him to enter Schofield's office. On the wall, next to the NYU Law and Rutgers undergraduate certificates, were photos of Schofield with JFK, LBJ, Reagan, The Clintons, and Barbra Streisand. Schofield was a full six inches shorter than his friend, a six-footer. Having been almost completely bald since his late twenties, he had been shaving the little remaining daily since the death by aneurysm of his last wife.

"You're looking a bit anxious, Fred."

"Cut the shit, Art. Of course I'm nervous. I'm on the radio because I hit somebody who's dying at the General."

"Sit down and tell me the story."

Klein relayed the events as he remembered them. He mentioned the whiskey and two wines, but didn't tell him about his anger over the food.

"I had to stop at the 7-Eleven to pick up Doritos and dip but my mind was occupied, so I drove two blocks past it. I realized what I had done so I made a U. A block later I felt a bump. I didn't hear or see a thing. It was real dark and she must have been wearing something dark. You know how these streets are in the City – no lights that do any good. My first thought was about the drinks and what my blood alcohol might have been. I wasn't drunk. I was in full control. You saw me when I got to the poker game. Did I look drunk? Huh?"

"You were a little, shall we say, out of sorts."

"What d'ya mean?"

"You know, Fred. Usually, you are a bundle of laughs when you walk in. Last night, you barely said a thing, even when you lost a hand. We talked about you when you went to the bathroom – what's wrong with Fred? I mentioned our conversation about your doctor visit and figured you were still pissed off."

"So you thought I was drunk?"

"I didn't say that – in fact, nobody brought it up. It certainly didn't occur to me. Just thought you were distracted.

"Shit, Art, what am I going to do? I may have killed that lady."

"Yes, you might have. That's the fact of the matter and we've got to do something about it."

"Why? Can't we leave it up to the cops to find me and maybe, just maybe, they won't? There are loads of Lexuses in the Bay Area. They don't have a license number or they would have come after me already."

"Come on Fred, you're smarter than that. You're not a hardened criminal trying to get away with your crime. You've gotta face the music and turn yourself in."

"Turn myself in? That's for murderers and bank robbers."

"Yeah, it is, but your crime could land you in jail for as long as one of them. Only by your cooperating is anybody going to even consider leniency. By the way, I'm no criminal attorney. We got to find you a specialist."

"Jesus, I'm 75. I'll spend the rest of my life in prison, won't I?"

Schofield ignored the question, buzzed his secretary and asked her to get Irving Greenberg on the line. Klein had heard the name before, in conjunction with a famous recent husband-killing-wife case in Burlingame. He sort of remembered that the husband may have gotten off with manslaughter.

Less than a minute later, the buzzer buzzed on the massive desk. "Morning, Irv. How about those Giants?" The local ball club was on a six game winning streak.

"Good stuff, but they need some hitters. What's up?"

"You know Fred Klein, from the Symphony?" Greenberg was a big-time supporter of classical music and Klein had served two five-year terms on the Board of Directors of the San Francisco Symphony, the last two years as Secretary/Treasurer. Since retirement, he had been the consummate volunteer boardsman, not only with the Symphony but also the Mayor's Cultural Commission, the Cancer Society, and a local hospice.

Klein couldn't tell if Greenberg knew of him. He was a bit surprised that Art had not put the phone on speaker.

"Yeah...good guy. He's sitting here with me right now. I've known him for a long, long time. Really good friend of mine. Never in any trouble – on the contrary, a real pillar of the community...He's in a bit of a stew now however. Did you hear about the lady who was hit and run down by a guy in a Lexus on California last night?"

After a pause which Klein took as evidence that not only Lawyer Greenberg, but all of the Bay Area knew of his crime, Lawyer Schofield spoke up, "My client thinks he did it. He was in the neighborhood and knocked into somebody getting out of a car – says he didn't see her – didn't know if it was a man or a woman. Says he had had a couple glasses of wine and a scotch in the two hours before – was on his way to a poker game. Says he thought that he only brushed whoever it was and that he left because he feared the cops would find booze in his blood."

Greenberg asked Schofield to put the call on speaker. "Mr. Klein – you there?"

"I'm here."

"I think we may have met before – maybe at a Bar Mitzvah?"

"Yeah, probably so. I go to a lot of them."

"Me to. I hear you've got a spot of trouble?"

"I guess I do. I was hoping that maybe they wouldn't find me."

"Sorry, Mr. Klein; there's not a chance that they aren't going to find you. As many Lexuses as there are, they will check all of them in your neighborhood and probably by tomorrow, you'll hear a knock on your door. Uh, can I call you Fred?

"That's fine. So, if they are going to find me, maybe I ought to find them before they do?"

"Goddam right you ought to. A hit and runner who keeps running is treated a lot worse than one who sees the error of his ways and goes to the police station groveling on his knees in apology. With your go-ahead, I'm going to call a friend at the DA's office and arrange to have you turn yourself in."

"Can't it wait 'til tomorrow? I've got to present the annual report to the Symphony Board tonight. We have a big shortfall and nobody else knows a thing about what the numbers mean."

"Fred, Fred. You're talking shortfalls when you're on the lam for hit and run and the victim probably will soon show up in the obits? Just picture yourself in the *Chronicle* when the cops come into your committee meeting at the Hall and put you in cuffs. We really want to limit the photo shoots to as few as possible."

"So you want me to do this today, huh? OK.....OK. But give me an hour to go home and tell Jennifer – that's my wife - and call the kids. I don't want any family member hearing this on the radio or TV."

"You're taking a chance, but I guess the odds are pretty good they won't find you in the next hour. Then, I am going to want you to meet me downtown. It's 8:45 now. We've got to be at the Central police station on Vallejo before noon. I've got another client down there right now. Meet me there at 11:45, and please, Mr. Klein, sorry, Fred, don't be late!"

On his way home, Klein looked in the eyes of oncoming drivers to try to detect if any of them was looking at his right front fender. Seeing none, he pulled up into his driveway, punched the automatic opener and started to go in. He stopped just before the grille crossed the threshold. Maybe I should hit the right side of the garage so that this damage is self-inflicted? He sat immobilized for a minute until it came to him that he'd already decided to turn himself on the mercies of the legal system; he fronted in, adding no further damage to his car.

The Kleins lived in one of the grand mansions in Pacific Heights. Fred had purchased the place for $600,000 when he moved up from LA several years before. He figured he'd done OK as houses not as nice as his in the neighborhood, were bringing up to ten million.

He loved the house. It had enough bedrooms for a family reunion for his three sons and 5 grandkids sharing. The furniture was mainly comfortable classic New England, including a couple of very valuable 18th century pieces. The rugs were expensive Isfahans and Turkish kilims. Whenever he entered through the kitchen, he recognized that it was retro, needing an upgrade as it had nothing stainless, no island, and an old white GE refrigerator with only one door. They had solicited bids – the lowest came in above eighty thousand, so refurbishment, stove, etc., went on the back burner even though they could well afford to do the work.

"Hey Jennifer!" Anyone coming in on the ground floor had to speak up to be heard as most of the day to day activity occurred on the third floor. When Fred was home and Jennifer was returning, even a shout didn't do it – Fred avoided hearing aids; his father's embarrassed Fred, even after he had made a name for himself.

"Yeah!"

"You've gotta come down here. We've got to talk."

"Give me a minute. I'm polishing my toe nails."

"Now, Jen. The nails can wait."

The creaky old wooden, uncarpeted steps and floors allowed him to count each stride of her descent. She descended with all deliberate speed.

"What's up dear? You look like you saw your mother's ghost."

"It's worse......Did you hear about the young woman who was hit and run into last night over on California?"

"No – what woman and why do you ask?" One thing that Fred found a bit irritating about his young second wife was that she had little interest in the news. She'd not be able to name her own congressperson, even though that person was Speaker of the House.

"It's not important who she is. I ran into her. Then I drove away to the poker game. I was afraid that I'd get arrested for DUI even though I know that I wasn't drunk. I just had that whiskey and a couple of glasses of wine."

"Jesus, Fred. What are you going to do about it? You've gotta turn yourself in don't you?" Jennifer had grown up a good Methodist; it wasn't every day she started a comment with the name of the Savior.

"You're right. I've already made that decision. I went to see Artie this morning and he got me in touch with a guy named Greenberg, a criminal lawyer. I'm meeting him at the police station at 11:45 this morning."

"Should I go with you?"

Before he could answer, the doorbell rang. Figuring that it was UPS delivering her online sweater purchase, Jennifer sauntered over. Two men in ill-fitting brown suits were at the entry. "Is this the home of Mr. Fred Klein?" asked the tall one. The short one, at least a decade younger than his colleague, nodded as if he agreed with the question."

"Yes it is. What do you want?"

Fred had made his way to the door, having heard the question and knew full well what this was about. "I'm Fred Klein. What do you want?" he parroted.

"We are from the San Francisco Police Department. We have a warrant for your arrest for vehicular manslaughter in the death of Teresa Spencer."

"Death! But she's in the hospital. I just heard it on the radio."

"I'm sorry sir, that's old news. She died about two hours ago." The short young one again nodded.

"My God...Why me? What makes you think I had anything to do with it?"

"All we can tell you, Mr. Klein, is that somebody got your plate number and called the cops, late last night. The description of the vehicle matches your Lexus."

The short cop began to read from his Miranda card. "You have the right to remain silent. Anything you say or do..."

"That's enough," said an irritated Fred. You don't think I know all that?"

"Sorry, Sir. I must read the entire thing. Anything you say or do will be held against you in a court of law. If you cannot afford an attorney..."

"Just look around you. You don't think I can afford an attorney? Matter of fact, I've already hired Irving Greenberg." He figured that dropping the name of a major player in local criminal law might impress. The two cops seemed to have no idea who Greenberg was, or at least didn't care. The short one finished his recitation.

"There's no reason for me to come with you. I'm meeting my lawyer at the station at 11:30. You can call over there; he's got it all set up with your people."

"Sorry, Mr. Klein but we'll be taking you. You can talk to your lawyer once you are booked. I'm also sorry to tell you that we are going to have to handcuff you."

"What the hell for? Look at me – I'm a sick old man. You think I'm going to run away? I couldn't run out of the house if it was burning down. I don't need handcuffs."

"Sorry," grunted the short one as he grabbed hold of Klein's wrists and cinched up the metal bracelet, his charge's hands behind his back.

"Get me my leather jacket, Jen." He was aware that one never left one's house in San Francisco without a wrap and he had seen enough TV news to know that alleged felons usually cover themselves with their jackets when being taken from the home or workplace in handcuffs. And, he wanted to make sure that any photographic record of the event included prime label, expensive clothing. He assumed that there were news photographers camped in front of his house. There'd probably be a bunch of paparazzi at the station too. His wife brought the Argentine jacket and draped it over his shoulders.

"I want to ride downtown with my husband."

"Sorry Mam, that's not possible. You'll have to drive down yourself and, frankly, you won't be able to see your husband for quite a while."

"I'm going anyway. Where can I park?"

"You'll have to figure that out for yourself Mrs. Klein." The tall one smirked, knowing that parking played a role in most every San Francisco discussion.

Fred, cuffed, was unable to get the jacket over his head, but his front yard was free of photographers and the only person visible was a Filipina maid pushing a stroller with twins. She paid no attention to the drama across the street.

Jennifer had walked tearfully to the curb, trailing the three men. "I love you, Freddy!" she said after the back door was slammed behind her husband. He was looking straight down and showed no sign of having heard her.

Frederick Aaron Klein was born in the early 1930s on the Lower East Side of Manhattan, the product of the marriage of Benjamin Klein of Vienna and Emma Pearlstein of the Ukraine. His parents had come to the US via Ellis Island in the first decade of the twentieth century with the great flood of Jewish immigrants from Europe. An academic musicologist who had done research on Mendelssohn, Ben thrived, relatively speaking, during the Depression on the faculty of NYU – that is to say, he stayed employed throughout the thirties. Emma mothered Fred and his older sister, Esther, spending untold hours schooling them after school. She was a lover of mathematics, English literature and Yiddish, expertly imparting those skills to her offspring. Both the Klein and Pearlstein families suffered devastating losses to the Nazis.

Esther graduated from Barnard, got a PhD at Harvard then returned to Barnard, joining the faculty there in English. She wrote a thesis on some obscure passages from Paradise Lost and stuck with Milton to earn tenure. She never married. She had a succession of exotic, younger female friends and associates. The word lesbian was never uttered by a parent or brother in the presence of another.

Fred, a lackluster high school student, deficient in social graces and athletic prowess, enrolled at the City College and graduated with honors 5 years later from NYU; he labored in the thought that he was only able to transfer downtown to NYU thanks to his father having a word with the admissions office. He never asked for help or for the answer as to whether or not he got it. Prior to university, he had only one close friend, Art Schofield. Art went on to Rutgers and Fred's sociability improved greatly at NYU; he ran for student body president, losing by a handful of votes.

His parents wanted him to major in math or science and follow his father into academia but he opted for business, specializing in marketing, and he excelled. He forsook the offer to get an MBA at Columbia, accepting instead an offer to join a small but growing advertising firm. Being out of school took from him the automatic exemption from the draft, so to his chagrin, he was drafted. The Police Action in Korea rekindled America's need for combat troops, making Klein a likely candidate for a government-sponsored trip to East Asia. He lobbied hard against that opportunity and was sent to clerk-typist school. He could have entered officer candidate school, but that would have obligated him to another two years in uniform. So, Klein typed, and typed accurately and quickly. He quickly rose through the cadre of male typists, landing a sought-after position in Headquarters Company of his brigade at Fort Dix. In that position, he typed personnel documents, based on decisions of officers, that determined where members of his brigade were to go and for how long they were to go there. One of the handwritten lists of transfers included the name Klein, Frederick. He was to be assigned to McArthur's headquarters in Tokyo. The job sounded cushy and even interesting, but it was all too evident that with the move to Japan came the very high likelihood of a transfer across the East China Sea to the land below, and above, the 38th parallel where he would be faced with the unpleasantness of bullets, mortar rounds, and deathly cold. He simply left his name off the orders, extending his tour of duty. His reputation was such that the orders were signed by the Major without a close perusal. Later, he found a way to get himself discharged a full six weeks before his tour was scheduled to end.

After discharge from the Army, he opted not to return to his previous employment but to seek an MBA, enrolling in Stanford Business School; weather was his primary motivation. Shortly after matriculation he met Barbara Ann Newman, a junior undergraduate on The Farm. She was the granddaughter of a rabbi and daughter of a cardiologist from Beverly Hills. In the fifties, there was little in the way of cohabitation of the unmarried; Barbara and Fred were not pacesetters. They overnighted on rare occasion; she kept her dorm room and he his studio apartment in Menlo Park. Both sets of parents were pleased that they did not stray from the faith, although Dr. and Mrs. Newman would have preferred their new in-laws to have come from a more presentable academic field than musicology – history or perhaps European literature. Days after he received his MBA, they were married at the Wilshire Boulevard Temple in LA; the reception took place at the recently constructed Beverly Hilton.

Barbara found a job in the fledgling field of television advertising, selling ads to Los Angeles super markets and auto painters – *Any car, any color, twenty nine ninety five.* As a recently minted MBA from Stanford, Fred was hot property. With some encouragement from his wife, he too went into TV, joining the administration of a newly created local station, KLAT, Channel 6. Within two years, he was elevated to chief financial officer and three years thereafter, with the financial aid of his father-in-law and some doctor cohorts from Cedars-Sinai Hospital, he bought out the owners of KLAT, kept it for a decade, making it the favorite of the burgeoning Latino community, and sold it for twenty times what he and his minority partners had paid. He gave large chunks of cash to the doctors and kept the rest for himself. Klein was rich.

He and Barbara added three male heirs during the first ten years of their marriage – Jason, then two years later, the identical twins, Phillip and Robert. Each graduated college in 4 years – Berkeley, Yale, and UCLA.

From the late sixties on, his work involved "husbanding his investments." With little outside advice, he invested well: Intel, Microsoft, Amgen and others enabled him to become one of California's wealthiest unemployed citizens.

The family fortune did not confer long life to his wife. Barbara started bleeding but did not seek medical intervention, assuming the blood was a result of her hemorrhoids that had appeared with the twin pregnancy. Eventually, the doctors at Cedars-Sinai discovered liver metastases when they confirmed the suspected colon cancer. Chemotherapy and surgery, if anything, shortened her life, making the four months between diagnosis and death terrible for her and her family. She was sixty.

Fred could not stay in Los Angeles. The sight of his in-laws, now in their eighties, instilled guilt. He assumed that they blamed him for not making her seek medical care earlier, although there were never words to back up the assumption. Jason, the eldest, lived nearby; he liked Jason, he didn't love Jason and he very much did not like, or love, Jason's Korean-American wife and their two success-at-any-cost children, 7 and 11.

The twins had long since moved to the Bay Area, Phillip to San Francisco, Robert to Piedmont in the East Bay. Both were doctors, Robert, ironically in view of his mother's cause of death, a gastroenterologist, and Phillip a radiologist. Both married Jewish girls; Robert and spouse had two daughters eighteen months apart. Phillip and his wife had a son. He had Down's syndrome. They opted against having more children. Fred decided that he'd rather live in San Francisco than in Southern California. He never considered any other state.

In San Francisco, he quickly bought the big Pacific Heights home with a view of Alcatraz and Berkeley. He moved to the area with his true love, his dachshund, Riley, and early on in his Bay Area tenure, met Jennifer Taylor, the Methodist, walking her pug, Bernie, in the park. She had recently divorced when her wealthy husband took up with a professional golfer. Fred asked Jennifer for coffee within fifteen minutes of their dog-specific first conversation. Then dinner, then a movie, then more dinners, more movies and more coffee. Conversations progressed from canines to politics to dead or departed spouses to loneliness. In spite of the three decade age difference, they clicked. Each enjoyed the other's company. Fred wondered why Jennifer, so much younger, so bright and funny, so attractive and so financially unneedy, had any interest in him, but he didn't ask. Four months after they met, they decided to move in together. Her house, only two blocks from Fred's, was a bedroom and lanai smaller, so when, another six months later, they settled on marriage, they sold hers and kept his. She had no kids to make these decisions harder. Both dogs died within a year of the move and were not replaced.

Jen and Fred showed up in the society pages of the *Chronicle* with regularity. He, like ninety percent of San Franciscans, was a Democrat – or at least not a Republican - and contributed handsomely to candidates for everything from governor to membership on the Party's central committee. Like so many rich men and women without gainful employment, he launched a bid for public office just a few years after moving north, running for County Supervisor in his silk-stocking neighborhood. He spent a not insignificant portion of his expendable monies on the campaign but finished a distant third to an Italian-surname woman native San Franciscan who lived two blocks away. Although not members of a synagogue, the Kleins were benefactors of Jewish/Israeli NGOs; Fred had served on boards or advisory committees of several. He was an outspoken advocate of silent auctions as a way to raise cash for charities; he bought trips, dinners, and paintings at outlandish prices and, not infrequently, gifted those purchases to other worthy causes.

Klein considered himself happy. He had resettled to a city with better art, better music, and better food than Los Angeles. He had married a gorgeous young woman from the sexual post-revolution and didn't have any of the libidinos discomforts of the pre-revolution; if anything, he consummated more frequently, with the help of pharmaceuticals, from seventy to seventy five than he did from fifty to fifty five.

Fred Klein never, for a minute, thought that he might ever be charged with a felony.

Jail

The blue Ford in which Klein was given his ride from Pacific Heights to the main police station needed upholstery work and a new muffler. The back cushion of the rear seat had been worn through, presumably by a succession of steel handcuffs and unclipped fingernails. A foul odor, combining those of urine and vomit, reeked; Fred wished for an open window but none was offered. The closed windows weren't tinted so he could see the homes of his friends and neighbors, including most of the wealthiest San Franciscans. He was pleased that he saw nobody that he knew.

South of Market, once the home of bars, brothels, fleabag motels and small business and industry, has been much gentrified in recent decades. There's no such up-scaling of the large police station and jail at 7th and Bryant. Klein's only pre-knowledge of the place came from the old TV show, The Lineup, which he watched avidly in the fifties in New York. Like the blue Ford, the place needed work. The stucco exterior hadn't hosted a painter in twenty years; the sidewalks around the place were unpoliced – trash, including whiskey bottles and beer cans, fast food boxes and Styrofoam containers, old *Chronicles* and empty cigarette packs, was everywhere. The short cop drove and took the car into the dark, dank garage. Fred removed himself from the car, the hand of the tall cop over his head to prevent his colliding with the roof. The short one talked to an ununiformed black woman behind a heavy screen while the short one held his prisoner by the chain connecting the two cuffs. Klein noted that he was the only person in the large room whose moves were controlled by a uniformed cop. It was, after all, about 1 PM, not the busy time for downtown arrests. He was guided gently to the screen.

"Name," growled the woman. Her stringy grey-brown hair barked for shampoo.

"Klein. Frederick Aaron Klein."

"Spell it." He rattled off the letters. When he reached the two A's she told him to slow down.

"Date of birth."

"January 15, 1930. Exactly one year after Martin Luther King." Fred thought there'd be something to be gained by the coincidence. His questioner was unmoved.

Klein responded to subsequent brusque demographic inquiries in a pleasant manner. He knew from TV the consequences of acting hostilely during early stages of the process.

After the initial paper work, Klein was handed off from the tall/short pair to a large white woman, this one dressed in police togs, but without a gun, club or radio. She led him into a square brown room where he was given bright orange pants and shirt. An ununiformed man watched as Klein took off his wool slacks, cashmere sweater and monogrammed silk boxers, recently gifted to him by his wife. His fear of being strip searched proved unwarranted; California had stopped doing that to non-violent arrestees years before. Fingerprinting and mug shots followed. He considered asking for a comb but thought better of it, running his fingers through his ample head of gray hair. He assumed that his picture would end up in and on the local media. He wanted to look innocent. He did not smile.

At some point in the process, he said to his handler, "My attorney, Irving Greenberg, is supposed to meet me here." His assumption was that everybody at the jail knew and feared Greenberg. The lady did not respond, verbally or non-verbally. Either she didn't hear or didn't care. He dropped it, presuming that Greenberg was on the other side of the walls getting things taken care of. He would be out of jail very soon.

Klein's guide marched him, now without cuffs, through heavy metal doors which she opened with a code – no jangling keys - to the holding cell. Another heavy steel door was the only entrance into the brick-walled room. In spite of the sparse assemblage of arrestees in the outer sanctum, this cell was packed. A good estimator of crowd size, Fred calculated there were 45 men in a space that could not have exceeded 25 by

15 feet. The periphery of three sides of the cell had tightly anchored steel benches that accommodated about half of the inmates. The rest stood or sat on the floor. He had no reasonable option but to join the floor-sitters. Holding cells were not created with the comfort of their inhabitants in mind.

Of the five senses, four – all but taste - were stimulated in their anatomically specific areas of Klein's brain. He saw that he had joined a temporary brotherhood of men – he was almost certainly the oldest. Gray hair was rare - his was the grayest. Most of his colleagues were young, teens and twenties. Latinos and blacks made up the distinct majority. Asians and scruffy Anglos more or less equally divided the remainder. Except for the Asians, most everybody else was bearded or in need of a shave. He heard very little; he was amazed by the fact that so many men could make so little noise. What verbal interaction he heard was mainly Spanish. Klein had once rated himself fluent in the language, thanks to college and travel, but here he understood very little. He felt enough bodies to make him uncomfortable. With so little space in the cell, movement was like that of an emptying, sold-out sports arena – one couldn't help bumping into others. Fearing violent reactions of his neighbors, he moved as little as possible. The sense most negatively abused was smell. The place stank. Obviously, no one had showered since getting incarcerated and, for most everybody, it had been some time before arrest that they last saw a shower or bath. Moreover, the two stainless steel toilets in the room had obviously not been cleaned for many days. Klein knew that he would accustom himself to the odors of the place, but that didn't make his initial minutes and hours any more tolerable.

An hour into his stay, he was approached from across the cell by a man who he assumed was the second oldest guy in the place – maybe 65 or a few years more. He was Asian, probably Chinese, but maybe Korean. His hair was black; chemicals had to have played a role in that. "What are you doing in this shithole?" the man asked, accentless and in a low enough voice to be inaudible to their fellow inmates.

"They say I hit someone with my car and left the scene."

"You weren't the guy who hit the woman on California Street that I heard about on the news, were you?"

"That's me."

"Jesus, you're in trouble."

"I've got a good lawyer. Why are you here?"

"White collar stuff. I'm being charged with taking money from the bank where I work. I did it but it was only about two thousand dollars. For my daughter-in-law. She's got cancer and they've got no insurance. But I've got a good lawyer too – name of Greenberg – always get a Jewish one when you're in big trouble."

"You mean Irving Greenberg? He's mine."

"That's him. Looks like we got something in common. He was supposed to get me out of here by noon."

"He told me to meet him here at 11:45. That must have been because he knew he needed to be here for you. He said he had another client to see here. But the cops came and got me first."

Time passed slowly. Klein did get accustomed to the smell, but he did everything in his power to resist his need to use the toilet for defecation. He had no desire to sit in the middle of a bunch of felons while he took a crap. Many of his mates had no such hesitation.

A small window several feet beyond the reach of the tallest inmate gave the men their only indication of the time of day; anyone with a watch was relieved of it at check-in. Klein had assumed that he'd be bailed out quickly after the door slammed behind him, but light gave way to dusk and it was clear that Greenberg wasn't going to be there either for him or his embezzler buddy. "Don't I get a telephone call?" he asked the decrepit old man who brought his evening meal of chicken soup and sourdough.

"Beats me. I just deliver the shitty food and mop the fuckin' floors."

"Ask one of the cops to come here so I can talk to him."

"Big chance that anybody'd listen to me."

"Just do it. Tell them that Fred Klein asked." He thought that there was at least a slight chance that the cop at the desk would know him from his community activities.

"Sure." It was obvious that the food guy wouldn't say a thing to anybody.

Dusk progressed to moonless darkness. Only two bare sixty watt bulbs, perpetually lit, offered any light to let the residents of the holding cell know where they could sit or lie and how they could get to the toilet. Klein saw a spot on a bench, rose from his seat on the floor like the old man he was and sat on it. Seconds later a black man fifty years younger, a hundred pounds heavier, and six inches taller than he, with biceps and triceps the size of pomelos, confronted him, "That's my seat, muthafucka. Just comin' back from da shitter." No amount of reasoning or pointing out that nobody has reservation on any seat was going to have an effect. Klein pushed himself up with his arms and returned to his seat on the concrete floor. He yearned for his iPod – no way was he going to get to sleep. The only inmates lucky enough to sleep were the ones that were boozed or drugged out. On second thought, he was glad he didn't bring his iPod recently given him by his granddaughter – it was pink, not a safe color in most slammers.

The New Widower

Mark Spencer, venture capitalist, was elegantly housed in a suite at the five-star Golf Hotel in Abidjan, Ivory Coast. Fearful of falling victim to the widespread and unpredictable violence of the beautiful but now lawless nation, his venturing out of his hotel room was limited to the times he could arrange body guards and an armored vehicle. He had been there only one day, but had made progress in trying to wrap up contracts for most of the cocoa production of a large portion of the northern half of the francophone West African nation. Hating the concept of eating alone in a restaurant, he'd order off the room service menu when he didn't have a business meeting. Occasionally on his foreign forays, he'd work it out with a doorman to have a young woman come up to his room for a bit of interracial frolicking. That night however he was too tired, having weathered the agonizingly long entry process at the airport the previous evening. He had long since recognized that the countries that you were not anxious to go to were the ones that made it hardest to enter. France and New Zealand were a breeze, Zimbabwe and Tajikistan hardly worth the effort. Dining alone, he was watching CNN International when his phone rang. He figured that he was going to hear about a pickup time for the following morning, but instead he heard the unmistakable voice of Jack Jensen, his brother-in-law, who to Mark's chagrin had recently moved into a home only a block from their Cow Hollow mansion.

"Mark, I've got bad news."

"What is it, Jack? Is it Meagan?" He always worried about crib death, even though his only daughter was well out of the crib.

"No, it's Teresa. She's been in an accident. She's at General Hospital in pretty bad shape."

"Oh, God. What happened?"

"Some asshole in a Cadillac ran into her outside her car on California Street."

"Huh, what was she doing there? When did it happen? How bad is it? Is Meagan OK?"

"Yeah, Meagan's just fine. She was in the car with Teresa. We don't know what they were doing. It happened early this evening – like about seven. Nobody knows why she was out of her car in the street. It's real bad, Mark. She's in coma."

"Jesus Christ! Did they operate on her? Is she going to make it?"

"I sure as hell hope so. The only operation they did was to put a drain in her skull to keep the pressure down. She has really bad swelling of the brain. Her coma's pretty deep – she doesn't respond to anything."

"Who did it? Is the son-of-a-bitch in jail?"

"The cops don't know. He didn't even stop. Drove right on. Some woman saw it from across the street and said he didn't slow down, or speed up – just kept on driving, almost like he didn't know anything had happened. Had to be a drunk, but a rich one. They'll catch him."

'Who's with her?"

"Maggie's been there since we found out late last night. Ashley's taking care of Meagan." Maggie, Jack's wife, was Teresa's older sister and Ashley, the Jensen's 17-year-old daughter.

"I'll get there as soon as I can find a plane out. They don't come into this war zone very often." For the first time since he left SFO, he thought about something other than getting even wealthier. "Give me your cell phone number and I'll call when I know when I'm getting in. And, Jack... don't let her die."

"We'll do whatever we can. We're praying."

Mark elevatored down to the ground floor to speak to a concierge; there was none as the desk stopped services at 6 PM. There weren't a lot of foreigners in Cote d'Ivoire to service, thanks to the political turmoil of the past two years. He considered himself fortunate to find an English-speaker at the check-in, check-out desk. There was nobody checking in or out. The hotel had only about 20 guests in its 300 rooms. The one employee was able to determine that an Air France plane to Paris was scheduled to leave early the following morning. There'd be no trouble getting on – flights in and out of Abidjan flew nearly empty. He'd be able to find a flight to the US easily when he got to De Gaulle. He arranged for a taxi to pick him up at four AM, four hours before the flight, reckoning that road blocks and snipers, so prevalent recently, were unlikely to post a threat at that hour.

The following morning he arrived before 4:30 at Houphouet Boigny International Airport, named after the beloved autocrat who served for decades after independence from France. Papa Houphouet made international fame by ordering and overseeing the construction of the largest church in Christendom in the dusty town of Yamoussoukro, in a country that has three times as many Muslims as Christians. Nobody was manning the counters. Nobody was there to sell a cup of coffee, let alone duty-free alcohol. Nobody was present to guard the security of people or things. Aside from the scores of non-traveling Ivoirians sleeping on chairs and floors to get a bit of safety from the lawlessness of the city, nobody was there.

At 6 AM, a shoddily uniformed young man with wings on his food-stained lapel showed up behind the Air France departure counter. He pushed buttons to first light up, then add information to, the Arrivals and Departures information board. FLIGHT 6 - PARIS – DELAYED. In the departure time column, 8 AM was replaced by 11:30 AM. Flight 6 was the only flight of the day to Europe on any airline. Between Spencer's arrival and the announcement of delay, some three dozen people, about 50/50 black and white, had arrived to check into Flight 6. Many lugged multiple suitcases; others dragged luggage while having infants strapped to their backs. All badly wanted out of the hell-hole and all expressed their displeasure on hearing the news of the postponement. The young airline employee was overwhelmed, unwilling, or unable to give adequate responses to the voiced and unvoiced anger. He left his post, going through an unmarked door behind the baggage belt, slamming it behind him and locking it. All the chairs outside of immigration were filled by the sleeping masses; no customs officials were present, for obvious reason – there were no flights. Therefore, there was no access to the plusher seating in the pre-boarding facilities. There wasn't even anybody, since the departure of the Air France man, for Mark Spencer and the other well-healed travelers to bribe. Luggage turned into makeshift chairs. Dirty clothes became pillows for those willing to lie on the filthy linoleum. And, as far as Spencer knew, his wife was dying and he couldn't get out of Africa to be with her.

At 11 AM, the flight was further delayed. No explanation was offered, either in French or English. There was no food available and Mark found the three toilets to all be in desperate need of the attention of a plumber. Rumor had it that the women's room was equally foul. At 4 PM, an Air France 747 landed; fewer than a dozen people from a plane that had a capacity of more than 300 deplaned. An hour later, Spencer was on his way to Paris, first class. It was policy at his firm, Spencer, Bowman and Clark to use only economy class but he calculated the circumstances warranted the expensive upgrade. It had been 20 hours since he learned of his wife's catastrophe. By the time he landed at De Gaulle Airport, it was nearly midnight in France, 3 PM in San Francisco. Not wanting to hear any news before he booked his way to the US, he approached the United Airlines desk and found he could take the first flight to San Francisco, at 8 the next morning. He took a room at the in-airport hotel and dialed his brother-in-law.

"She died this morning. Meagan's with us."

Jason Klein, Fred and Barbara's first-born, appeared on the scene at Cedars-Sinai Hospital, a building considered by LA's Westside Jews to be the spiritual near-equivalent of the First and Second Temples of Jerusalem. The couple battled over a name – she lobbied for Abram, after her late grandfather who died in Dachau; he preferred Ethan Klein which he figured would facilitate his acceptance into the Ivy League and set him up should he opt for a career in film. Neither accepted the other's choice; Jason, a name then beginning to appear on the top fifty lists, was the eventual compromise.

Bar Mitzvah by his own choice, he pleased his parents religiously but was less successful academically. A public high school graduate – the folks thought the Westside LA schools to be more than adequate – he had a good, not great, GPA, and lacked the skills to compete on any of the high priority athletic fields. His SATs were excellent, giving him some optimism about his chances of being accepted to a top university. Rejections came from Harvard, Yale, Princeton, and Brown. He made waiting list at Cornell and Penn but had heard nothing more by the time he needed to accept or decline an offer from UC Berkeley. He chose yes, a fortuitous decision as his wait-listed name was not reached at either Ithaca or Philadelphia.

He did well at Berkeley and was very glad that he had not ended up on the East Coast. He was only a bit jealous when Robert, one of the twins, two years after Jason's rejection, was accepted at both Yale and Brown. His grades were good and he learned that he could score with women, both Jews and goyim. During the holidays of his junior year, he brought home a Cohen, first name Deena. The parents were ecstatic, both sets, but it didn't last. He told his folks that it was a mutual decision, but they suspected otherwise when they learned that Deena became Mrs. Weinberg the following summer.

Jason applied to law schools – again, he was turned down at both Harvard and Yale, but had a variety of high level acceptances, ultimately matriculating at Columbia Law. There he met a classmate, Chan-sook Park, known outside her immediate family as Emily. She made Law Review; he did not, but they fell for each other and he took her home to meet the parents. She certainly was no Deena Cohen and their immediate reaction was lukewarm. Knowing better than to speak disparagingly about his choice, they said nothing. Jason interpreted the silence as negativity but dismissed its importance and three months later he and Emily announced their engagement. The summer after graduation, the Park parents, wealthy by way of the chemical industry, put on a huge fete in Newport, RI. The already diminishing bright skies of familial relationships began to become partly cloudy in Rhode Island. Father Park was a Republican of few words and the words of Mother Park were laced with saccharine that overwhelmed the taste buds of Fred and Barbara alike. The father shook his counterpart's hands with a manly grip accompanied by a barely perceptible upturn of the lips, his best attempt at a smile. The mother, with previous coaching by her daughter, hugged both Kleins, welcoming them to their manse and talked at great length about the wonderful past, present, and future of the betrothed couple. A record hot spell rolled into coastal New England the day before the big day. The oppressive heat put a damper on what the Parks, and the Kleins, hoped to be a crowning occasion, the pairing of the only child and first born. Nonetheless, the extravagant meal and wedding went off without embarrassment; in fact, a fine time was had by all. A Korean Presbyterian minister and a Reform rabbi mutually officiated. The second series of handshakes and hugs followed the lavish reception with both parental couples assuming that there would not likely be any follow-up meetings, at least until an offspring was christened, named, confirmed, bar- or bat Mitzvah, or graduated. The Kleins did not know what their son and future daughter-in-law planned in terms of a religious upbringing for their future kids; they said to each other that they didn't care, but both did.

Emily accepted a clerkship with a Federal Appellate judge in Washington. Jason did not aim that high, knowing that his chances of hitting the target were low, and took a job at the Justice Department in the Office of Legislative Affairs. There he honed his schmoozing skills dealing with congressional aides, most of whom were his age or younger. After Emily's two year clerkship concluded, she had a wide scope of options in both DC and the nation at-large. She was disturbed by the preponderance of Democrats in the District of Columbia and silently held at least some interest in seeking elected office. Jason was congenitally a Democrat, but learned early in his relationship with Emily to temper his overt enthusiasm, keeping his view on the major issues of the day to himself. He had no problems with her desire to leave the land inside the

Beltway; his father had the best of Southern California connections and, as Emily could essentially write her own ticket, they decided to take their talents to Los Angeles. Both joined prestigious law firms that owned conjoining tall buildings on Wilshire Blvd. Hers specialized in mergers and acquisitions, his in entertainment. Both took home handsome salaries, but they had not accumulated enough to put a down payment on a home equal to their status-to-be. The father of the bride offered to pony up the full sum, but the Kleins did not want to be outdone and negotiated a deal whereby each pair of parents proffered a sizable chunk of cash, readily accepted by the young marrieds. Repayment documents were neither requested nor offered. The purchased property was a five bedroom four bath Tudor place in Holmby Hills, a block from UCLA and a short walk from the Playboy Mansion. It was ten minutes by car from the Kleins, five and a half hours by plane from the Parks. The gross inequality of distances was to prove problematic.

Houdini

The morning after the incarceration began, the food guy, while collecting the paper plates and plastic utensils from breakfast, called out, "Fred Klein?" It was almost 9 AM.

"Yeah, that's me."

"Your lawyer is waiting for you. Somebody'll come get you in a couple minutes."

At 9:45, a uniformed woman appeared, called for Klein and led him down the hall, through the heavy iron door to a small, unadorned room with a table and four chairs. A portly, mostly bald man dressed in a suit that Klein recognized as Italian and exclusive, sat at one end of the table. He stood as his client entered, extended his hand and made definite eye contact. "Fred, I'm Irving Greenberg."

"Where were you, sir?" Klein responded to this man, at least two decades younger than he. "I'm not real happy having been locked up with those stinking slime balls for an entire night. I couldn't sleep…"

"I'm sorry Fred. I couldn't get here yesterday. I had an MRI yesterday afternoon. Just after you and I talked, my doctor called and told me there was a problem with my blood tests – they thought I might have a liver tumor. Thank God they were wrong. Sorry to say that I was so freaked out having cancer that I forgot everything about coming over here. Plus, I've got another client in lock-up – did you meet him?"

"Yeah, I did. He's really pissed."

"Let's get you out of here. We'll go before the judge who handles this stuff. I'd predict you are going to have to come up with three hundred thousand bucks, as this involves a death. They are going to charge you with vehicular manslaughter and that's the number listed on the bail schedule of the county. I'll try to get her to lower the bail, but am not optimistic. Can you write a check for that?"

"Hell no, I can't. Can't I just give them a deed to my house or a bunch of stock certificates? I'm not a poor man – three hundred G's is not a big deal. I just don't have it in cash."

"We better work through a bail bondsman – arranging something with your house or your securities would take a few days and you'd have to stay where you are."

"Me and a bail bondsman? They are all scumbags who work for even scummier crooks, no?"

"Some of their clients are innocent, some are scumbags, and some are both. And then there is a group of reasonable citizens that are not innocent."

"Me."

Greenberg grimaced, glancing at the four corners of the room implying that his client should say nothing that he'd regret hearing later. "We go to the bail hearing in ten minutes. You should be out of here soon. Just don't argue your case in front of the judge; she's only going to set bail and you don't want to piss her off. Keep your hands at your sides, not in your pockets and not folded in front of you. 'Yes, your honor. No, your honor.' That should be the sum total of your testimony. I'll do the talking."

Resplendent in his orange outfit, un-cuffed Klein, Greenberg, and the uniformed woman walked to the elevators and on to the courtroom where there were about a dozen men, half of whom were in cuffs, and two women, all in orange, plus four or five suited individuals who had presumably all passed the California Bar exam. Klein rightfully assumed that there were fewer lawyers than arrestees because many of the latter were represented by the same public defender. Judge Katherine Wang brought to his mind his daughter-in-law Emily - young, attractive, and mean; he had a viscerally negative response. He could feel his heart thumping on his rib cage and he had pain in his chest, minor but no doubt real. It was minutes after he entered the court room that he noticed his wife seated in the gallery. She was dressed as if she were going to the opera. Greenberg approached her as she and her husband communicated without words. She handed him a folder of papers, presumably attesting to their financial stability and his lofty role in the community.

Klein thought he'd be first to be called because he was such a pillar – clearly he had more to do outside than his fellow inmates. Such was not the case as his name was not announced until nine others had been, occasionally through interpreters, assigned bail, told that they would not be bailed, or released on their own recognizance. "Frederick Klein," intoned the bailiff. Klein and his lawyer bounced to their feet and approached the bench. "You are charged with vehicular manslaughter, a felony. How do you plead?"

He was not prepared for the question, Greenberg having not told him that this was likely to happen. The lawyer leaned over with whispered instructions. "Not guilty, your honor."

"The court understands that you have no previous record and are active in community affairs. Therefore, I see no concern that you'd be a flight risk and therefore are eligible for release on bail. The standard bail for the offense with which you are charged is three hundred thousand dollars."

"Your honor," said Greenberg before his client had a chance to respond. "My client is, as you say, a well-respected person in San Francisco, a highly regarded philanthropist for many local causes, owns a fine home, and is happily married. There is no risk whatever that he will not return for further appearances. We would ask that bail be waived or at least that it be diminished to a considerably lower sum, say fifty thousand dollars."

"Mr. Greenberg, you are aware that the event for which these charges are levied resulted in the death of a young mother. There is no way that I could approve release without bail. I, on the other hand, am not opposed to a somewhat lower bail and set the figure at two hundred thousand dollars.

"Thank you, your honor."

They were taken to the clerk's office and met by a bail bondsman, a fiftyish male, looking the part in his too-tight black T-shirt, too-gaudy pinstriped pants, and penny loafers. He was the owner and only representative of his company, Houdini Bail Bonds. "So you need two hundred large, huh? You give me a check for twenty grand and I write a guarantee for the rest."

"How much of the twenty do I get back when I show up?"

"Zero, zip, nada. I'm taking the gamble, you pay to get out."

"Screw that. I can come up with two hundred grand, can't I Jen?" he asked his wife as she entered the room.

"Yes, dear, we can get the money. We don't have the cash – remember you just had me buy more Google stock. We'll have to sell most of it to raise that much."

"Fred, that's going to take a couple of days at least," said Greenberg. "Do you want to spend another two nights in the holding cell?"

"Houdini – can't you do it any cheaper? Just look in the paper – I'm a solid citizen – your chance of a default is zero, zip, nada."

"Sorry buddy. It's ten percent whether you're OJ or the King of England."

"OK, goddamit. Jen – write this son-of-a-bitch a check for twenty thousand. And sell some of those shares tomorrow."

He was out of jail in less than 24 hours. It seemed like 24 weeks.

"All the kids are waiting for you at home, Freddy."

There were no yellow ribbons hanging from the trees when Jennifer drove up in her BMW SUV with her now-indicted septuagenarian husband. His clothes, having been placed in a sack during his short incarceration, were embarrassingly wrinkled. The embarrassment resulted from the modest crowd of neighbors and press people on his lawn and sidewalk. Under more propitious circumstances, he would have probably asked those treading on the grass to move back, but his legal status made that a poor idea. He walked in the door, Jennifer taking a step back to allow him to enter first. There were no "Welcome Back Grandpa" posters or cake. A return from jail, with guilt or innocence not yet determined, was different from coming back from Viet Nam or Iraq. While there was no food, there was a large turnout of family – all three boys, and their wives, plus the three grandchildren from the Bay Area and one of Jason and Emily's two kids. Their older child, the eleven-year-old, stayed back in Los Angeles to prepare for an upcoming lacrosse tournament. Art Schofield was the sole non-family member of the gathering.

The twins, Phillip and Robert, as children were impossible to distinguish. As adults, it was still difficult, although Robert appeared to have grayed faster than his brother. Their personalities were nearly identical although their vocabularies differed some, presumably based on the Yale and UCLA educations. Neither was anxious to open the discussion when Dad entered the room, wrinkled and droopy-eyed from unsuccessfully trying to sleep on a linoleum jail floor. "Hey Dad." Fred didn't know or much care which of the boys spoke.

"Grampa, Gramps, Poppa," three grandchildren shouted out. Mickey, the Down's child, was silent.

Not a lot of touching went on in the Klein household – never had. Each of the twins tendered a low-pressure hug to their father; he accepted with some hesitation. A shake of the hands was exchanged by Jason and his dad. The twins' spouses each hugged the returnee with more gusto than their husbands while Emily did not make a move toward her father-in-law. She looked in his direction and smiled coolly while her husband ducked into the kitchen to get a beer as his father came through the door. Their seven-year-old was hunched over thumbing a video game.

"Welcome home, Amigo," Schofield muttered. He offered the only heart-felt physical greeting, tightly wrapping his arms around his companion of more than sixty years.

Fred plopped into his lounge chair. Initially, no relative sat down on either the leather sofa or the stuffed chairs a couple of feet away. An anxiety filled the space. After too many long seconds, Phillip gently lowered himself on to the sofa. "Dad, I hate to do this, but you've got to look at the paper."

Philanthropist

Beneath the fold on the front page of the day's *San Francisco Chronicle* appeared the headline:

LOCAL PHILANTHROPIST ARRESTED IN DEATH OF MOTHER, 28

The paper rarely featured anything but local news on its front page, having given way on distant matters to internet editions of the *Times, Post and Journal*. Above the fold was an article on bus drivers' pensions and below an expose on restaurant cleanliness. A recent photo of the hit and run victim, with baby in hand, graced the left side of the lower front page. Fred Klein did not read the article in which he was one of two main characters. He refolded the paper and handed it back, burying the relevant newsprint and saying nothing to his son. He had not felt such grief since the oncologist told him that further chemotherapy would be of no value to Barbara.

Less than half an hour after his father's arrival Jason finished his beer and said, "We've got to go, Dad. We've got an early plane in the morning – gotta find a hotel room. Let us know how we can help." He, Emily and the 7-year-old left, having offered no advice or uttered anything of sympathy or love. Their premium rental pulled away silently.

"What next Honey?" inquired Jennifer.

Her husband responded only with his eyes. A tear rose and fell through the crevasses of his cheek and chin.

Humor was the standard basis of communication between Kleins; none was to be heard, although Phillip and his brother tried to lift the gray cloud. Eventually Robert chimed in, "Come on, Pop. We've got to know what's happening so that we can help. For sure, our kids are going to be asked questions when they go to school tomorrow. It could get pretty ugly unless they're ready."

"OK – here's what I understand. Irv Greenberg is supposed to be the best criminal attorney in the City. He tells me that the Grand Jury will meet in three or four weeks and decide whether to take me to trial. Not much chance that I won't be charged. Right, Art?"

41

"Yeah, right. It doesn't look promising for you."

"What if he pleads guilty, Art," asked Robert.

"He could do that, but there's no way the DA's office won't demand some jail time. Only way we avoid that is convincing the judge, or the DA that you aren't healthy enough."

"Did your stepmother tell you about my visit to the doctor yesterday?" Fred asked the twins.

"Yeah, she said you went for a physical and everything was fine – you were well."

"Hell no, I wasn't well. The bitch told me that I had to change everything I ate because I had a cholesterol problem. That's what was pissing me off so much when I did what they said I did…I did. I killed that woman. She got out of the car on the wrong side and I didn't even see her. Even after the collision, I didn't think I did anything but brush her back."

"So, why did you leave the scene?"

"I was afraid that they'd find I had been drinking. I only had a whiskey and a couple of glasses of wine and I was perfectly capable of driving, but those blood tests and line-walking ones are not always right. They could have accused me of drunk driving. And, goddamit, I wasn't drunk!"

"I'm sure you weren't Dad, but the problem you have now is a whole lot worse. How are we going to solve it? There's no way we convince the judge that you can't go to jail with a high cholesterol, is there?"

"Afraid not," answered Schofield.

"It's up to Greenberg, said Fred. And it's going to cost me a shitload of money. I already had to shell out twenty grand to that asshole bail bondsman."

Robert continued, "Dad, you have a shitload of money – please don't worry about that. So, bottom line is that you are home until a trial or 'til you cop a plea. You prepared to spend some time in prison?"

"Hell, no. I'm 75 – there's no way I could survive. I'd be raped before the first day was over."

"Come on – you're not exactly the sort of dude that those rapists have any interest in.

"Yeah, maybe you're right, but I still couldn't live through a sentence. The stress would get me in a week. Shit, I had chest pain in the holding cell and the courtroom."

"Holding cells are a whole lot worse than prison cells, Pop," said Phillip.

"So, you guys think that I will end up behind bars, don't you?"

"Hopefully not, but you gotta be ready for it."

The doorbell announced the arrival of the pizza delivery guy that Jennifer had arranged before getting home. What with the unexpectedly rapid departure of Jason, et. al, there was more than enough.

That same night marked the monthly meeting of the Mayor's Cultural Committee. Klein was Immediate Past President, a position of some continuing importance. Do I go? Of course not; they just let me out on bail for killing somebody. But then again, why shouldn't I? Especially if I'm pleading not guilty. I'll go and show the bastards.

Robert, Phillip, and families, knowing that he was going to attend the meeting, went to a movie. Jennifer, as expected, supported her husband in his decision to go. She offered to drive him and return to take him home. She figured that driving was the last thing he'd want to do considering the newspaper headlines, the TV coverage, and the detailed and nuanced report on the local NPR affiliate. "Fuck 'em. I can drive just fine." Eschewing his usual whiskey and wine, he ate left-over sausage and mushroom pizza, cold, drove the Lexus with its dented right fender and found a space on the street three blocks from City Hall. To spare himself the embarrassment of coming in when most of the others had already seated themselves, he arrived twenty minutes before the 7 PM starting time, with only the two-member staff in the ornate conference room. He had worked closely with both of the young staffers during his recently concluded presidency, considering them friends. They simultaneously smiled on his entry. "Good evening, Mr. Klein." "Hello, Sir." Klein knew that both were well aware of recent events and was not surprised by the fact that neither mentioned it nor inquired about his health. Over the next quarter hour, those members who usually came, came; those who accepted membership on the reasonably prestigious committee but usually found more important obligations on meeting nights, didn't. All acknowledged Klein with either a nod of the head or a simple hello. "How Are You?" was not part of the evening's vocabulary; nobody shook his hands although some did with other members. It occurred to him, before the gavel fell, that the incumbent committee chair, a retired prima ballerina with whom Klein had a mutual lack of admiration, might ask for a moment of silence in honor of Teresa Spencer. She didn't; she was not that nasty.

The agenda was not particularly controversial or burdensome in its length. The City's support for opera, ballet, and symphony was, as always, on the month's agenda; the amount of money from the public coffers to each continued to drop, now to essentially zero. The committee held sway over the public cultural events in Golden Gate Park, so the Park people were represented. Klein despised the fact that almost all such events were now rock or bluegrass and that Shakespeare and classical and big band music had nearly disappeared from the annual schedule. In the past, he would have made a mini-ruckus, extolling the value of real culture; tonight he'd remain mute. The community attendance for these meetings generally did not exceed the number of people who had requested time on the agenda. At this meeting, there was what could gently be called a crowd – maybe 25 people in all. Klein assumed that several were there only to see the alleged killer. He convinced himself that most eyes were focused toward him as he sat silently in the seat next to his successor, the Board President. He voted with the unanimous majority on the several occasions when a vote was called. Voting required only a raise of the hand; normally voluble, he said not a word for the entire two hours. By custom, the members and the staffers retired to a nearby pub at the conclusion of the meeting; Klein was looking forward to the camaraderie that always followed the bickering, but to a man, the others pled reasons of fatigue, other social obligations, or the common cold for not joining. He braved the foggy walk to his car and, noticing the dent, kept walking.

Jennifer was not worried when her husband had not arrived at home by ten. She was aware of the gatherings at the pub and knew he was smart enough not to drink and drive under the circumstances of the day. She had been buoyed by the presence of the twins and the grandchildren after all returned from the movie, and took advantage of the kids' bedtime and early departure of the daughters-in-law to discuss Fred's situation with her sons-in-law. She was glad that Jason wasn't there, even though he, as a lawyer, might have been able to offer concrete legal information, of which she and the doctors were ignorant. She did not have the same problems with Jason, Emily, and the two achievers as did her spouse, but she and they had never established any great warmth.

"So, how do you see all this playing out?" said one twin. "Do you think he'll end up with a jail term?" queried the other. They both saw their young stepmother as bright, reasonable and, while no Barbara, not a bad looking woman.

"I'm really worried about your father." She relayed the overreaction to the news of his hypercholesterolemia and need for dietary manipulation that immediately preceded the episode. "I'm afraid that this will kill him. He's never had anything bad happen to him."

"Uhm, Jen, he did lose our mother, horribly."

"Oh, I'm so sorry – of course that's true. I guess what I mean to say is that nothing's happened since we've known each other." The twins were assuaged.

"I don't know if you ever heard the story, but he beat himself up pretty bad when she died," said Phillip.

Barbara was the perfect philanthropist's wife – smart, energetic and willing to do anything, anytime as long as she thought she was helping the underprivileged or undiscovered artists and musicians. She was on twice as many non-profit boards as Fred, spending at least two nights per week away from home. She loved charity balls and banquets; she usually was the one who bought out a table for ten and found other couples, gay or straight, to occupy the other eight seats. She was perfectly happy with the title of Mrs. Frederick Klein.

Her father, the society cardiologist, made sure that she did everything she could to prevent coronary artery disease. She did not rebel, running frequent 10-kilometer races, avoiding trans-fats and checking her serum lipids at least annually; she prided herself on her sub-200 cholesterol level. Her radiologist-son offered her free mammograms which she gladly accepted every year as a birthday present. Her gastroenterologist-son, on the other hand, never discussed esophagi, anuses, and rectums with his mother. She had been bothered with hemorrhoids since her first pregnancy and attributed the intermittent bleeding to them – she never mentioned the blood to the twin. She'd read about colonoscopies but justified her ignoring published advice by pointing out to herself that there was no family history of any cancer, let alone colon cancer. She, on a few occasions, told her husband about the blood; he accepted, without questioning, her hemorrhoidal explanation. He had not had a colonoscopy, fearing the discomfort, and was buoyed by her emphasis on the importance of family history. He had learned that he could not get away with advising his wife on health issues. "You take care of your body and I'll take care of mine!"

On her 59th birthday, Barbara opened her annual present by having her yearly breast X-ray. Her radiologist-son was perceptive enough, recognizing the folly of doctoring a loved-one, to have the films read by one of his office mates. The mate, also named Barbara, saw a thickening that concerned her just a bit. An ultrasound was ordered and done immediately, a response that only another doctor or the radiologist's mother would receive. Barbara was called into Barbara's office to be told that the thickening was of no significance. No biopsy was indicated. "Let me ask you a question," said Barbara Klein. "My hemorrhoids have been bleeding a lot – more than they ever have. Do you think I should have them operated on?"

"When did you last have a colonoscopy, Mrs. Klein?"

"Please call me Barbara, Barbara. I've never had one. I didn't see any reason to; there's no cancer in my family, not even any polyps."

"That doesn't make you immune to colon cancer, Barbara. Why don't we set you up for a colonoscopy?"

"OK, but please don't say anything to either Robert or Phillip or my husband."

"I'm not sure that makes any sense, but you make the call."

Three days later, the colonoscopy was done "You've got something in there; I took a biopsy and we'll know by tomorrow. Frankly, it doesn't look good." The gastroenterologist, a member of her son's partnership, was direct and honest and scared the hell out of her. There was good reason to be scared. She had a large, ugly cancer.

Barbara notified the family as soon as she was given the diagnosis.

"Christ All Mighty – Why didn't you do something about this before?" yelled Fred.

"I don't know. I thought it was the hemorrhoids."

Recognizing that there was nothing to gain by castigating her further, her husband turned optimistic. Colon cancer is usually curable – surely, she'd just get the damn thing taken out and be fine.

The CAT scan suggested that the liver housed metastases, lots of them. She wasn't going to be fine. A surgeon removed the primary tumor, confirmed the grim findings of the CAT scan and sewed her up. There were too many pockets of evil in the liver to remove them all. Maybe chemo would buy her, and them, some time.

The twins rallied round. Both they and their wives spent significant hours at the hospital and were there when she came home. Both cut back their schedule of patients to commiserate or sit silently with Barbara and with Fred. Jason was in the middle of a trial when the word came through. "I'll get up there next week." Emily couldn't come at all.

Chemotherapy hit her like a pack of wolves. After two full courses, her oncologist told her how superbly effective the drugs were – the tumors in the liver hadn't grown. They hadn't shrunk either. Barbara decided that she'd had enough, in spite of the protestations of the boys and the tears of her husband. She died three months later, jaundiced, pain-wracked from lung metastases and uncommunicative. Nobody remembered her last words as they were uttered several days before she died.

The boys' protestations led to incrimination. Wrongdoing was attributed to the doctors and the widower. The deceased – innocent.

Jason was the most vociferous. He berated his father mercilessly as they left the synagogue after the funeral service. "Why didn't you get her to the doctor sooner? Why did you let them do the surgery when they already knew that the tumor had spread to the liver? Why didn't you take her to Sloan-Kettering or MD Anderson? Everybody knows that San Francisco is a wasteland in cancer care." Fred's tears covered his cheeks, but he could not otherwise respond. He walked away from his first-born, toward the twins, like a defeated regiment would retreat behind breastworks. "I've got to understand this! Tell me why?" his eldest son yelled as his father retreated.

"Lay off him, Jason," pleaded Robert.

"Tell me you don't think Mom would be alive today if Dad had paid a bit more attention rather than going out to meetings and poker every night."

"That's not true! What was I supposed to do, tie her up and take her to a doctor? She knew she was bleeding. She was convinced that it wasn't anything serious. What could I do?"

Jason, having no answer to the logical question, kept at it. "Then, tell me about you and the secretary!" There had been a short term dalliance with a girl-Friday many years earlier, brought out in the open between spouses and, after some counseling, put behind them. Fred assumed that none of his boys had known about it.

"Goddamn you," said father to eldest son, who left the house, retreating to the security of his talented family.

Hennessey VSOP

Aware that he wouldn't be cavorting with his fellow boardspeople, Fred continued walking down Eddy Street in the heart of the notorious Tenderloin District, so close but so far from the magnificent City Hall. The Tenderloin houses, feeds and liquors-up the downtrodden of San Francisco. Klein was certain he'd benefit by some liquoring up and entered a bar, any bar. There was nothing elegant, handsome, pretty, historic or even OK about the place. It smelled bad – cigarettes, booze, stale fried snacks and distinctly, urine. It looked bad – dark, dank, unswept and unmopped. Behind the bar, a surprisingly sprightly woman, dressed in jeans and a man's dress shirt, no tie, spent most of her time washing glasses and juggling the order of the bottles under the huge, faded black and white photo of the Bay Bridge and the City as it had been in the 60s, including the long forgotten Embarcadero Freeway. Fred did notice that the bar totally lacked colors other than off-white, gray, brown and black. Even the Johnny Walker Red label looked gray through the smoke filled air. He couldn't tell if the bar lady was a blond or a brunette, as the part in her hair looked darker than the sides. He assumed she was a bleached blond; the closer he got to her, the less sprightly she looked. His original estimate of her age being 30 climbed two decades as he sat on an unbalanced stool near her sink.

The establishment was more crowded than he would have guessed. Fred was not a frequenter of bars, especially in his home town. He occasionally stopped in one when he was on business travel elsewhere, to watch football or basketball. A real fan, he despised watching alone in a hotel room. At the bar, every second stool was taken – five patrons, 3 men, including him, and 2 women bent over their beers or cocktails, looking up at the TV when the baseball announcer's voice made it sound worthwhile to do so, not speaking to anyone except the barmaid and then only for refills. Two of the half dozen booths had patrons. One, the furthest from the entrance, was occupied by a man in an expensive suit, a hand-painted tie, loosely knotted and pulled down, a crocodile brief case by his side and a much, much younger woman, probably blond, across. She looked young enough to require carding; he certainly would have qualified for AARP membership. They both drank white wine; a bottle of a Grand cru Chablis that Fred recognized, and was surprised to find in the Tenderloin, was nearly empty. Midway down the row of booths sat a group of 4 white men, also cardable. They were uniformed in that they dressed alike - tight jeans, tighter tee shirts, mainly off-white and menacingly scuffed shit-kicking boots. All had lighted cigarettes in spite of local ordinances to the contrary. The bar lady made no effort to have them cease or go outside. In spite of the quietude of the rest of the room, they spoke as if they needed to be heard at a rock concert. One of the four was the alpha. He didn't look any different from his mates; in fact his biceps and triceps were on the puny side. He sported only a single visible tattoo, while the others were more densely decorated. His alpha status was seemingly a result of his ability to craft a coherent sentence with limited numbers of fucks, shits and cunts. Plus he spoke more softly, and much less frequently, than the rest. It was simple to see that his cohorts bowed to his wisdom and sought his concurrence on the rare opinion that they proffered, invariably with more'. "How 'bout those fuckin' cops bustin' that bitch for leaving her kid in the car? She's good shit, that one. I know her and her kid's an asshole – always screamin' and shittin'. Kid didn't fuckin' die – the motherfuckin' ambulance got him to the ER in time." "Yeah," said the other two betas in *sotto voci* and the alpha nodded his approval.

Klein ordered cognac. The bar didn't offer the great XO's that he would always buy duty free when he returned from foreign travel. But they did have a Hennessy VSOP and even had a short rack of brandy snifters. He ordered a double, which he consumed without sniffing or sipping. He swallowed it in three mouths full. Then he ordered another and another. He wanted to get drunk but to do it in style, or at least as stylistically as one could do in a dive like this. He gave not a soupçon of thought to how he might get himself and his dented ride home.

After his third double Hennessy, his senses blurred, producing an even greater grayness to his immediate environs. His hearing, on the other hand, became more acute and he could not but avoid hearing the nastiness that emanated from the table of the four manchildren. Saying nothing to her, he made eye contact with the bent-over woman two chairs down, exchanging their mutual disgust for the language and the intensity of noise from the booth. "Shit-eating Raiders don't fuckin' belong on the same field as the Niners. No team with a spook at QB should be allowed in the fuckin' stadium." The betas talked, the alpha nodded and smiled or frowned to send his message of approval or disapproval.

Klein had had enough. The barmaid was certainly not about to do anything to quiet the boys down. Both women at the bar non-verbally expressed their unhappiness, so somebody had to take a stand. The accused felon, the events of the last two days suppressed deep in his cortex, chose to be that somebody. He got off his stool and spent a few seconds establishing his balance; he knew that a fall would make his effort to make change less likely to succeed. His head was swimming from the fine cognac but he knew that once he started walking, he could negotiate the several steps between the stools and the booth.

"Gentlemen, would you be so kind as to keep your voices down a little bit? There are ladies here that you are making very uncomfortable."

"Fuck the ladies. We're just having a good time. You know, Mr. Suit, you're in the Tenderloin, not Nob Hill. There's plenty more bars around – you don't like our talking, get the fuck outta here."

"Neither the ladies nor I want to go anyplace else. Would you just be a little quieter and stop the swearing."

"Hey, aren't you the guy I saw on TV this afternoon. The guy who killed the woman with the kid on California?" asked one of the betas, looking first at Klein and immediately thereafter at the alpha.

"Good call, Jackie, "responded the alpha. "That's the motherfucker, or should I say mother killer, ha ha. You're the Jewguy, aren't you?"

Klein didn't hesitate. "Yeah, that's me, Jewguy, but I didn't kill anybody and that's not what we're talking about here right now. I, and my friends over there, want you to be just a little quieter."

The biggest and youngest beta responded, "You and your friends can just go fuck yourselves." As the decibels of discussion rose, the mismatched couple with the Chablis and one of the men at the bar made their way around the discussants and left for the safety of the mean streets of late night blighted Central San Francisco. The barmaid kept washing glasses and juggling bottles.

Klein could never remember having been in such a situation. Of course, he couldn't remember much of anything as a result of his drunken state, but being in circumstances where his rational persona could not deal effectively with unthinking thuggery was a novelty. He could turn around and return to his stool and have a couple more doubles. He could leave the bar. He could threaten to call the cops. He could plead with the barkeep to exercise her responsibility and solve the dilemma. He, at 75, could act like a retired pugilist and try to scare them into submission. He did none of those. He collapsed to the floor as if he had been shot in the head.

The trauma group on call for the night shift at San Francisco General Hospital ER was made up of a fourth year resident, a first year resident (nee, intern) and two medical students. Like every night, the ER had been busy. Two teens badly broken from driving a stolen car into a light pole in the Mission District, but alive and likely to stay that way. A gunshot victim, no more than 16, from the Western Addition, DOA. A nonagenarian who broke her hip, while buying gloves at Macy's. But around midnight, there were a few quiet moments, allowing for donuts, coffee and some teaching. There's no such thing in the trauma center as time for napping. Before the first donut was down and the first mnemonic memorized

(Never Lower Tillie's Pants, Mother Might Come Home – the first letters of the bones of the wrist), a city ambulance radioed in.

"We're five minutes out with an old guy picked up at our favorite Eddy Street establishment, out of it, but responsive to pain and to yelling in his ear. Pulse real low. 34. BP is 140 over 90. Respirations OK. Stinks of booze. Big bump on the head. Pupils responsive and equal. Heart and lungs good except for the pulse. Guy's got no ID on him. Bartender thinks he may have been robbed by one of her customers after he fell. She says that there was no fight – at least no fisticuffs. He was in a verbal battle with some punks when he just went down."

The hoar-frosted triage nurse called the 4th year resident, a tall looker in his late 20s who reminded her of Dr. Kildare from the 60s. "Ralphie, we got an old drunk coming in from the Tenderloin – big bump on the head and bad bradycardia – 34. Got no ID, but is probably one of our regulars." The Tenderloin was more than adequately represented at the ER and most of the diagnoses had to do with alcohol – DTs, liver cirrhosis with bleeding, heart failure, stab wounds, gunshot wounds and damage induced by "blunt objects."

"Hey, you two," Ralphie shouted out to the third year medical students on their first night in the ER. Both students were female, short, slim, and Asian. "Get a quick look at this dude. Make sure there's nothing going on with his chest or legs and let X-ray know that he needs to be CT'd stat. …Quick, before he gets here. What causes a heart rate of 34?" The two Asian women, already standing straight, straightened even more. "Third degree heart block from AV node disease or an MI. Drugs like digitalis and beta blockers. Hypothermia." They knew the lingo, and the science.

"Good. Now save this drunk's life." The two young women assigned themselves tasks.

"I'll do the physical, you do the EKG and call X-ray."

Precisely five minutes after the radio alert, the ambulance pulled up and the ER techs jumped into action. Door open. Gurney extracted from the vehicle. Wheels lowered. IV bottle secured. Oxygen flowing. Wheel him in.

The patient and staffers sped past the front door and the desk of the triage nurse. "I don't know this guy – I'd swear we've never seen him before." She'd been the one who differentiates not sick from sick from very sick for more than 25 years; she wore a pin to prove it. The quarter century of experience licenses her to call senior residents Ralphie. "Hey, get a load of the suit – our regular visitors don't dress like that."

The techs rolled the gurney into the ER trauma bay, pulled the suit jacket off, unzipped the pants and yanked them down, covered him with a gown and cut the underwear off, saying nothing about the silk boxers. The expensive looking suit was unceremoniously shoved into a bag and the undergarments tossed into the recyclable waste. They took off his shoes and socks last. One of the techs looked inside a shoe – "Bruno Magli! This old guy's got something in common with OJ. I bet these things cost him five hundred bucks." Nobody else responded but the comment registered.

"So, what have we got?" asked the senior resident of the students. The first year resident stood right behind her charges ready to jump in if needed. One of the young women quickly took control of the physical examination and the other slapped on the electrocardiogram leads, printed out a tracing and went to the phone in the exam room to set up the CAT scan. The examiner shouted out in a voice as loud as her diminutive stature and cultural background allowed.

"Pupils both reactive and same size, but the right one is sluggish, suggesting possibly early problems in the brain. Pulse still in the mid-30s and regular. Breathing normal. BP OK. Chest is clear – no evidence of pneumothorax (an air leak around the lung but in the thoracic cavity.) I don't hear any murmurs or rubs. Reflexes intact and he moves appropriately with painful stimuli. EKG shows complete heart block."

"How about that thing on his head?"

"Oh, sorry. He's got a four centimeter hematoma over the right temple. Skin is intact. And, by the way, his mental status shows severe obtundation – he groans but can't respond to commands."

"And, why do you think he's obtunded?

"The bradycardia, maybe?"

"Not usually. A slow pulse doesn't very often stop you from talking and responding to commands. How would we find out?"

"Not sure, Doctor."

"How would we make his heart go faster?"

"You could give him atropine."

"Yeah, I could, but that probably wouldn't speed up the ventricle with third degree block. How about a pacemaker?"

"Oh, right. A pacemaker."

The resident nodded at the charge nurse who got out the external pacer and slapped the pads on the patient's chest. She had the rate set at 80 and immediately the pulse rate, felt at the wrist and confirmed by the monitor, was 80 beats per minute.

"See how that worked on his brain."

The student yelled into the patient's ear. "Wake up! Open your eyes! Squeeze my fingers! Nothing happened, Doctor."

"What does that tell you?"

"Maybe we haven't given him enough time to wake up?"

"Huh-uh. Increasing the pulse should reverse any neurological issues of bradycardia right away."

"So he's got something going on in his head?"

"Good. It's either that or something toxic. Doesn't look like narcotics – he's got no needle marks and people with expensive suits and Bruno Maglis don't usually shoot up heroin. And, when the ambulance guys started the IVs he was given Narcan – it's policy when they find a patient that's out of it for no known reason. The anti-opiate would eliminate, again almost immediately, any confusion or coma from narcotics."

The time between the beginning of the exam by the student and the placement of the pacer was about 90 seconds. The next moment, the radiology technician came into the room and wheeled John Doe, his official name until he was tagged in the system with his real one, off for his CAT scan. Following in his wake was a cardiac nurse and her crash cart, containing a defibrillator and all the other high tech meds and gadgets to be called on if he tried to die.

The resident received a call no more than 10 minutes later. "For once, Ralphie, you sent us one that didn't waste our time and our stuff. Mr. Doe, here, has a huge subdural on the right side; there's got to be 100 cc of blood in there. Plus there's a sizable skull fracture under the hematoma on the scalp." The surgical and radiology residents had been sharing patients and insults for several years.

"How's he looking now?"

"Same as he did when you sent him to us. Groaning and doing a bit of kicking, more on the right than left. Nurse Knockers tells us that his heart is doing OK. Pacemaker is capturing fine. BP stable." Knockers was neither the nurse's maiden nor married name.

"I'm glad I didn't embarrass myself in front of the two medical students. I told them we'd find more than just a slow pulse to explain his neuro. Guess it's time to call the always upbeat and never ungrateful neurosurgical team, the dirty bastards."

One of the bastards grumped on the phone, "You sure you've got him worked up completely? I had just fallen asleep after fixing that guy you sent me with the C-spine fracture. You are aware, are you not, that the C-spine didn't have a urinalysis on the chart?"

"Yes, Milo, your first year reamed out our first year on that subject. A little subtlety might go a long way."

Doe, all worked up, and his gurney and Nurse Knockers and her crash cart rode the elevator to the second floor operating room, bumped through the easy-open doors and disappeared to a place where only those in blue scrubs dared tread.

Ernesto

Ernesto Contreras was born outside Guadalajara 37 years earlier, to a single, basically uneducated, mother of 17 years. Four years later, mother and son and infant daughter were transported across the Mexico/Arizona border abetted by a costly coyote. Mother got a job as a "housekeeper" in a ritzy Pasadena Arts and Crafts house and Ernesto entered public school, where he picked up English in a flash, excelled at every grade level, and earned an acceptance, with full scholarship, to USC, in the days when Latinos were not always required to show papers. He majored in business, did well academically and socially and was employed after graduation at a midlevel in a San Pedro shipping company. He developed a penchant for women co-workers older than he. When they expanded northward, the company transferred him to another midlevel slot in San Francisco where he encountered a higher class of sexually experimental middle age women. Less than two years after opening their doors, the company recognized that San Francisco was no San Pedro or even Oakland. There simply weren't enough ships in port so they battened the hatches and let go of all employees, with a tiny severance, but without offering Ernesto or anyone else a chance to return south. He had difficulty finding another job. Eventually, he signed on as a salesman at an auto dealership peddling Subarus and was pretty good at it, selling a bunch of station wagons to Spanish-speaking family folks. He quickly got bored however and left the agency for a position as a waiter at a high-end downtown steakhouse where, between a modest salary and large tips, he, the only college graduate on staff, succeeded.

Jennifer Taylor was three yours older than Ernesto Contreras, he 31, she 34, when they became lovers. Mrs. Taylor was then into the early decline of her first marriage to Randy Taylor, a multiple franchisee. He owned two of each of the following - fast food joints, movie theaters, tire outlets, car washes and gyms - plus one check-cashing establishment and a nine-hole golf course. Ernesto and Jennifer met at one of Taylor's car washes and started talking when they noted that they both had black Subarus. Coffee one day, sex the next, and the next. It was not hard to cuckold Mr. Taylor. Constantly in motion and rarely home thanks to his multiple holdings, he also took on an ever-increasing importance in his church, serving as its representative on the regional council of the United Methodists. He was away more than he was home, and since Jen didn't work, at his request, and had opted against offspring, she had plenty of free time for foreplay and fornication. Ernesto was glad to oblige and for the first several months the dalliances occurred weekly or more. Occasionally, they would smoke a joint that he would come up with from sources about which she never inquired. Jennifer had been a somewhat more than occasional user of the weed at high school in New Jersey, but had switched to beer and wine following college. After a year, plus or minus, of the frequent adultery, she developed a modicum of guilt. She wasn't prepared to get divorced. Old man Taylor wasn't mean to her and his combined income from all the franchises made them more than comfortable. The marital sex was, to put it in as kind a way as she could, awful. She didn't want to give up the affair, but felt it would be more morally acceptable if the get-togethers occurred less often. They would continue to talk on the phone as often as either desired, which worked out to almost every day, but would copulate at a lesser frequency. Jennifer loved to talk to Ernesto about life, her unhappiness at home and sex, and loved to lie with him; she didn't think she loved him and she had no interest in leaving one husband to marry the immigrant, although she could not give voice to a reason. Perhaps it had to do with the fact that he never asked her to do so. She suspected that she was not her lover's only lover, but made no attempt to prove or disprove the suspicion.

    The Taylor's called it quits about two years after Ernesto surfaced. Shockingly for Jennifer, the breakup resulted not from her affair but from his. He came home one afternoon after working on the books at the golf course and notified her that he was in love with the pro, a gentleman who Taylor said had a swing like Arnold Palmer. The split was surprisingly amicable. He offered her one each of the franchises of which he had two and the check cashing store; she insisted on and was given lots of money instead. With it she bought a fine, but small, home in Pacific Heights and the pug Bernie, the whelp of champions. Jennifer and Ernesto had systematized their lovemaking. They coupled twice a month, usually on Tuesday, until she met and married Fred Klein who spent most of his time at home. At that point, they had to work it out to suit her new husband's philanthropic and poker playing schedule. The occasional, rewarding relationship had continued for the entirety of her second marriage with, to her knowledge, no suspicions at home.

It was well after midnight and Fred had not returned from his cultural committee meeting. The twins and their charges had gone to bed, comfortably ensconced into two of the three guest rooms of the mansion, adults in the queen beds, kids on air mattresses on the floor. At the time they retired, there was minimal concern about his whereabouts. An hour later, Jennifer decided to call Ernesto, her closest confidant and her personal font of wisdom. She, by then, was close to panic, fearing that her husband had committed suicide; she sought both reassurance and advice. She was not particularly close to her stepsons and had an underlying fear that they somehow blamed her for his predicament. She didn't want to call the police, fearing that it would only aggravate them and make his chances for judicial leniency that much less. Calling the lawyers, either Schofield, whom she knew well, or Greenberg, whom she had met only the previous day during the transaction with the bail bondsman, did not seem wise.

    Ernesto knew only what he read in the papers and heard on local news broadcasts. His lover's spouse was in major trouble. He felt sympathy for her and even for her husband. On the other hand, he was not totally upset by the circumstances as they might greatly simplify, and possibly embellish the still torrid affair. Jennifer's call was answered quickly but sleepily. She started as if he knew nothing of the events, an illogical thought as she knew Ernesto to be always aware of what was going on internationally, nationally, and locally. "Fred killed a woman."

"I know, I know. I heard about it yesterday and they just had a story about him getting out on bail on the 11 o'clock news."

"He went to one of his board meetings even though he just got out of jail and, now, he hasn't come home. He was supposed to be here more than two hours ago and he hasn't even called. He always comes home when he says he will. If he's stuck in traffic, or his meeting goes longer than planned, he calls me, even if he's only going to be ten minutes late. It's the only time he ever uses a cell phone. I'm really worried about him. It's just not like him."

"You know, he's gotta be stressed, really stressed. He's not going to be acting like usual. Think about what he might be doing that's not normal."

"I guess he could be drinking with somebody from the committee, or one of his poker buddies. He doesn't drink much but I did hear from his kids that he hit it pretty hard when Barbara died."

"Barbara?"

"His first wife." She was sure that she must have told Ernesto about her and that she had almost certainly used the name lots of times over their later years together. "So, what should I do?"

"Did you try his cell?"

"He never turns it on unless he's going to call me. I tried it anyway. No answer. Just voice mail."

"I guess you are going to just have to wait 'til he comes home or calls. If it would make you feel better, why don't you call the hospitals and find out if he checked himself in or was brought in?"

"They would have called me. If he was dead, or not able to talk, they would have checked his wallet; he carries business cards even though he doesn't do business anymore."

"But why don't you call anyway. It'd make you feel better."

"Would you call for me?"

"OK. I can do that. I'll call the private hospitals. Can't imagine he'd go to County or the VA. I'll call you as soon as I know anything."

He got the series of numbers from 411 and called the emergency department of California Pacific, St. Mary's and St. Francis. "I am looking for a Mr. Fred, or Frederick Klein. He might have been admitted tonight." In each case, he was given some variation of no. To be even more complete, he called the ERs at St. Luke's, San Francisco General, Seton in Daly City and Marin General Hospital. Nobody had a Klein on the list.

"Good news, *mi amor*. None of the emergency rooms in the area saw anybody named Klein tonight."

"I guess that's good news. But I'm still really scared."

"You'll just have to wait a while. I'm sure he'll come back soon, maybe drunk as a skunk." Jen recognized the irony of the possibility that he would drive himself home inebriated.

Robert shuffled into the den, having heard the phone ring, seeing that it was almost 2 AM and knowing that when he went to bed his father hadn't come home.

"Was that about Dad? Is he OK?"

"That was a friend who I asked to call hospitals. They haven't seen him in any of the emergency rooms. That's good, I guess, but I'm still worried."

"Jesus – would he have done something to himself? Could he be lying dead in the park? Oh God, could he have jumped off the bridge?" The Klein's did not own a gun and they didn't have any pills that could kill you. Fred had always seemed fascinated by jumpers, questioning their sanity. No way that he'd be one of them. "I guess we should call the police. They'll know who we're talking about."

When Robert, now with his twin brother at his side, called the SFPD and got through to the appropriate extension, Sgt. Gallardo, the on-call cop, indeed knew the name Fred Klein. "Is this the same guy who is charged with the hit and run that killed the woman on California?"

"Yes, sir, it is."

"We haven't heard anything about any jumpers recently. The hospitals would know if any bodies had turned up; the ambulance takes 'em all to SFGH for pronouncing. Give me your number and we'll call if we hear anything."

Evacuation of a subdural hematoma, a collection of blood between the thick lining of the brain and the brain tissue itself, is a quick procedure. It can be done in a minute or two, through a burr hole in the skull in an acute emergency. A more definitive operation can be done in half an hour or less. Doe's surgeons, the dirty bastards, were, in spite of their nasty disposition, efficient. The blood was removed and drainage established in twenty minutes, relieving the pressure on the brain, and he was moved to recovery, a breathing tube in place with a respirator connected. The effects of the anesthesia and the residuals from the swelling kept him under; he was still John Doe.

After the blood was removed from around his brain, his heart became the subject of greatest medical interest. His blood tests showed that he had had a heart attack. The myocardial infarction was obviously the cause of his complete heart block and, as a result of damage to the electrical conduction system in the heart, the critically slow pulse. As a consequence of the slow heart rate, the brain didn't get enough oxygen, causing him to fall which, in turn, led to the subdural hematoma. A temporary internal pacemaker would have to be placed via a big vein to replace the less reliable external one that had been attached before his surgery. That was straight forward for the cardiology fellow who had been standing by in the operating room. Doe was stable and after an hour in recovery was moved to the ICU where he began to thrash.

Two hours later, he stopped thrashing and was clearly awake. The tube in his trachea prevented him from speaking and the nurses were unprepared to wake the surgeon for an order to take out the tube. The dirty bastards had been up all night on the C-spine case and Patient Doe. She handed the patient a clipboard and a ballpoint.

Where am I?

Philanthropist

"San Francisco General Hospital – you are in the intensive care unit and just had surgery.

What kind of surgery?

"Surgery to take blood out from around your brain. You fell in some bar because of a heart attack and hit your head on the floor. By the way, can you tell us your name? And, where do you live? You didn't have any ID on you when you came in."

I'm Fred Klein. I live in the City.

"Are you married? If so, what's your wife's name?"

Barbara.

"We'll call her. What's your number?"

I don't remember.

"Hey. You aren't the same Fred Klein that ran into that mother the other day, are you?"

He shrugged his shoulders. No.

A nurse's aide had heard the question, took a look at the patient and was sure he was the same guy whose picture she had seen the day before. "That's the man. Let him die," she said loud enough for the patient to hear. She was the mother of a three-year-old.

The nurse knew that she had a unique problem on her hand. She needed advice from on high. She called the Supervisor of Nurses for the night shift.

"Should I just call the wife? He tells me he's married to someone named Barbara."

"'Are we sure this is the same Fred Klein?"

"Hard to say with all the bandages and tubes, but he sure looks like the guy I saw on TV. Natasha thinks it's him too."

"We better call the cops first. This could be real sticky."

They reached Sgt. Gallardo, the SFPD person who two hours before had been talking to the Klein household and told him about Fred Klein, John Doe and his saying that he lived in the City and was married to a Barbara. She included the fact that he wore a designer suit, now bagged in paper, and well shined Bruno Maglis. "Yeah, I gotta presume that's the same Fred Klein. His family has been trying to find him – left home and didn't return. We have no other candidates behind bars or in the morgue and the son said that they had checked the ERs. I'll call them and try to tie it together. But as to what we need to do if it is the same Klein, probably nothing. If it is the same guy, he's out on bail and it doesn't seem that he's going any place real soon with all the tubes and catheters and IVs you put into anybody unlucky enough to end up in your shop. Plus, we don't have any spare cops right now to sit outside his room. I'll call the family. I just happen to have their number right here on my desk."

Jennifer picked up the phone on the first ring. "Hello, this is Sergeant Gallardo from the San Francisco Police Department. Is this Mrs. Barbara Klein?"

"Huh. No, Barbara Klein doesn't live here anymore. She passed away several years ago. Why…why are you calling? Aren't you the same officer that talked to my son-in-law two hours ago?"

"Yes, Mam. But you say Barbara died years ago? Who are you then?"

"I'm Jennifer. I'm Fred's wife now. Stop. Just a second, speak to my stepson." She was sure she was about to hear that she was a widow.

Robert took the hand-off. "Hello Sergeant, this is Doctor Robert Klein."

"Doctor Klein, how you doin'?"

"OK, OK. What? Why are you calling? My stepmother seems very upset."

"We may have found your father. He's in the ICU at San Francisco General Hospital, but he says his wife is named Barbara. He's pretty sick – something happened to his heart and to his brain. They say he'll probably survive but they're not sure."

Robert gave a thumbs-up to Jennifer and continued talking to the Sergeant. "Barbara was our mother. She's dead – long time ago. He's married to Jennifer now. If, as you say, something happened to his brain – I presume that means a stroke – he may have lost his short term memory."

"Could be. Doctor, do you know if he had a pair of Bruno Magli shoes?"

"No, I have no idea what kind of shoes he has. Jen – did Dad have Bruno Maglis?"

"Yes. I think he had them on when he went to his meeting. Why?"

"Yes he has some. And…"

"I heard her. Then this has to be the same Fred Klein."

"Can you tell me anything more about his condition? How did this happen?" Robert asked.

"All I can tell you is that he's at the General in intensive care. They say he had a fall and a heart attack. They found him in a bar in the Tenderloin. He needed some sort of surgery on his brain, but he's doing a little better now."

"How can he be there? We called the General Hospital Emergency and they said there were no Fred Kleins. And our father doesn't go to bars in the Tenderloin. Hell, I've never heard of him going into any bar."

"Sorry. I can't tell you anything more about that. The ambulance brought him in from the bar. No ID. Maybe he was robbed after he fell. They signed him in as John Doe. That's why they told you he wasn't there. After they operated on him, he couldn't' talk 'cause of the breathing tube, but he wrote notes saying who he was and that he was married to Barbara."

"Can we go see him?"

"The nurse said you better wait 'til morning. They're gonna take the tube out and clean him up. He was pretty smelly when he came into the ER – booze."

"What does this do to his legal situation, Sergeant?"

"You're talking to the wrong guy, Doctor. I'm just a cop on the beat. Talk to his lawyer. I read that he has Greenberg. Good choice. He gets some real scumbags off, as long as they've got the dough to pay him."

Robert hung up without saying goodbye and relayed the information to the others. Jennifer, relieved, excused herself to go to the bathroom and used her cell phone to bring her lover up to date. His reactions were mixed.

General Hospital

Mark Spencer landed at SFO at the same time that Fred Klein was attending the Mayor's Cultural Committee meeting, before he consumed too many double cognacs. Meeting Spencer as he arrived at baggage claim were his brother-in law and sister-in-law, Jack and Maggie Jensen. Their faces were long; Maggie's tears had stopped flowing but her scarlet eyes gave away her grief. It took half an hour to get the suitcase as Mark had been unable to get a first class seat across the country.

"How's Meagan?" was his first question after the heartfelt and comforting hugs that he had never before appreciated, in fact found unpleasant, for as long as he knew his wife's kin.

"She's doing fine, Mark. She's with Ashley and she's been eating and sleeping OK. She calls for her Mom and we've been telling her that she's gone for a while. We decided that you should be the one who tells her the bad news."

Mark was glad to hear of their decision although he hadn't a clue as to how to tell a two-year-old that she'd never see her mother again. The last thing he thought he'd be was a single father. Teresa was always so healthy. She ate all the right fruits and vegetables, went to the gym four days a week and made sure she had her Pap smear every year. Mark was the one who would not have surprised anyone with an early demise; he ate all the wrong red meats and refined sugary delicacies, never exercised, whored around on business trips and was as much an A personality as anyone could be.

"Did the cops find the guy who did this?"

"Yeah, they did. We heard about it on TV last night – this is all over the news. You are going to have hundreds of calls on your answering machine. We've had plenty ourselves and everybody asked us to let you know they loved you and will do anything they can to help.

"The guy is somebody you may have heard of – name of Frederick Klein – he's got to be at least 70 – lots of money, LOTS of money. He lives six blocks from your house. You may remember him – he ran for Supervisor in our district long before we bought the house –lost badly, even though he put big bucks into his campaign."

"Is he in jail?"

"He was but he's out on bail. Two hundred thousand – ridiculous amount – he probably carries that much around in his wallet. The judge who let him go so cheap was that Chinese one that Schwarzenegger appointed – she's tough with low-lifes but a real sieve when a rich crook's in her court room. Originally, she was asking for three hundred thousand. His lawyer, Greenberg, said fifty and she caved right away at two hundred Gs."

"Greenberg? That's the guy that got the Google VP off after he punched out his wife. Klein isn't going to jail – he's got too good a lawyer and the DA's got no money – they'll probably send a lawyer right out of law school…Jesus, how can I be talking like this when I have a daughter who lost her Mom? Let's get out of here and go home. Is she at your place or ours?"

"Yours. We wanted her to have all her toys with her. And she cries when Bob isn't in the same room with her."

"Bob?"

"That's your dog."

"Oh, right."

The ride from SFO to Presidio Heights could take as little as 30 minutes. Thanks to an accident on the freeway, it took the Jensens and the new widower nearly an hour. Maggie had gotten in the back so that Mark wouldn't be sitting alone. She and Jack noticed an almost complete lack of emotion on Mark's part. He commented on the traffic and the cool weather, comparing it to the swelter of West Africa. He did not cry. They knew their brother-in-law well enough that he probably would never let anyone see him shed tears. Or maybe he just couldn't cry.

Finally, Jack pulled into the Spencer garage. The three walked into the home through the entry hall and into the family room. Sitting on the ground, playing with dolls were Meagan and Ashley with the beagle asleep on the sofa nearby. Mark had to call out her name to get her to turn around to see that he had returned.

"Daddy, Daddy!" Smiling broadly, she picked up, and showed him a Barbie doll that he had not seen before – he hadn't seen it because Maggie had purchased it for her just after she learned that Teresa didn't make it. "Mommy? Home?"

He paused. He thought, until his last night in Abidjan that he knew how to respond in almost any situation. But he had no clue how to convey the idea of death to a two-year-old. He was sure that there were experts out there that could help, but a question had been asked that couldn't wait for expert opinion. He couldn't talk of God or Jesus – she had had no religious input, although Mark and Teresa had decided that they would bring her up Catholic, as they had been. He couldn't lie and say that she'd be back later. He obviously couldn't say she'd died, as a two-year-old would have absolutely no ability to understand what that meant. She had not lost any grandparents that she knew. Both of Teresa's parents had passed before she and Mark were married and his had not come west from Nebraska since she was less than one. Mark had a house full of siblings; his parents now had 15 grandkids in 4 states. They simply didn't have the resources to visit them all.

"She's gone, my love."
"Oh, OK. Where?"
"A very long way away.
"She coming home?"
"No Meagan, she can't come home."
"OK – Daddy play with dollies?"

"Of course I can, honey." He sat down on the floor and did his Type A best to establish relationships between himself, his daughter and several six to twelve-inch plastic children, adults, cats, dogs and animals from the barnyard and the jungle.

Four hours later, late afternoon, Mark had taken a short nap while Meagan was taking hers. He awakened before she did and went out to the living room where Maggie was watching TV. Jack had gone back to work; he was a laboratory tech at Cal Pacific Medical Center, a major private hospital near his home. Maggie had stopped teaching third graders when Ashley was born and hadn't brought money into the family since. They were clearly living beyond their means; just the taxes on a smallish house in their part of San Francisco set them back over ten thousand per year. They could only have afforded the purchase price of the house because they had sold a larger place in Noe Valley, which they had purchased for a song just after they got married. Though Noe Valley was now the au courant San Francisco address, their buttons burst when they moved into the upscale Cow Hollow neighborhood by the Bay, paying cash.

"Unbelievable!" Maggie cried out as he entered the room. I just saw the most incredible thing. Klein, the same Klein who killed Teresa, is at General Hospital. He had brain surgery and a pacemaker. They found him on the floor in some bar in the Tenderloin and I guess he almost died, but now they say he is stable, critical but stable.

"Why didn't they just let the son-of-a-bitch die? It would have saved the State a ton of money and wiped that creep off the face of the earth. He's an old man who would die anyway and he killed my wife and Meagan's mother. He doesn't deserve to have brain surgery and a pacemaker. You know what's worse? He's at the General, not some private hospital. You and I and all the taxpayers are going to pay for keeping him alive. What a waste!"

"You're right, but there's nothing we can do about it. They'd have to treat Hitler if he was brought in by ambulance needing brain surgery."

"You said he's at the General didn't you? Isn't that where they took Teresa after he hit her?"

"It is."

"Do we know who the doctor was that took care of her? I'd like to find out what happened. Whether she said anything, like what she was doing in the car and why she got out of it."

"A nurse named Smith, or something common like that, called me to tell me that she had come in and was in coma. He suggested that we not come in but to stay by the phone. That's when I called you in Africa. Smith didn't say anything else. He'd tried to get you but obviously, nobody was home. I don't know how they got to me – she must have had her address book in her purse. It was hours after the accident that they called us – we were asleep – after midnight – and the accident happened around seven. A couple of hours later, they did call us and told us that she had died. I decided not to call you back. You'd learn soon enough."

Mark called the hospital ER. He was directed to the Head Nurse, a woman not named Smith. He was told that, indeed they had a male night nurse named Smith but as it was afternoon, he had not come on duty yet. She didn't know if he had been on when Ms. Spencer had come in, but presumed he had. Mark decided to go to the hospital after change of shift to talk with Nurse Smith.

The Spencers, in the name of energy conservation, had only one car. Mark's wealth did not get in the way of getting to and from work on the #1 Muni bus which traversed the California St. corridor. Teresa had been the primary Nissan driver. He was, as a result of tragedy, now the car's only operator and decided to drive himself to the General. Having never been to the Potrero St. hospital, he had to get directions off his phone and felt uneasy with the idea of driving alone into a part of town that he felt wasn't any safer than downtown Abidjan. Parking was not simple – he ended up three blocks from the emergency entrance and scurried down Potrero, wishing he had had somebody like his Ivorian bodyguard at his side. On entering the ER, he was greeted by the triage nurse, the same gray haired veteran who had been the first to see Klein the night he was admitted.

She triaged Mark Spencer to a room meant for quiet discussions between patients' families and staff, usually to deal with an unexpected death. Two minutes later, DeSean Smith, RN, an African-American man of at least six and a half feet and at least forty years, entered the room and sat with Mark at a small table in the center of the undecorated, beige-walled room. His head was clean-shaven and a gold stud shone from his right earlobe. "How can I help you, sir?"

"I think you were the nurse on duty when my wife, Teresa Spencer, was brought in three nights ago after she was hit by a car. She's the one who died after the madman ran into her and left without stopping."

"Yes, sir, I was the one. And I was the one who called your relative with the terrible news."

"That wasn't my relative. It was hers. What can you tell me, Mr. Smith?"

"Not much. And my condolences for your loss."

"Thanks." Mark knew the nurse was obliged to say it. Not doing so would have been a breach of etiquette. Saying it added nothing.

Smith continued, "She was only with us a few minutes before they sent her for a CT scan. We heard that she had suffered massive brain trauma and that there's was nothing to be gained by operating. She came back after the X-Ray and we just watched her while they waited for a bed in ICU to be cleared. She was here about five hours when her heart stopped. The doctors did everything they could, including CPR and putting a breathing tube in her trachea – all to no benefit. The chief trauma doctor pronounced her dead at about 2 in the morning."

"Did she say anything?"

"Not a word. She was in a deep coma when she arrived. She never woke up. I'm sorry."

Spencer could say no more. He wished that he could cry but couldn't. "Can you tell me where the ICU is?"

"It's on 4 East Ward. Go to the elevators, up to the fourth floor then turn left."

Spencer entered the elevator alone, pushed 4 and exited to a busy, almost hectic scene of couriers and messengers pushing carts with bottles of IV fluid and toting X-Rays, and med students with their attending physician strolling down the hall, learning on the run of the latest about infections or drugs or how to differentiate levels of shock. He turned left and found massive double doors with ICU in eight-inch bold blue letters on both. He tried to open them but they were locked. He spotted a buzzer on the side that invited him to push the button for entry. "How can I help you, Sir?" A surveillance camera above the doors pointed down at him.

"I would like to see Mr. Fred Klein."

"Are you a relative of Mr. Klein?"

"No, I'm his friend. I'd like to just say hello for a minute."

"I'm sorry, only immediate family members are permitted. I'd be happy to tell him you came by. What is your name?"

Mark Spencer, venture capitalist, widower, and single father, turned away from the speaker and camera, having not identified himself, returned to the elevator, got off outside the ER and walked the three moonless blocks back to his car.

The three Klein sons joined their stepmother for breakfast in her gourmet kitchen. She laid out half a dozen boxes of dry cereals, all heart-healthy, and three renditions of bagel with low fat cream cheese. Orange juice was freshly squeezed and the coffee was Peet's. Jason, who had, to the surprise of the other three, come at 8, offered to drive his rental to General Hospital for their first visit with their husband/father. He had sent the family on alone. All accepted the offer even though his reputation in the family was that of a second rate driver. Phillip thought about using the Lexus with Jennifer at the wheel, but remembering its central role in the drama at hand, said nothing. A brief note in the *Chronicle* describing Fred's status and the legal machinations downtown was read aloud by Robert without comment from others. Fred Klein had quickly fallen off the front page.

The advice the family had received late at night was to come at 9. With a quarter-hour hunt for parking, they arrived at the door of the ICU exactly at that hour. The voice on the speaker queried about who they were and, learning of the four-person visiting party, said that only two could enter at any one time. "Why don't Phillip and I go in first?" suggested Robert. "We are more used to ICUs than you two. It could be pretty ugly in there."

It wasn't ugly. Their father had had the breathing tube taken out and his head bandaged. One catheter was connected to a bag that allowed for hourly measurement of his urine output and another one drained fluid from inside the skull to prevent the pressure around his brain from reaching dangerous levels. The external pacemaker had been removed and the line from the internal one was thin and covered by the patient gown. The twins could interpret the monitor to determine that his blood pressure was well in the normal range and the pulse was 80 and completely regular. They could see the electrical blips on the screen, proving that their father's heart had not taken over control of its own rhythm and that the pacer was keeping that rhythm regular at a perfectly acceptable rate. But Fred was asleep and he was not responsive when they simultaneously tried to let him know they were there. The Filipina nurse at his bedside explained that he had been agitated and confused after waking up the night before and that the neurosurgeons had elected to sedate him heavily using large doses of intravenous narcotics. She said that it would be several hours before he'd be awake and making sense, even if everything went well. She suggested that they return in the early evening. The two doctors left, satisfied that their father was going to survive all of this. Jennifer was upset that she had come all that way and not been able to see her husband, but accepted their suggestion. Jason was angry but recognized he couldn't do anything about it.

Ten hours later, the foursome returned. Jennifer spoke to the anonymous intercom and was told that she and one other could come in. Jason made it very clear that the one other was going to be him, even if he hadn't gone to medical school. Not wanting to go through a Jason rant like they had seen so many times in their many years together, the twins relented.

Jen had never been in an ICU. Jason had the experience of his mother's death and the meningitis of his first child, so had enough familiarity with very sick people to be able to act as if he understood. They walked into Fred's small electronically-rich room. A young chestnut-haired nurse in scrubs was at his bedside. "Look who's come in, Freddy! Your first visitors."

"He doesn't like to be called Freddy," said his wife. "Perhaps Mr. Klein would be more appropriate considering the circumstances." The nurse did not ask which of the circumstances she meant, but nodded affirmatively.

"Who is it? Is that you, Barbara? I can't find my glasses." He had not had glasses when he was brought in to the ER. They presumably had been lost during the events at the bar. His vision was bad enough without them that he could not distinguish one person from another.

"It's me. Jennifer. And Jason's with me. The other boys are out in the hall waiting their turn. May I give him a kiss?"

"Of course. We're not too worried about infections. Just make sure you use a hand cleaner or soap and water every time you come in."

Jennifer buzzed him on the cheek. "Hi honey. I'm sure glad you're OK. We were worried."

"Hey Dad. You're looking good – a whole lot better than I thought you'd look." Jason extended his hand to shake his father's. Only then did he notice that his father's arms were restrained.

"Your father has been pulling out his IVs and tugging at his urine catheter. We had to restrain him. We were afraid he'd go after his pacemaker wire and take it out too. As you can tell, he's still a bit confused."

"A bit? He thought I was his first wife. She's been dead for years."

"Let me get the doctor in here." Seconds later, a very young, very serious looking South Asian man in scrubs entered the room and offered his hand in welcome to both visitors. He didn't offer his name; his tag showed that both his first and last names were too long to pronounce, let alone remember. The well-traveled Jason rightly guessed that he was from Sri Lanka.

"Let's step out of the room for a minute." They moved in the direction of the nurses' station. "I don't like talking close to a patient when he's confused. Your husband is doing well – probably better than most people his age after suffering both a heart attack and bleeding around the brain. But he's not a young man. Elderly people, when they are hospitalized, especially after big surgeries or trauma, or in his case, both, get confused. It's almost surely something that will get better. But for the present time, keep your visits short and don't expect to have any meaningful discussions with him. He's not going to remember any of this. But come by as often as you can. The more people that he sees that he knows, the faster the confusion will clear up."

"How long will he be here?" asked Jason. He had to get back to LA as soon as possible. He had to prepare for the closing on the finances of a blockbuster movie but didn't want to look like he didn't care about his father.

"It's impossible to say. Usually, the confusion clears up in a day or two and shouldn't leave him with any long term mental problems. But he'll need to get a permanent pacemaker. Because of the heart attack, his heart can't beat often enough on its own. That's really nothing big. Millions of people have pacemakers."

"Thank you Doctor," Jason said. "Perhaps you know that my father has some, shall we say, legal problems."

"Yes, everybody here in the ICU knows about that."

"What does this mean for him in the future? Will he be able to tolerate a trial? Will he be able to be taken care of if he has to go to jail?"

"I'm sorry, sir. I cannot answer those questions. You'll need to talk to somebody who knows a lot more about such things. I'm only an intensive care resident. We don't deal with what happens after our patients leave the unit. Incidentally, a few hours before you came in, somebody who says he was your father's friend asked to come in to see him, but wasn't allowed because he wasn't a member of your family. We asked for his name but he left without telling us who he was. If you know who it was, please offer our apologies. We only let in immediate family."

"My father has lots of friends. Probably one of the guys he plays poker with. I'm sure we'll find out who it was when we get home."

As Jason exited the unit, Jennifer returned to the bedside. "I love you Fred. Get better fast, OK?" The patient had fallen asleep and showed no sign of having heard what she said.

The twins were allowed in and heard the similar though medically-specific description of his condition from the nurse and prognosis from the doctor. They were impressed by the quality of the care in the public hospital. They had expected worse.

When the four arrived back at the big house in the Heights, there was, among many others, a recorded message from Maggie, telling them to look at SFGate, the *Chronicle's* on-line service.

FRED KLEIN HOSPITALIZED FOR HEART ATTACK AND HEAD INJURY
PHILANTHROPIST, ALLEGED FELON, ON CRITICAL LIST

Noted San Francisco philanthropist Fred Klein, out on bail for allegedly having driven the hit and run vehicle that killed Teresa Spencer, two-year-old, is in critical condition in the intensive care unit of San Francisco General Hospital. Unconfirmed reports have it that he was in a Tenderloin bar and fell to the ground, injuring his skull. There were reports of a verbal conflict between Klein and four young men before the fall, but no evidence of a physical fight. He was operated on by the hospital's nationally famous neurosurgical trauma team. He was also discovered to have had a heart attack, but the association of the fall and the heart attack are not known at this time. His condition is critical, but according to a hospital spokesman, he is expected to survive.

Klein is well known as the one-time owner of television station KLAT in Los Angeles and is presently active in a host of cultural and Jewish charities in the Bay Area where he has lived for 15 years. In 2003, he was an unsuccessful candidate for County Supervisor in the district that includes his mansion in Pacific Heights.

Ms. Spencer was 28 years old and married to wealthy venture capitalist, Mark Spencer of Cow Hollow in San Francisco, who was reportedly on a business trip in West Africa when his wife died. The Spencer's two-year-old daughter Meagan was in the car with her mother at the time of the accident, but was not injured.

Between paragraphs, there were two pictures, one of Fred and Jennifer as seen at the recent Black and White Ball, a fund raiser for the SF Symphony, and one of Teresa, probably a wedding photo. Teresa was beautiful; Fred was not particularly handsome.

"Wouldn't you know that they'd bring up the fact that Dad's Jewish?" snarled Jason. "That's not going to make him any more popular in Pacific Heights. Just like with the blacks, any time a Jew is involved in something terrible, shit comes down on all of us."

"Come on, Jason, lighten up. This is San Francisco, not Houston or Atlanta," responded Robert, with an approving nod from Phillip. Internecine verbal battles in the Klein household almost invariably found the twins on one side and the eldest son on the other.

Frequently, Jennifer took a mediator role, as had her predecessor, Barbara. "Come on guys; let's not worry about this stuff. We've got bigger things to figure out than whether your father's Jewishness is going to cause him and us trouble."

Mark Spencer also had big things to figure out. He'd need to work out child care, including someone to be in the house when he took work trips. They'd have to decrease in frequency and duration, probably to almost zero, but no way could he not travel at all. He made his reputation by finding jewels in shitholes. Who else could they send to the Ivory Coast or Uzbekistan or Cambodia to find the product, and then corner the market on ores, lumber, fruits, and berries? He'd need to find a lawyer to sue the bastard that made him a widower. He'd need to learn something about how to run the house. He knew that he couldn't tell the difference between the washer and the dryer – he knew only that what Teresa had called the laundry room had two large white boxes that disturbed his TV watching when they were running. But first he had to bury his wife.

The autopsy, required by law in such a case, had shown nothing abnormal except the skull fracture and massive brain contusion resulting from the collision with the concrete curb. Her arteries were clear, her liver shiny and her heart strong and fat-free. Her body was picked up by whichever mortuary was on call that night as neither Jack nor Maggie had any reason to pick one over another. Mark and Teresa had never discussed what the other should do if one died unexpectedly. They were young, prime of life, why talk about such depressing things?

So, Mark had to make decisions without any guidelines from the deceased. Catholic or non-sectarian? Burial or cremation? Open or closed? Who'd come? When? Where? Why? Why? Why?

Both Mark and Teresa had been brought up Catholic, she more Catholic than he. She went through the catechism; he, as a child, attended mass at Easter and Christmas and when grandparents were in town. Both, upon leaving home for college, a non-Catholic one, severed any meaningful relationship with their Church. They were married by a priest, at the insistence of Teresa's parents, but didn't see the inside of a house of the Lord again until Meagan's baptism. They grew no closer to the church afterwards, although they planned to give their daughter a Catholic education. Mark, after deliberation and discussions with his in-laws, his lawyer and his accountant, opted against a funeral in the neighborhood church. He didn't want a full-fledged funeral with a mortician. Instead, he chose cremation and a memorial service. He had never heard his wife utter the word cremation and assumed therefore that she would not object. Plus, these choices spared him the grief of a visitation and a religious ceremony with prayers with which most of his friends and business associates, Protestants, Jews, and Atheists, would not be familiar. The date and place for the service were published in the short obituary in the *Chronicle*, written by Maggie with the approval of the widower. Neither noticed a brief report in the local news section of the same day's paper describing the slow but steady improvement of alleged felon Fred Klein.

The event occurred three days after Mark's return to California. He expected a handful of acquaintances and associates, plus a few relatives from both sides. Her parents weren't coming as her mother had advanced Alzheimer's and was housed in a skilled nursing facility and her father had died, ironically, in an auto accident during a South Dakota ice storm ten years ago. His parents, in their eighties, begged off due to the difficulties of getting to San Francisco from the family farmhouse in Nebraska where they did everything possible to keep one another out of a nursing home. Two of Mark's five siblings came. Some of the others sent flowers. Four of the five had never moved out of central Nebraska; the fifth had taken his wife and military pension and moved to Acapulco. Mark had no real friends. He knew most everybody and most everybody knew him; some liked him, a few disliked him; most had no opinion – such is the plight of the nouveau riche.

In spite of the lack of relatives and friends, the mortuary's great room was jammed. The memorial service for Teresa Jane Spencer had become a political event of importance. The event was noted on the front page of the Bay Area section of the *Chronicle*. Mothers Against Drunk Driving mentioned it in a brochure although there was no public evidence that Klein had been drinking. The Mayor was touring Mongolia, whose capital Ulan Bator is a sister city of San Francisco, but he sent the Vice Mayor and three of his young, politically aspiring staff. Four members of the Board of Supervisors attended as did the CEOs of more than a dozen non-profits and profit-making corporations. The *Chronicle* and the *Examiner*, the *Oakland Tribune* and the *San Jose Mercury News* all sent reporters and photographers. Among the attendees were several who knew both Mr. Klein and Mr. Spencer. Present were two of the poker players who had, five evenings earlier, noted the strange behavior of their buddy Fred. They were investors with the financially astute but emotionally distant Mark.

Teresa's body had been cremated earlier in the day. Her ashes were deposited in an expensive yellow ceramic urn on a Victorian table directly in front of the podium from which Maggie delivered a moving, tear jerking, laugh provoking, and lengthy eulogy. Her sister's life had been all too short and, frankly, uneventful for a long eulogy, but Maggie made the most of their early sisterhood and Teri's (called that only by first degree relatives) hi-jinx in high school and community college. She praised Mark to the skies, telling the assembled what a wonderful father he had been and would surely continue to be. A line of photos showing the deceased from her birth to the birth of her only child proved to all that she had been a staggeringly handsome woman. Mark still hadn't cried.

On the Mend

As reported in the short *Chronicle* blurb, Fred was on the mend. A permanent pacemaker had replaced the temporary one; there was no expectation that his rhythm would revert to normal on its own. The pressure in the brain cavity had remained low for two days so the drainage tube could be removed. He was able to transfer, with helpers, to a lounger at the side of the bed and even took steps around the room. His bladder catheter made frequent trips to the toilet unnecessary; a bowel movement was greeted by the caregivers like a present from Santa. On the negative side of the ledger, his brain, though bathed in low pressure uninfected fluid, wasn't working so well. He could talk and all the words were enunciated in his usual educated manner, but strung together they didn't make much sense. He had gotten over thinking wife two was wife one and recognized each of his sons. The twins came in at least daily, never at the same time for fear that their identicality would confuse their father; first-born Jason had returned to LA for his signings. The wives of Robert and Phillip brought cookies and magazines; Jason's Emily did not set foot in the hospital. Fred had never before been an avid TV watcher, in spite of his fortune having been made in the industry. In his private room on the neurosurgical ward, he was usually found by his family, glued to sitcoms, cop shows or baseball. But he was not capable of discussing present day reality. He had no recollection of the events of the days leading up to his hospitalization. Why am I here? Who is Irv Greenberg? Who is Teresa Spencer? Jail. Me. Never. His ultra-short term memory was fine. He could name the killer and victim in the thriller he had just seen. After a Giants game, he could talk garbledly of the relative merits of the present center fielder and Willy Mays. His long term memory was fine; he remembered well his middle school teachers from the Lower East Side. His recent term memory was anything but fine.

The Iranian neurologist who had followed Klein's case after the evacuation of the hematoma told the family that it could take up to six months for full recovery and, even then, he may not be the intellect that he had been before the trauma. The Vietnamese psychologist who oversaw a battery of tests identified the temporal lobe as the area of damage – something that was diagnosable as soon as he had his CT scan in the emergency room. The Latvian physiotherapist prescribed a series of exercises to help him with mobility and marched with him through the vast halls of the General Hospital, while the Argentine occupational therapist sat with him as he attempted to assemble a thousand piece puzzle of the Grand Canyon.

Medicare pays hospitals a flat sum for a patient's stay based on that patient's diagnosis. In other words, the facility usually gets the same amount of money from a patient who comes in with a heart attack plus a subdural hematoma if that patient remains in the hospital for three weeks or dies on day one. The doctors and the ancillary therapists are paid by the visit, but the vast amounts of nursing care, the X-rays, the lab tests and the social worker are all part of the global fee offered by the US Government for the specific diagnosis. Given this system, Klein was not a great patient for the General Hospital's bottom line. He was utilizing a massive amount of resources. Ideally, he'd have been discharged within a week, but the combination of his substantial wealth and his fame and infamy made it difficult to go against the wishes of the family, especially Jennifer, to keep him in. Furthermore, there was nobody who identified him- or herself as "his doctor." He had the neurologist, the neurosurgeon, the cardiologist, the internist and the urologist, but not the doctor. Klein's generalist, Allison Jamison, had not visited. Nobody called her, so unless she read the papers and listened to the radio, she might not know anything about it. No one was willing to force the issue and say, "He's gotten all he can out of being an in-patient." The social worker offered the suggestion of a skilled nursing facility for rehabilitation. Jennifer approved and the sons didn't object. But to Fred, a SNF meant a rest home and he vividly remembered the disgusting odor of the repulsive edifice that housed his mother during the last four years of her life. "No." An attempt to have him distinguish a place for rehab from a place for death preparation was unsuccessful; success would have required better cognitive function.

Some two weeks into his hospitalization, three lawyers, all in dark suits, entered his hospital room simultaneously. Fred recognized his friend, Art Schofield and his son, Jason, who had come up from LA for the meeting. The third man, he'd swear that he'd never laid eyes on, was his criminal attorney, Irving Greenberg.

"Jason, great to see you, finally. How'd you know I was in this place?"

"I was here when you had your surgery. I was staying with the twins at your house when the police didn't know where you were. Then, Dad, I had to go home to LA – I'm involved in a new film project."

"What the hell do you mean I didn't know where I was? I knew damn well where I was. I was playing poker with this SOB," he mumbled, pointing at Schofield. "Who's your friend with the expensive suit?"

"I'm Irv Greenberg, your criminal attorney. Don't you remember meeting me when you were bailed out of jail?"

"Nope, don't remember a thing about that. Jennifer – she's my wife – she told me that I had been arrested for killing somebody with my car. I've got no memory – none at all – about such a thing. Am I going to prison?"

"That's what I'm here for, Fred," said Greenberg. "The DA has a pretty good case against you. You know that you admitted hitting somebody and leaving the scene of the accident."

"Huh. I did? And he died?"

"She, not he. She was a young mother who was married to a very wealthy man – Spencer by name. There's a lot going on in the media and they're yelling for your scalp. There was a big funeral last week with lots of politicos and reporters there. Even the mayor said something about making sure you spent a long time in jail – and he wasn't even in town."

"Yeah, the mayor. He's a good friend of mine. He put me on that committee – you know I was president of the board. I gave him a lot of money when he ran."

"Yes, you did, Dad."

"So, why does he want me in jail?"

"It's all politics, Dad. You don't make any friends when you take the sides of an old rich guy who has accidentally killed the mother of a two-year-old and then left the scene. There's talk that you might have had too much to drink."

"I'm no drunk. I never drove when I had been drinking more than a glass or two of wine. That's bullshit! But I killed somebody, huh?"

"Yes, you did, Dad."

"I'm tired. Thanks for your visit. I'm gonna take a nap."

Schofield suggested that the three have coffee in the hospital cafeteria. He started the conversation, "I'm no criminal lawyer, but it seems pretty obvious that our client is in no shape to have anything to do with his defense, right, Irv?"

"For sure. I had no idea how bad his mind was until just now. He'd be no more able to defend himself than a four-year-old would. And, there's no certainty that this will ever change. I talked to a neurologist who I've put on the stand a bunch of times and he tells me that predicting the amount of improvement an old person with a head injury might have is a fruitless effort. He could be back to normal in a month, or he could spend the rest of his life confused like he is now."

"So, where do we go from here?" asked Jason.

"I'll call the DA's office and let them know what's up. They're under a lot of pressure to get this case to trial, or at least get a plea which puts your father in jail for minimum of a few years."

"You can't plead out a confused old man who just had his brain operated on, can you?" chimed in Schofield.

"Of course I can't. Can you imagine putting somebody who doesn't remember that he was involved in a crime into jail for that crime? It won't happen. But we've got to let the DA see our patient. They have to make sure that he really is disabled. Too often accused criminals, especially white collar ones, act like they've lost their mind to get off. This isn't your usual case of mental competence where the perp is the same guy before and after the crime. Here, our guy was obviously fine before, out of it after.

"He's supposed to go to court for a preliminary hearing in three weeks. The first thing I'll do is request a continuance. Again, that'll take a visit from the DA to see Fred before they'll buy into it."

Going Home

"I miss you so much! It's been a month. Can't we meet, at least for a drink? I know I can't come to your house, but maybe at the Clift?"

"Ernesto, you know that I want to see you. I miss you too, but it can't happen. We get dozens of calls. Reporters phone and even come to the house. Sometimes I think I'm being followed."

"Why the hell would anybody follow you?"

"God, I don't know. You've seen the papers. I don't think there's been a day since Fred was involved in his accident that there hasn't been something in one of the papers or on TV. Just think of what would happen if one of them found out that you and I were fucking."

"Who said anything about fucking? I just want to see you...and talk to you. Let's meet downtown this afternoon."

"No, my love, it's not going to work now. Later, maybe."

"When?"

"After this settles down. Fred's coming home in a couple of days. He's not making any sense still. The hemorrhage caused him to lose his memory."

"It could be months before it settles down. I can't wait that long."

"You're just going to have to. I'm so sorry."

Ernesto hung up, saying no more.

Klein was finally released from General Hospital, almost a month from his ER appearance as John Doe. The neurologist who OK'd his discharge suggested an ambulance to get him home; the discharge planner, a social worker agreed, but Klein refused. "Hell no. Goddam ambulances cost a mint. One of my sons can pick me up."

"Your insurance will pay for the ambulance. No need to worry."

"I told you, I'm not riding in any ambulance. I don't want my neighbors to think I'm an invalid. I'm just fine. I've got a huge house on Jackson Street. This pacemaker will keep me going 'til I'm a hundred."

"All right, Mr. Klein, whatever you say. I'll call your home to make sure somebody comes over tomorrow – they've got to be here by 9 AM."

"I'll make sure they are here by 8. Get them on the phone for me. I don't remember the number."

The twins and Jennifer all showed up in Fred's room well before 8.

"Let's get you out of here, Dad," said one of the boys. Jennifer had chosen an appropriate traveling outfit for her husband – oversized aqua polo shirt, black lounge pants with a white streak down the legs, flip-flops and an orange and black Giants baseball cap. "Where do we sign out for Mr. Klein in 212?" Robert asked the charge nurse. He had a sense, having had years of hospital experience, that this might not be as easy as it should be.

"He can go as soon as we get an order from his doctor. He should be here any minute," she answered, not looking up from the medical record on which she was charting the vital signs of another patient. Robert had plenty of experience in the matter of signing the discharge order. Teaching hospitals, like San Francisco General, are highly demanding of the time of their attending physicians, the ones who are in charge of deciding who gets to go home and when. They teach, they round, they operate, they schmooze. "He should be here any minute," is a comment that rarely has any relationship to the facts.

Eight AM came and went. So did nine AM and nine-thirty. Fred showed no evidence of knowing what time it was. He showed no concern. Jennifer had total respect for the medical profession and was sure that whatever was holding up the attending from getting to the floor to write the order must be much more important than this. The twins, radiologist and gastroenterologist, were pissed off. "I know damn well that he could just call in the order or send one of the residents. I wish that I had privileges here – I'd write the order myself."

"We could just sign out AMA (against medical advice)," said Phillip who himself wrote discharge orders almost every day and made a point of not making his patients wait – that is unless he had a polyp to remove or an esophagus to scope.

"I don't think it would be a good idea to do that. Your father isn't just an ordinary patient. We don't want the *Chronicle* to write that he violated a hospital regulation."

"You're right, Jen. We'll just have to wait. I've got an office full of patients in the Berkeley office this afternoon – I may have to leave before the doc even gets here."

"That's OK Phil," said Robert. "I can stay with Jen – I can always read films later – my partners can cover my special procedures." Jennifer never stopped being amazed by how the twin boys cooperated with one another and how poorly both got along with Jason.

A twenty-something Latina first-year resident finally arrived in Fred's room shortly after 10. She made a cursory apology, without an exculpatory explanation. She had heard from the nurses that there was anger, at least among the medical professionals in the room with the famous patient. Ignoring the anger, she went down the discharge plans. She could offer nothing prognostically not already known by the family. She listed the medicines that he was to take at home. Pain pills – only if needed. Stool softeners – only if you take the pain pills. Multi-vitamins. Statins to keep your cholesterol down – you don't want to have another heart attack. Sleeping pills.

"How about giving me some Viagras, doc?"

She blushed. So did Jennifer. "Your doctor didn't mention them. Maybe you better ask him that when you come in for follow up. And that reminds me – you've got to call and set up appointments with the cardiologist in one week, the neurologist in about ten days, and the neurosurgeon in a month – he wants to check the scar. And be sure to go see your primary care person sometime. We have Dr. Jameson down as your primary. I don't know him."

"Her, not him," injected Jennifer.

"Any questions for me before I go – they need me in Emergency." She was out the door before any question could be asked.

A three-hundred pound orderly pushed a wheel chair into the room. He had only one hand – the other was absent with the left forearm being half of its normal length. "My name is Oumar. I am here to escort you to your automobile. Might I carry your valise? Do you have your medications?" he asked in a West African accent.

The family was impressed by his demeanor, his vocabulary and his willingness to carry a valise and push a wheel chair with a single hand. "Where are you from, sir?" asked Robert.

"I'm from Sierra Leone – I was a surgeon there, but my license isn't accepted here – I'd have to go through my training all over again. Plus, I don't think I'd be a very good surgeon with only one hand."

"I don't need any goddam wheel chair," blurted out the now discharged patient. "I can walk just fine. Why else did I pay for all those physical therapy treatments?"

"It's policy, Mr. Klein. Everybody who comes in here goes out in a wheel chair. I know that you can walk perfectly well – probably faster than me. Please sit down here."

"You didn't have to pay for your physical therapy, Dad. Medicare pays for it – it's all part of the bill." Klein sat in the chair.

Jennifer had gone down to the parking lot to get the Lexus, pulling it up to the passenger loading area outside the ER.

"How'd that dent get there?" asked Fred as he was loaded into the back seat on the right.

Tonic Water and a Slice of Lime

The Redwood Room at the Clift Hotel in downtown San Francisco is as close to New York as anything in California. Smoke free and thirteen bucks for well drinks – Johnny Walker Black, Bombay, and Remy Martin.

Ernesto Contreras finally convinced Jennifer Klein that the time had come for them to get back together. It had been two months since Fred had returned home; he had become accustomed to the full-time Filipinas and no longer put up a stink when Jennifer would leave the house to shop or go to the gym or visit with a girlfriend. He was fairly mobile, having developed the skills necessary to get around with his walker.

Ernesto and Jennifer had never had any embarrassing encounters at the Clift in the dozens of times they had reconnoitered at the up-market Geary Street establishment. They had their own favorite obscure corner table next to the kitchen entrance - refused, for traffic reasons, by most patrons and therefore nearly always available. Jennifer would always sit with her back to the room; she was far more likely to be recognized than he. Not once in the three years that The Clift was their first choice in meeting places had they seen anyone that they knew, and no evidence ever surfaced that they had been unknowingly seen. The closest they had ever come to discovery happened shortly after they stepped up to the Clift from a sleazy place in Chinatown. As the lovers were leaving the main door of the hotel, the husband of one of her neighbor friends was entering. She could tell he knew that he knew her, but probably didn't know from where. He said hello, she did the same and both went their own ways. Thereafter, she and Ernesto made sure that they entered and left the hotel, and the bar, separately.

The last time they had been together was a Tuesday, ten days before the felony and eight before Ernesto had been the designated-caller of emergency rooms. For the next two months he had persisted in his pleas to rekindle their affair. She declined, not out of lack of desire, but out of guilt and fear. Guilt for obvious reasons, fear for something ending up in the paper. Before her husband's accession to infamy, she recognized that the worst that could happen was that Fred would learn of her adultery. That she could handle; he never said anything to make her think that their gap in ages was not considered by him a free pass to an occasional tryst. He hadn't said "Go for it." But he had not said not to. But Fred Klein had become a Bay Area household name. Discovery of spousal infidelity would be headline stuff. Early on in adulthood, Jen would have loved to be famous. But she couldn't sing and couldn't dance and, while attractive enough, was no Marilyn Monroe. She did a course at City College in acting, and got an A: the teacher offered no real encouragement, favoring others, so Jen did not enroll in Acting II. She gave up the quest for fame some years ago; she now feared it.

Eventually, Ernesto's persistence paid off and Jennifer accepted a date at the Redwood Room. "Let's get there early so our table is empty."

It was empty. In fact, only a handful of the two dozen tables was occupied. The maître d' knew them from earlier meetings, but said nothing about how good it was to see them back after the long absence. He took them to their accustomed perches although there were many better tables available. Jennifer tipped handsomely.

Their usual afternoon waitperson approached the table, using no names. "One Tanqueray and tonic and one Sam Adams draught, I presume?"

Contreras nodded affirmatively to the offer of beer. Mrs. Klein said, "No, just bring me a tonic with a slice of lime."

"Huh?" queried Ernesto.

"I don't drink anymore outside my house, unless someone else is going to drive me home. One criminal in the household is enough."

"Next time I'll drive you home."

"Right," snickered Jennifer. "How will I get here? I'm not about to take a bus. When I leave the house, Fred knows how I go - my car, or someone else's. He may not remember but he is getting better. He's going to be asking questions soon and I don't want any that I can't answer."

"How about, 'who were you with?'"

"I don't get that one. As I've told you a hundred times, I think he's OK with me sowing oats, as long as he doesn't know where they are sown and with what farmer."

"Speaking of sex, I've made a reservation upstairs. This is a pretty special occasion, getting back together after all that time apart." Special occasions like birthdays and Christmas had in the past, been excuses for booking a room in the elegant hotel, to be paid for by the Klein millions but covered by the Contreras Master Card. They'd square up with cash.

"No, my dear. It's too early for that. I'd love to go to bed with you. But I've got a disabled husband at home. I can't do it."

"You said he was OK with that."

"He was OK with it, but that was before brain damage. He may get back to where he was before, but until then, I'm not going to cheat on him."

Ernesto came as close to pouting as she had ever seen, but said nothing other than, "All right." After the drinks arrived, she told him about the little bit of progress made by her husband, plus the inadequacies of the care givers and the attentiveness or lack thereof shown by the three sons and their families. Gradually, the tension of the renewal of the relationship subsided and the two long-time companions lapsed into their meaningful meaningless discussions that kept them together for nearly two decades. They held hands above the table, comingled feet below.

Ten minutes later, that comfort was interrupted. "Jennifer, my love, don't turn around."

"Why, who's there?"

"I'm not sure, but I think it's one of your stepsons. The older one maybe." Ernesto had never met any of her step family, but she was incessant about taking out her smart phone whenever they were together.

Philanthropist

She would document her stories with photos, so he had seen pictures of each of the family members multiple times. As Jason and his crew were the object of more stories than the other siblings combined, he was the easiest to remember.

Jason Klein, Esq., had indeed entered the bar, with two men, both older than he and both dressed like he was – dark suit, blue button-down, power tie. They had to be fellow members of the California bar. Jennifer used the full range of motion of her eye muscles to identify her stepson out of the side of her eyes. "Oh, shit," she mouthed. Jason, et al., were seated at a table no more than ten feet from her plush chair. He had taken the seat facing the entrance to the room so that he didn't look directly on her table, nor did he look directly away. All it would take was a single ninety degree twist of the neck to the left for him to have his stepmother in his direct line of sight. Were she to go to the ladies' or were she and Ernesto to get up and leave the establishment, there would be no way for her to not be noticed. "Oh, shit," she repeated silently. Her best bet was for him to require a trip to the men's.

The lovers, who had role-played a couple of times for their unlikely discovery by friends or family, talked stocks. Ernesto was the broker, Jennifer the client. They spoke softly, but not so soft that drinkers at neighbor tables could not, if they paid any attention to the handsome Latin and his female friend, avoid hearing that the discussion centered on equities. "Should I sell the Amazon?" "...index funds?" "... ETFs?" "...long term capital gains?" Jennifer knew more about the subject than did Ernesto, so the more audible comments came from her. He mostly nodded or uttered single word affirmative responses.

Half an hour went by. Jason showed no evidence of a full bladder or sticky hands. He remained seated, involved in often heated negotiations with his colleagues. To Jennifer's knowledge, he had not seen her and had not heard enough of her voice to pick up on the fact that the wife of his father was ten feet away. She and Ernesto had no pieces of paper that they could pass back and forth to suggest that their reason for being there was strictly business. They could only mention specific publicly traded companies so often before it became ridiculous. They had to escape; their antagonist wasn't showing any sign of wrapping up his conference. They waited until one of the unknown lawyers handed Jason a thick document which he started to peruse, at which point they stood up, aiming themselves toward the front of the barroom.

"Your check, sir." The waiter had come out of the kitchen and saw his customers leaving, having not requested a bill. He had known them for as long as he'd had his job and assumed they just forgot.

"We were going to pay up front," responded Ernesto.

"No problem, Mr. Contreras."

Jason looked up from the hefty document. "Jennifer, is that you?"

"Oh, hi, Jason. I didn't know you were in town." Jason had not announced his arrival to his father or stepmother or brothers. He didn't want to have to try to talk to his father. It had been hard enough to have a discussion with him before the brain damage. Since Fred's episode, he was even more willing than before to tell his first born how much he didn't like his wife and kids. In the weeks since Fred had been home from the hospital, this was Jason's third trip to San Francisco, two of which were unannounced.

"I'm just up for the day – I've got to prepare for a couple of depositions. Meet my colleagues." The two men, both more than six foot two, stood.

"This is my stockbroker, Ernesto Contreras." Hands were shaken all around.

"Good to meet you, Ernie. Who do you work for? One of the bigs?"

The two hadn't role-played anything to do with brokerages and Contreras was no expert on the field. In fact, the only name he could come up with was one from a TV commercial that he remembered fondly. "EF Hutton." Jennifer cringed.

"I thought they were long gone," Jason responded. "Didn't they get taken up by Citigroup and then became part of Smith Barney and then Morgan Stanley?"

"You're right. I'm with Morgan Stanley, but there are still a few of us from the old Hutton days that can't give up the name."

"Can't believe that the Morgan Stanley guys would be very happy you advertising yourself as a part of a failed company like EFH."

"Yeah, true. I got to get over that."

"Got any hot tips, Ernie?"

"Come on, Jason, you know he can't do that. You're not a client." Jen was barely able to hide her anger.

"No, no hot tips. I'm an index fund guy."

"You can't make any money selling index funds. No commissions there."

"Ernesto and I have to leave. Your Dad was having a pretty good day and I want to see if there's been any more progress. Shall I tell him you might come over?"

"No, don't mention that I'm here. He might get upset. And we sure don't want to upset my father, do we?"

Ernesto and Jennifer headed to the bar to pay the bill. Jason called his stepmother back out of the others' earshot. "Do you always hold hands with your stockbroker, Jen?"

Fred had been home a bit more than a month. A hospital bed had been rented and a staff of care-givers hired. The former had all the electronic answers to modern ergonomics and the latter were all from the Philippine Islands. A physical therapist made twice weekly visits. An occupational therapist came once as did a speech therapist. Visiting RNs came every other day, although they did little more than check the pulse, monitor the blood pressure and examine the now-healed incisions on the head and the chest. A wheel chair had been waiting for him on his arrival but he had not spent a single second on it. He did use his 4-wheeled walker. His in-hospital therapy had been successful; he and his family prided themselves on his ability to get to the bathroom, the dining room and the TV room, where he continued to watch intently his sitcoms and cop shows. He had become a walking, talking TV Guide. He watched far more programming than he did when he was CEO of KLAT. "Hurry up," he'd say as he finished dinner. "CSI is about to start. It's a new one."

One afternoon, in his second week at home, the doorbell rang at a time when no professional was expected. Jen was fairly certain that it wasn't one of his friends – none, except life-long alter ego Art Schofield, had visited since the episode(s), either at the hospital or at home. She was not expecting anything from FedEx or UPS.

Upon opening the front door, she saw two unknown people, a very tall African-American male and a very short Asian female. Both were dressed as if they were going to church in the 50s. "Hello, said the woman and she and the man offered their photo IDs. "I am Katherine Ng, assistant District Attorney and this is my aide, Mr. Carson. We are here to interview Mr. Frederick Klein. Are you related to him? His daughter perhaps?"

"I am Jennifer Klein, his wife, thank you." The tone of the thank you made it clear that she was not happy with Ms. Ng's guess.

"My apologies, Ms. Klein. You look so young. May we come in?" Seeing no immediate reasons not to let them enter, she motioned them into the living room where they were seated on the antique chenille-covered loveseat that Jennifer had recently purchased at an estate sale.

"I have spoken to Mr. Klein's attorney, Mr. Greenberg and he told me that it would be OK to come over and interview your husband without him – Mr. Greenberg, that is – being here. Our only purpose is to determine whether he would be capable of partaking in a trial, or whether legal proceedings should be placed on hold while he recovers from his surgery. There will be no fact finding in terms of his recollections of the automobile accident. Mr. Carson is trained in psychology; he will be asking most of the questions."

"In all due respect Ms. Ng, I'd prefer to hear that this is OK from Mr. Greenberg himself." Jennifer, miffed, went to the kitchen and called the office. To her surprise, he was not only in the office, but available to take her call. She explained the situation.

"Don't let them see him until I get over! I did not tell that little twerp that she could do that without somebody being there. I did say that it didn't have to be me – just someone from the office. I knew that they'd send over a rookie – I guess that's good news – we're not up against the first team, at least not yet. But I better come over rather than make them come back later. We don't want to piss 'em off. Have them wait for me – I'll get there in 45 minutes."

Jennifer came back from the kitchen with a short stack of magazines, mainly Rolling Stone and House Beautiful, setting them in front of the visitors and telling them they had to wait until the attorney arrived. Ng's expression showed her unhappiness but she made no comment. She took her Blackberry from her purse and pushed buttons. Carson scouted the room, looking at the 20 or so paintings and prints on the wall and the books on the shelves. He picked up and examined knick-knacks off tables and display cases, careful to return them safely to their original positions. Jennifer returned to the TV room to sit with Fred as he finished with Seinfeld and launched into Fraser.

Greenberg rang the bell half an hour after he had hung up from his call from Jennifer. "Amazing – there was an empty space right across the street. Where are the people from the DA's office?" To Jen's great surprise, the distinguished barrister appeared in Levis and a Grateful Dead T-shirt. She escorted him into the living room where Ng was thumbing a text and Carson was looking at the bottom of a piece of English silver to determine its place and date of origin. Introductions were made; Ng and Greenberg had never met but had talked on the phone to deal with the issue of Klein's competency. Carson explained his role and his educational bona fides. At Greenberg's request, Ms. Klein brought Mr. Klein into the living room without the aid of his walker, gently holding his right arm to guard against a fall.

"Please proceed Ms. Ng, but remember our agreement that you will not ask questions about the episode."

"I do remember, Mr. Greenberg. Mr. Carson will be asking most of the questions. Do you have any objections to our using this recorder?"

"Indeed, I do. You can take notes, but nothing is to be recorded."

"OK." She wasn't really sure why she couldn't make a permanent record but didn't want to embarrass herself by asking. This was her first big case since graduation from the University of San Francisco law school in the middle of her class.

"Good morning, Mr. Klein. My name is Johnny Carson. I work with the District Attorney's office and am going to ask you a few questions. Will that be all right?"

"No problemo. Johnny Carson, huh? Any relation?"

"No relation. That's not the first time I've been asked that. Tell me about yourself, sir."

"What do you mean? Where I was born, my parents?"

"Whatever you want to tell me."

"I'm from New York – the City. My Dad was in music. I went to CCNY then Columbia then Stanford. Got my MBA here and ended up owning a TV station – Latino station. Sold it and have lived off the profits since. Married twice. First wife died of cancer then I married this beautiful young woman – same age as my kids. Got three kids, all boys and a bunch of grandkids."

"How many grandchildren?"

"Uh…three or four. How many, dear?"

"You have five grandchildren my love, two in Berkeley, one in San Francisco, and two in LA."

"Yeah, right – five. Yeah, one of them has Down's. But he counts too."

"What do you do to keep busy? Got any hobbies? Do you work?"

"No, living off the profits. I trade stocks – or at least I used to trade stocks. Did real well in the 80s and 90s – no need to work anymore. I'm on some boards – the mayor – what's his name? – appointed me."

"Hobbies?"

"I play the banjo and go dancing. Love to dance."

"My dear, you haven't taken me dancing since our wedding day. And you got rid of that banjo when Barbara got sick."

"I did – why did I do that? I play a pretty mean banjo."

Carson continued. "How old are you Mr. Klein?"

"Hell, I can never remember that. 77 maybe?"

"You just turned 76, dear. Don't rush it." said his wife.

"What is your birth date?"

"March 6," he answered. Jen nodded.

"What are the names of your children?"

"The eldest is Jason. The others are twins. But their names don't rhyme like most twins."

"Are your sons married? If so, what are their wives' names?"

"Jason is married to a Korean woman – not a very nice person. I like the other two wives – both Jewish."

"Are you Jewish, Mr. Klein?"

"Why do you ask? That's none of your business."

Katherine Ng chimed in, "I think we've asked enough questions. Mr. Carson and I have to get back to the office. Thank you very much, Mr. Klein. And you too, Ms. Klein. Mr. Greenberg – thank you for coming – I know you are a busy man." They headed for the door.

Carson stepped toward one wall on his way out. "Ms. Klein – is this an original Chagall?"

"Oh, it's just a print, but it's signed. Fred has had it for many years."

"Yes sir. I bought that in Geneva in 1964. Cost me sixty bucks."

"How did I do, Steve?" asked Klein.

"It's Irv, not Steve. You did just fine Fred," responded Greenberg."

"Oh yeah, Irv. Sorry. I had a high school buddy named Steve Greenberg. Big ladies' man. Made me jealous. So, am I going to have to go to jail?"

"Fred, I can't tell you anything now. You certainly aren't going to be behind bars any time soon." He turned toward Ms. Klein. "There's no way the DA could bring him to trial the way he is. They've got to put off the preliminary hearing. No doubt, he's better than he was when I saw him in the hospital, but no jury would ever convict someone who answers questions like he does now. My guess is that I hear from the DA himself, not his lackey, in the next day or two and he'll tell me that they want your husband to undergo a psychiatric exam in a few months to see if the improvement has gone far enough to proceed with the case. In the meantime, the case will cool down. We won't be seeing his name in the paper or hear about him on TV. That can only help our odds of a good outcome."

Fred broke into the conversation "Anybody know what time it is?"

"It's five 'til four, dear."

"Oh oh. I got to go back to the TV. Judge Judy is on at four. I got to get ready for my trial." He chuckled at his joke.

Three hours later, Greenberg called Jennifer to tell her that he had, as predicted, heard from the District Attorney in person and was told that the case was not being dropped, only postponed. Ng had obviously let him know that he had a loser of a case if he took it to trial with the defendant like he was today. And, obviously no judge would allow the case to proceed. But they figured there was a good chance that his cerebral function would improve with time. "And by the way, Counselor," the DA said in conclusion, "when the time does come for your client to see a shrink, don't give him acting lessons. The psychiatrist will see right through it."

"Mr. District Attorney, that comment was unnecessary." Greenberg had a reputation to keep. He was not about to portray an intact man as demented.

Megan Turns Three

Life in the Spencer house was taking on a routine. Five days a week, Meagan went to a pre-school three blocks from their home. Fortunate to have husbanded his income well, Mark could afford everyday help for the house and for his daughter. The nanny/housekeeper, Carmen, came via a recommendation from a client of his. She had been employed by the family for two years before they had been transferred to Singapore at the same time Mark Spencer sought domestic help. Born in Mexico, she had presented papers to her previous employers so Mark saw no reason for her to give him the same. He trusted her from the first moment she came to the house for an interview. The fact that she was strikingly handsome did not dissuade. Her English was accented but educated. She was hired immediately and had not disappointed. The house was cleaner than it had ever been under Teresa's supervision – his late wife had had help only one day per week and paid little attention to the details. Meagan took to Carmen straight away. A joyous child to begin with, her smiles became wider and her laughter more infectious. Carmen was always available when Mark had to spend the evening, or a day or two, out of the house. He compensated her well and bought her a reasonably new Toyota, paying for its gas, its upkeep and its insurance. Mark made no attempt to get to know about her personal life. He assumed that she was not attached and that she had very few interests other than reading and classical music, both of which she seemed to devour with deep devotion. Symphonies and concerti were a near constant when he came home and books, generally substantive paper backs, often lay open on a table.

    Mark's work was very much changed by his becoming a widower. Nearly all trips to faraway places like Ivory Coast were put on hold; he was able to mentor less experienced members of the firm on how to negotiate and close deals in developing nations, particularly those with autocratic leaders and sycophantic sidekicks. He devoted his greatest energies to deals close to home. Agriculture, as practiced in the third world was his specialty but robotics and nanotechnology tickled his fancy; he found ample opportunities for investing less than two hours' drive from the City, both south to Silicon Valley and north to Napa and environs. The future of robots and tiny things was not as certain as that of African cocoa beans but the major players were a whole lot easier to deal with. There was no concern about greasing palms. At least what greasing there was in the US was far less overt than that in the Southern Hemisphere. Spencer spent every weekend at home, priding himself on his previously unrefined skills as a father. He became competent in putting together meals fit for a toddler – mac and cheese, over-boiled string beans, yogurt and cinnamon toast. He learned the nutritional benefit of adding a couple of teaspoons of chocolate syrup to milk and thrilled his daughter at least once weekly with trips to the ice cream store.

Meagan was to turn three about four months after losing her mother. A party was required. Mark put himself in charge of making out a guest list. He delegated the real party planning to Carmen with Teresa's sister and niece, Maggie and Ashley, as unpaid consultants. The guests were drawn from other kids at the day care, three toddlers from the neighborhood that Carmen had met through their nannies, and a handful of children and grandchildren of his co-workers at the firm. Maggie ordered the cake and Ashley decorated the downstairs room that Mark and Teresa had identified as a playroom for their three planned children. All gathered on a Sunday afternoon – some fifteen kids and an equal number of adults came. Bob, the beagle, who Mark felt had become morose after the disappearance of the woman who had fed and walked him since puppyhood, perked up at the sudden appearance of a mass of people unlike he had seen in months. Carmen had arranged for the appearance of a clown to make balloons and take pratfalls to the delight of the youngsters.

As the children played and ate under the watchful eyes of Maggie and Ashley, most of the adults retired to the patio for wine and finger foods. The day was much nicer than Weather.com had predicted – mid-sixties, more sunny than cloudy and barely a touch of wind. All-purpose Carmen, having left the clown to entertain the children, kept the plates of hot hors d'oeuvres coming and the glasses of pinot, chardonnay, and pale ale freshened.

The grown-up discussion started with the future of the 49ers and the past of the Giants, the incompetence of the wildly leftish Board of Supervisors, the exorbitant cost of local houses, then the unpredictability of the Municipal Transit Authority. When that led to a lull in the discussion because no one at the table except the host had taken a bus ride in years, one of the fathers, clothed in tennis togs, turned to Mark and asked about the legal matters surrounding the death of Teresa.

"Nobody tells me anything," he said. "I used to learn about Klein's status by reading the paper, but there hasn't been anything in the *Chronicle* in weeks."

"Don't you have a lawyer? Aren't you going to sue the bastard?" asked a prematurely gray mother.

"Yes, I do have a lawyer – top personal injury guy named Sullivan – Harvard grad. But he told me to sit tight until the criminal case is resolved. He filed a case, but said we don't have to do anything until we hear what the criminal jury decides."

"That could take an eternity. From what I hear, his brain damage is pretty severe," responded the same mother. "You do know that they postponed his hearing, don't you?"

"Of course, that was the last thing I read in the paper. But I also heard that he is improving and that the doctors expect him to get back to the way he used to be. Then they could get the criminal proceedings going again."

"The way he used to be?" said a different father who looked like he belonged in a freshman seminar. "I sure hope that they take his license away from him. I don't want him killing anybody else." The others looked at him incredulously, saying nothing.

A pathologically thin mother with her arm in a sling asked Mark what he knew about Klein as a person.

"Not much. I've talked to people who know people who know him and he has a pretty good reputation as a generous contributor to a bunch of charities. But they also say he's a cheap bastard who gives lousy tips at all the best restaurants.

"I haven't told anybody this before, but I tried to see him in the hospital. I had gone to talk to the doctors that treated Teresa and he was in the ICU at General. They wouldn't let me in."

Another father, bald and previously silent, asked, "What were you going to do? Turn off his ventilator or yank out his IV?"

"I really don't know why I wanted to see him. But that's all I wanted – to look at him. I guess that I hoped to see him suffering. I certainly wasn't going to try to kill him although I really wanted his surgery to be unsuccessful. It wasn't. I never went back, although I probably could have gotten in his room once he was out of the ICU. I didn't want to talk to him or have him talk to me. Last thing I wanted was an apology from the shithead."

"Do you want one now?" asked the dad that had made the inappropriate comment about the license.

"What good would it do? She's dead and he's alive."

One of the other mothers, who had obviously had her child near the end of her prime breeding years as her hair was silver and her neck wrinkled, spoke up. "I know Ms. Klein, Jennifer, his wife. She and I were in the same book club for a while. I hate to say it, but I really like her. She's smart and she bakes great desserts. A couple of times, she hosted the group – she does a lemon bar to die for. I never met the husband."

That mother's husband, younger than she and wearing a bright yellow Caterpillar cap, said, "She's a real looker. She came over to our house once when I was home. I can't understand why she'd go for an old man like him. Then again, maybe I can. I hear he's loaded."

His wife responded, "She'd been married before to another rich guy. I don't think she needed more money. Maybe she loved him?"

"Uh-huh. Sure."

Philanthropist

The party lasted another hour after the clown departed. Presents were opened, a piñata was obliterated, candles were extinguished, and cake was cut and smeared on the children's faces. The families filed out to their SUVs or vans. Quiet returned to the Spencers'.

Carmen restored order from the post-party chaos. Meagan fell deeply asleep.

"Mr. Spencer, may I sit down and talk to you for a moment?" Carmen had never been so bold.

"Yes, of course." He assumed that she was either going to seek a raise, or say that she was quitting her job. As generous as her salary and perks were, her intelligence was such that she could well have been offered something much more meaningful and lucrative than her present position. Or maybe she was getting married. She had never discussed her private life with Mark. He did not know if she even had a boy- or girlfriend.

"Sir, I am sorry to say that I overheard some of your conversation when you were with the adults."

"That's no problem. We had nothing to hide. I can't ask you to cover your ears when you are serving drinks and food. Did somebody say something that bothered you?"

"No, not really. But one of the mothers did mention Jennifer Klein. I knew that your wife's accident involved a man named Klein but I had never known that his wife was named Jennifer."

"So, what? That's a common enough name."

"I know, but what I also know is that Jennifer Klein is having an affair with my brother, Ernesto. They have been, he says, lovers for years, long before she married Mr. Klein. He tells me everything about his life – I don't think he has many other friends."

"That's very interesting information, Carmen. Thank you very much for letting me know. What else can you tell me? What does your brother do? Have they lived together? Have they had children?"

105

"No children. I don't think they lived together. When she got divorced from her first husband, he spent lots of time at her house, but he always kept his house in the Excelsior. He's a waiter – a waiter in an expensive restaurant in the Financial District – I don't remember its name. I've never been."

"Maybe you can get the name for me. Are you telling me that the affair between your brother and Mrs. Klein is still going on even after his surgery?"

"I don't know sir. I don't talk to him very often and when I do, I don't ask anything about his women friends."

"By that do you mean that he has affairs with more than just the one woman – not just Jennifer Klein?"

"Oh yes. He has always had lots of girlfriends. Almost all of them were *gringas* – not Mexicans or Salvadorians. And most of them were rich; a few married but most divorced. He never told me me that they had money, but when his good friend from Mexico was here once, he told me about it. I guess that he was getting money from them. Can't be very much money because he lives in an ugly little house."

"So, why do you know about Mrs. Klein especially?"

"She's the only one he'd tell me about. I think he sees her more than the others. I don't remember him ever telling the names of any of the other women. And, I think he's probably in love with her, 'cause he talks about her like she's his number one *novia*."

"Carmen, can you find out for me if your brother is still seeing Mrs. Klein?"

"I don't know, sir. I don't want to get him in trouble. He'd be very mad with me if he had to go to court."

"There's no way that he'd have to go to court. Your brother had nothing to do with Mr. Klein's accident."

"Yeah, you are right. I'm having dinner with Ernesto Sunday – next week, I see him. I won't tell him about our talk today, but maybe I can find out what is going on now."

Philanthropist

Superior Court Judge Louis Gasparini had drawn the case of the City and County of San Francisco vs. Frederick Klein. He had not had many high notoriety cases in his twenty years on the bench and he was thrilled to see his name in the papers early on as adjudicator-to-be in the matter of a major player on the San Francisco scene charged with being responsible for the death of a young mother, a young rich mother. Although he could not possibly admit it to anyone, even his wife, he was praying that the case wouldn't be pled out – he wanted, desperately wanted, a trial. Like so many of his brethren in the San Francisco legal community, he was a product of the local Catholic high schools and the Jesuit University of San Francisco, both for his undergraduate degree and his JD. He had a stint with the Public Defender and then a half dozen years as a criminal defense lawyer before Governor Wilson appointed him to the Municipal Court, which shortly thereafter was amalgamated into the Superior Court. Gasparini was well liked by his colleagues and attorneys who argued before him. He was fair. He much preferred the criminal calendar to the civil one but by the luck of the draw, drew none of the capital cases or high profile white collar ones. Fred Klein was his first big fish.

Irving Greenberg called Jason Klein, having decided that the eldest son of the accused was the best contact with the family when decisions had to be made. He was not particularly enamored of the brusque LA-based lawyer, but at least the communication was efficient. He didn't have to explain the legal niceties of an issue.

"Jason, we've got a pissed off judge. Gasparini's pissed at both me and the Assistant DA, that Ms. Ng. We stepped on his toes. His take is that decisions about putting off hearings, let alone trials, are up to him and not to the lawyers. He is saying that we, meaning I, should have sent him something about how your father's condition would make it impossible for him to help in his defense. It's not a matter of whether he can tell the difference between right and wrong. It's whether he's competent to speak up intelligibly when necessary."

"Intelligibly is not a word that pertains to my father. So, what does this mean for the case?"

"I'm just relieved that Gasparini's mad at Ng, too. He is not going to make us do anything like go to a psychiatrist at this point. He took my word that Fred would not be competent at trial, at least for the time being. He's put the case off for the same two months that Ng and I had talked about when she saw him. But then, if we think he's still out to lunch, we'll have to get a shrink to see him. That won't be cheap."

"Don't worry, Irv. He's got cash."

Jason called his brothers as soon as he got off the phone with Greenberg, telling them of the not surprising news that their father wasn't going to be going to trial any time soon. He asked Robert to pass the word on to Jennifer and added, "We've got to get together in the next couple of days. Something's come up that may affect him, and all of us."

"What is it?"

"I don't want to talk about it on the phone. I'm going to be coming up tomorrow for a deposition. Let's meet at Mel's Diner on Geary at 6."

Jason rolled into Mel's at 6:20, his brothers having made it on time. He offered no apology. The twins had chosen a magenta Naugahyde booth in the rear. The best of 50's doo-wop was available to them for a quarter a song at their seats, but they declined. Jason perused the plasticized menu and opted for chicken pot pie. Robert and Phillip both planned dinner at home and ordered only beer.

"So what is such a big deal that we need to all meet up? Aside from the time Dad was so sick and when he got married, we haven't been together in years." Robert and Phillip and families met at least monthly; they liked each other. The same could not be said for relations between them and their older brother.

Jason launched into a description of what he had seen the week before. "I was in the City last week preparing for the deposition that's going to happen tomorrow morning. Two guys from the firm that we are using as our on-site lawyers in the case and I went for a drink at the Clift, the Redwood Room. We got a table in the back, near the kitchen, figuring it would be quieter as we had to come up with questions I'd be asking. It's a great big case – probably 30 million bucks involved." He hoped that his brothers would be stimulated to ask what the case was all about. They didn't.

"And next to our table are two lovebirds, holding hands. The woman's back is to me. I can't make out anything about her except for her red hair. The guy is a good-looking Latino, got to be forty or forty-five, dressed in khakis and a sport shirt. I didn't pay much attention to them – they started speaking so that we could occasionally hear that they were talking about investments – stocks, I'm thinking. It was funny – they stopped the hand holding right after we sat down. Maybe fifteen minutes later, I'm engrossed in some documents and they stand up. I look up and who do I see but our stepmother."

"Holy shit!"

"Yep, Jennifer Klein in the flesh. She acted nonchalant saying she didn't know I was in town and introduces me to her friend who had some Spanish name – I don't remember. She said he was his stockbroker. I chatted him up, asking who he worked for. He was obviously not prepared and what does he come up with – EF Hutton. They haven't been around for a long, long time. I pointed that out and he then brought up Morgan Stanley and City. The guy knows less about the stock market than my eleven-year-old. So, we drop the topic and they leave to pay the check and I ask her if she always holds hands with her broker. She left in a huff."

"Unbelievable Jason," spurted Phillip. "It never crossed my mind that our stepmother could be cheating on our father. But I guess I shouldn't be too shocked. She's a whole lot younger than he is and you don't have to know calculus to work out that all of her needs weren't supplied at home. So, what's it mean? What do we do with this information?"

"She knows that I know. So confronting her doesn't result in anything positive, while it could cause big problems. Last thing we could handle is her leaving him – she's got plenty of money from the first guy and would get a load from Dad also – so the incentives to stay aren't that strong, and they'd be worse if we made an issue of the cheating. And, bottom line – how bad is it that she'd got something on the side? Who suffers here? Not Dad, not Jennifer, for sure, not us. Why not just let sleeping dogs lie?

"Do you think we ought to tell the lawyers, Jason?" asked Robert.

"Yeah, we probably ought to tell Greenberg. No reason to tell Schofield – he's Dad's good friend and he's not really involved in the criminal case. We might have to if there's ever a trial on the civil case."

"Civil case – that's maybe a bigger deal than the criminal one," said Phillip. "There's no way that Dad, at least the way he is now, is going to go to jail. But how he is now, or any other time, isn't going to be important in deciding whether he owes the Spencer family money – right, Jason?"

"Right. Big money. And, the woman was young and married to a rich man. A jury is likely to come down with a very large award. My guess is we're going to see a great big settlement offer the day after we learn whether or not he goes to prison."

Brunello Di Montalcino

"My name is Ernesto and I'll be your server tonight. Still or sparkling?"

Beef, Ltd., the renowned steakhouse in the financial district was small, dark, and crowded. Sound proofing was excellent so the diners did not encumber one another. The tables had paper, not cloth covers. French china, English sterling silver flatware, and German steak knives attempted to justify the $50+ tab for dry aged beef.

Ernesto Contreras asked the Brooks Brothers bedecked Mark Spencer and his somewhat smart-casual brother-in-law for drink orders. Mark selected a Tuscan Brunello from the lavish list of wines; Jack requested a rum and Coke.

"So that's Carmen's brother. Pretty amazing that he's our waiter, no?" offered Jack.

"Look around you. There are only three waiters in the place. The odds were fairly good that he'd be ours. I was prepared to ask to change tables if he wasn't."

"Good looking guy, don't you think?"

"Yes, he is. I'm not surprised. Carmen is a dazzler. Plus, his skills as a lady's man would require that he not be a dog. From what we've heard about Jennifer Klein, she'd have a wide selection to choose from."

Ernesto returned to the table with the Cuba Libre and the expensive bottle of Tuscan red. "Gentlemen, let me tell you about our specials tonight." He told them about the Chilean sea bass and the vegetarian plate, a must in San Francisco, but almost no one ate anything but rib eye, filet, or New York strip at his restaurant. They chose meat, rare for the widower and medium well for his dinner guest. Ernesto marveled at the wisdom of their choices and suggested baked rather than french fried, plus a side of creamed spinach to share. The diners were most impressed by the

Larry Hill

service as well as the meal. The pacing was impeccable, the presentation perfect. Mark adored his rib eye. Jack waxed enthusiastically about his filet mignon, especially after he found the courage to ask for A-1 Sauce.

At no time during the unrushed but well-timed dinner did Mark bring up to Ernesto the facts surrounding his coming to the eatery. There was no mention of his being the employer of the waiter's sister, let alone was there any hint of Mark's knowledge of the relationship between Ernesto and Jennifer Klein. Mark ordered a cheese plate to follow the meal; Jack chose cheesecake. Both finished off the evening with a non-vintage but expensive port.

"So, bro, what was the purpose of all that?" asked Jack outside the restaurant, after Mark had paid the bill, left a tip well above the expected 20%, and asked for a take-out bag for the leftover Brunello.

"You know, Jack, I really don't know how to answer your question. Just like I didn't really understand why I tried to go into the ICU to see Klein when he was so sick. I had no plans and I don't know what I'd do with the information that I got, either then or now. I'm no criminal – I'm not going to do anything myself, or hire a hit-man. Sure, I'd like to see Klein suffer, but you know, he's probably suffering plenty already. As for Ernesto, I guess I am going to try to get to know the characters in the story of how my wife died. By the way, Jack, please don't tell Carmen that we came to her brother's restaurant."

Mark Spencer had been conceived on a farm. He wasn't born on one. His parents were Nebraska farmers at the time of his birth and he was delivered in a twenty-five bed hospital in Grand Island, the nearest city with an obstetrics department. Corn, soy beans, and alfalfa were the source of what little wealth the Spencers and their six children – Mark had two sisters and three brothers – lived on. Dirt poor would be too strong a description. Dirt lower middle class fit the bill a bit better. The family had an old station wagon and an older tractor. They had two milk cows – Jerseys - and half a dozen Suffolk sheep. Chickens and ducks had free reign, offering a continuous supply of eggs and poultry for the table, plus entertainment for the two generic farm dogs. The family was not without its own entertainment; they had a 27-inch color television and a VHS tape player on which they watched only G-rated movies. Mark, unlike most of his siblings, was not the kind of farm kid that stayed home from school for planting or harvesting. Mr. and Mrs. Spencer believed in education even though neither of them had finished high school, but recognized that they lacked the resources to pay for college for all of the children. Mark did well as a student; he was the most academically gifted of the six. He proudly brought home report cards with more As than Bs, and no Cs. In high school, he excelled in math and science and starred on the school's six-man football team, where he was quarterback on offense, backfield on defense. There was no doubt that he'd go on to further schooling. With the help of a generous scholarship, he enrolled at Hastings College to be close enough to home to help on weekends and less academically burdensome weekdays. At Hastings he met Teresa McElroy, a freshman when Mark was a junior. They studied, they went out, they went to movies, and bought tickets to the few rock concerts that were held in the plains of central Nebraska. They necked. They did not have sex. Teresa, like Mark, a product of a Catholic upbringing, took to heart the proscription against seriously fooling around before marriage. She was the offspring of a pharmacist and a housewife in the small city of Hastings.

Majoring in agricultural economics, Mark was academically prepared to return to the soya beans and corn, but academic preparation did not equal emotional readiness. He simply did not want to farm. He decided to go to business school, having been, to the surprise of himself and his professors, accepted to Stanford. To the knowledge of those who were likely to know such things, nobody from Hastings College had ever even applied to Stanford Business, let alone matriculated there.

As much as anything to get beyond the sexless dilemma, Mark and Teresa married in a traditional Catholic ceremony just prior to their Western trek for enrollment in Palo Alto. She gave up her nursing studies, knowing that she could always enroll later in a two year program at a California junior college. He happened upon the revered Stanford B School in the days that venture capitalism was a fledgling profession, with, by far, its deepest roots in the Silicon Valley. He was, after graduating in the top half of his class, able to hook onto one of the smaller firms and discovered that he had an inherent skill at identifying opportunities. His earliest hits were in the field of agriculture, especially in developing nations. Visas from Kazakhstan, Laos, Burkina Faso, and Zambia dotted his first passport. His greatest hit was the Ivory Coast cocoa market, where he helped put together a consortium of landowners in a uniquely verdant sector of the northern part of the once stable country. After five years as a successful underling, he and two other juniors split off to form their own firm. He could not take clients with him, but managed to spot and sign contracts with another bunch of Ivorian cocoa growers. After a few major scores in West Africa, Mark and Teresa had become very wealthy. Their future was assured.

Fred had an appointment with his cardiologist. The Kleins spent a not insignificant number of hours in the weeks and months after his long hospital stay going to and from and waiting in the offices of doctors. In fact, Fred did little else outside his home in Pacific Heights. He'd occasionally take a walk around the block. Although he rarely saw neighbors, when he did, the interactions were brief – a nod of the head, a comment about the wind and the sky, but nothing of depth. He was pleased that they were brief, as his ability to communicate had fallen drastically. The neighbors, who before the events tended to verbosity, were pleased that they didn't have to make more than small talk with a neurologically-handicapped, alleged felon.

The Houston-trained cardiologist had not been involved in the placing or early monitoring of Fred's pacemaker because he was the heart doctor for the upper crust. He spent no time in the County Hospital. His office featured Salvador Dali prints on the wall and Foreign Affairs and New York Review of Books on the coffee table. Fred was quickly ushered into the examining room where he instantly disrobed from the waist up when the nurse told him he was to have an EKG. The doctor was euphoric about how well the pacer was working. He wouldn't comment on Fred's good cholesterol level; that was a job for the primary care doctor. "Come back every three months and we'll run a check on your battery."

The Boston-trained neurosurgeon, who, as a clinical faculty member at San Francisco General, had been in phone contact when the hematoma was evacuated, was thrilled by how well Fred's full head of hair had obscured the rough edges of the craniotomy scar. "No reason for you to come here anymore. Just don't hit your head again. Ho ho ho."

The New York-trained neurologist bragged about his practice's total lack of Medicaid patients. He, like the cardiologist, had taken on Klein's care via a referral from the neurology clinic at the General. If there is a main-man for a patient with Fred's medical history, it's the neurologist. The heart, the liver, the lungs, the kidneys and the skin and bones – they can all be going at full throttle, but to what end if the brain is out of whack? On each monthly visit, the doctor's assistant administered tests of ambulation, fine and gross motor function, and most importantly, memory.

"Mrs. Klein, I don't want to sound overly optimistic, but Fred is getting better. Last month, he couldn't remember three simple objects for over a minute. Now he can. Look at these drawings of circles and squares – compare them to last month…not bad, huh?"

"Thank you so much, Doctor. I thought that he was improving but then figured it was just me getting used to the way he is and always would be after the accident. He's gotten more interested in things other than TV. The other day, he asked for the sports section – he wanted to read about the 49ers. He hasn't looked at a paper since before he was arrested. But he's not the Fred of old. Is he going to be?"

"I wish I had a crystal ball. There's just no way to know. But we can say that things are going in the right direction. Where it ends up is anybody's guess. Let's see him again in six weeks."

"Why six and not four?"

"Sorry. I'm going to be at our place in Provence."

"Ready for this, Fred? Your cholesterol is 165!"

Allison Jameson, the primary care lady, hadn't seen her patient since the day she told him that his cholesterol was 260. What an improvement! Of course, since then, he'd been arrested for manslaughter, suffered a heart attack which required a pacemaker, and had his brain function damaged by head trauma and neurosurgery. She didn't allude to any of that.

"So, can I eat steak again? And fried eggs?"

"Of course you can, Sweetie." He did not react to the name. "Jennifer, I think you can probably let up on the diet restrictions a bit. Those statin pills are doing what they are supposed to – even better than we expected."

"He's been eating steak and fried eggs since he came home from the hospital. I guess he just wants your approval."

"He's got it." Jameson proceeded to listen to Fred's heart and lungs, feel his abdomen, and check his ankles for swelling.

"You taking your baby aspirin?"

"Yep, every day."

"How are your spirits, Fred?"

"Spirits? I haven't touched a drop of booze since they sent me home. One of the doctors told me not to."

She didn't know whether this was sophisticated humor or confusion. She doubted his brain's capacity for sophistication.

"Not that kind of spirits. I mean how do you feel? Are you sad? Depressed?"

"You mean, do I want to kill myself? No way. I've gone through all this shit with the surgery. I gotta get my money's worth. Just look at this gorgeous wife of mine – why would I leave her so that she could hook up with some young dude? And, I've got to find out who those idiotic Republicans are going to nominate."

"Not everybody who is depressed wants to kill himself. You don't sound depressed. What do you think, Jennifer?"

"No, Fred's pretty upbeat. A lot more upbeat than I'd be in his situation. I guess that's an OK side effect of having a brain that's not working at 100%"

Fred did a double take. "What do you mean, not working at 100%? My brain is just fine thank you."

"Come on, dear. Your memory still isn't what it was before the surgery. You can't even name your grandkids."

He named them and came up with their ages, give or take a couple of years.

"Not bad, Fred. You couldn't have done that two weeks ago. Doctor Jameson, I guess you're right. He's better."

"Good news...that's really good news. Keep up the good work, Fred. Keep taking those cholesterol medicines and the others and come on back in a month."

"Why do I need to do that?"

"I guess you don't really need to. How about three months?"

"Make it six and you've got a deal."

"Six it is."

Fred stopped at the receptionist's desk on the way out. "The doctor wants me back in a month. Give me a nine o'clock on Thursday. I've got lots of meetings that week."

The burly buxom reservationist at Beef, Ltd. called across the room. It was 3 PM. The place was empty of lunch diners and setting up for dinner diners. "Ernesto, phone call for you."

"Hello, Ernesto. This is Mark Spencer. You may remember me from last night. I was the guy who ordered the expensive Brunello and the other guy drank rum and Coke."

"Yes, I do remember you." He remembered the big tip more than he did the bar order. He assumed that Spencer must have lost his credit card. Rarely would a customer call the waitperson at a restaurant where he had eaten the previous day for reason other than a forgotten card. "How can I help you?"

"I just wanted to say how impressed I was by the service we received last night. Let me tell you about myself. I am a principal of an investment company here in the City – Spencer, Bowman and Clark. Often, I am looking for talent. What I mean by that is I look for men and women who might fit into slots in companies that I invest in. And, right now, I am involved in something new that needs an intelligent and persuasive Spanish speaker. I don't mean to be presumptuous, but am I not right in assuming you speak Spanish? Your accent certainly suggests you are from South of the Border."

"Yes, I do. I was born in Mexico."

"Would you be willing to talk to me?"

"Yes, I guess I would. Where? When?" He didn't ask why.

"Why don't you come over to my office tomorrow morning at ten? I assume that Beef, Ltd. doesn't serve breakfast," he chuckled.

Spencer's firm was on the 14th floor of the most recognized symbol of post-1970 San Francisco, the Transamerica Pyramid. His office's 270 degree view looked at both bridges, Alcatraz, and the East Bay. On about half the days, he could see the Campanile at UC Berkeley. Every day was casual Friday at Spencer, Bowman and Clark. Mark sported a Thai silk sport shirt and chinos over Air Jordans when Ernesto Contreras was brought in by the critically handsome male secretary. Ernesto was dressed as if he was a waiter at a fancy dining establishment – dark suit, white shirt, subdued blue tie. He was offered coffee, tea, or San Francisco tap, declining all.

"How kind of you to come, Mr. Contreras. May I call you Ernesto?"

Ernesto had never been asked the question before. "Yes, just don't call me Ernie."

Mark grinned broadly. "Tell me about your background." He received an abbreviated history of his having come to the US with his mother and sister, his education at USC, his citizenship success and his employment at the shipping company. "Have you ever been to South America?"

"No, Mexico and California – nothing more."

"Married?"

"Never. But I'm not gay."

"No problem. Gay, straight – we don't worry much about that here. You have a girl friend?"

"Not really. I see a few women."

"Let me tell you about this company that you might be just the right guy for. A few months ago, I was introduced to a cattle man in Uruguay. I don't know if you, as a steak guy, know anything about cattle in Uruguay. There are four times as many cows as people – the biggest herd compared to population in the world. Most of the farms, and there are thousands of them, are small – just a few acres – and they raise their animals and slaughter them like they do in the US or Argentina – nothing special. Well, this guy I met wants to get into a new niche – he wants to get a Kobe beef thing going, like Japan – you know about Kobe beef?"

"Sure, I've heard to it, but we don't sell it at Beef. Those are the cows that are treated better than the waiters who serve it."

"Right you are. Kobe beef is from the Wagyu breed of cattle and the mother and calf are together, in a tight shed, for their entire lifetimes. The beef tastes like nothing you've ever had in your mouth. It's incredibly expensive – you can spend over a thousand dollars for a steak. The farmer I learned about outside of Montevideo has purchased some Wagyu cows and bred them to Angus bulls and is planning to raise them in the traditional Japanese way and then sell his meat on the world market. The Japanese almost never let any of theirs get out of the country. Our guy thinks that there's a big market for Kobe beef in the US, Europe, and especially the Middle East. He may not be able to use the name, got to call it Kobe-style or something like that.

"And, why me?"

"As I told you, I need a Spanish speaker who knows something about beef. I could tell by the way that you were with us the other day that you get along with people and are smart. Your job will be to grease the skids."

"Huh?"

"Sorry. I mean that you will be our go-between – you will use your people skills to make our guy there think that our firm is the way he should go.

"We supply the business information – that's what we sell at the firm. And, we can pay you more than you are getting at the restaurant – lots more. Of course, we pay all expenses of getting there and staying there – nothing but five star hotels and business class seats."

"That's all pretty cool. When would the job start?"

"If you go for it, we'd probably take you on in a couple of weeks – there's a training program. First, we've got to check you out. Can't afford to have somebody without papers, no? You are OK with that, aren't you?"

"Yes, Sir. I've got my citizenship – have for years.

"Good. Our personnel girl will need to see some documents. We teach you the business of venture capital. We'd have to send you out to UC Davis Vet School and have them give you a crash course in cattle care. You gotta have the right vocabulary. Our guy speaks fair English but none of the guys around him does, so you'll have to learn the Spanish for this stuff. It'll be a couple of months before you take your first trip to Uruguay. You interested?"

"Sure, I'm interested. I have to think it over for a few days at least. Let me get back to you by the end of the week."

Mark shook his head. "I need an answer by tomorrow at noon. In this venture capital business, we've got to make our decisions fast – if we don't do it, somebody else will. And, by the way, don't tell anybody about your being here – don't mention my name or the firm's name. If you are talking to your girl friends or mother or sister, it's OK to talk about a new job and the possibility of travel to Latin America, but not a word about Kobe beef or Uruguay or Spencer, Bowman and Clark. Agreed?"

"Agreed. I'll call you tomorrow morning." As Contreras left, Spencer observed dark patches of sweat under both arms.

"Jesus Christ, Jack. You won't believe what I've done with Carmen's brother! And, I don't even know why I'm doing it. You know that deal I was telling you about with the Kobe beef in Uruguay? I've offered him a job as our man in Montevideo. I can't believe he won't take it – I told him he'd be making a lot more dough than he is at Beef."

The brother-in-law, who had invited Mark over for a drink, was not surprised. "You trying to mess with the Klein lady's mind? There are probably ten thousand Spanish speaking smart people in the Bay Area who would grab a job like that in a heartbeat, and you go out of your way to pick the lover of the wife of the guy who killed your wife. You are a sick son-of-a-bitch, Mark."

Ernesto lived in the Excelsior District, as far south in San Francisco as one can go – just above the Daly City line. Excelsior houses tended to be considerably cheaper than most parts of the expensive metropolis. The common languages of the street were Tagalog, Spanish, and Cantonese. Street crime was high and street trash was everywhere. One rarely went more than five minutes without seeing a SFPD black and white pass by.

Jennifer had been to his place only once, some ten years earlier when the affair was just getting under way. Hotels, motels, her place – venues for their escapades until Fred's issues took away her place as an alternative. After the encounter with Jason at the Clift, she was more than a bit apprehensive about meeting her lover in public places. It was her idea to suggest a return visit to his place when he called saying that he absolutely had to see her that day.

Her newish SUV was one of the more impressive rides in the neighborhood. She found, much to her shock, a full size space immediately in front of his house. She could tell that the house hadn't been painted since she last visited a decade earlier. The cracked stucco recalled to her the map of a big city subway system. The window frames peeled paint and the concrete steps had turned a mildew-green. She knocked on the door, in need of either cleaning or replacement, and she regretted not having put an alcohol germ killer in her purse to slather on her knuckles. She could not believe that her lover, so clean of person and dress, would accept living in such a hovel.

Ernesto opened the door looking as handsome and spotless as ever. They hugged but to Jennifer, the hug lacked its usual passion. She felt like he hugged her to prevent the consequences of not hugging her. The living room was no more a candidate for a House Beautiful photograph than was the exterior. The walls screamed for paint. The carpet, a sickly green not very different from the steps to the front door, showed signs of spilled liquids and too many years of use. The chandelier, once the only real sign of class in the room, had lost several of its crystal pieces, while the furniture, non-matching sofa and easy chairs, plus a coffee table of oak-like veneer, needed a trip to Goodwill. Unframed posters of Mexican tourist sites alternated with old photos and a plaster of Paris icon of the Virgin and Son as decorative highlights. There was no sign of a book, magazine or newspaper in the room.

"So, why the urgency, my love?"

"I need to talk to you about something. You're the only person I know that can advise me. A weird thing happened to me a few nights ago. A couple of men came into the restaurant and had steaks. Nothing unusual about the encounter – nice enough guys. One was obviously richer than the other and he left me a very big tip – the biggest I've gotten since the rapper left five hundred dollars a few years ago – you remember. The next day I get a phone call at work from the rich one – he wants me to come to his office and talk about a job. So, I go the next day, yesterday, and he says he wants someone who speaks Spanish to work on a big deal in South America. I had to promise that I wouldn't say who he is, where he works or what country in South America. Says that it's too risky and that maybe the information would get out and they'd lose the deal."

"What's the job?"

"I'm not really sure. All I can say is that it involves beef – he must think that since I work at Beef and I speak Spanish I'd be just right for it."

"Did he ask for a resume or for references? Did he talk to your boss? How does he know anything about you based on your serving him a steak?"

"Damned if I know. He can't know anything about me. I guess he thought I looked pretty good and seemed smart. He didn't even ask me where I was from. I did tell him about the shipping job that I used to have and that seemed to turn him on a little."

"Does it mean you'd be moving?" she asked with a dollop of anxiety.

"I don't think so. He said I'd be flying in business class and staying in five star hotels. That sounds like I'd be here most of the time. Who knows, I might even keep waiting tables. But he did say he'd pay me a lot more than I'm making now."

"This whole thing sounds really weird to me, love. Pretty strange HR procedures for the boss to offer big money and flights to South America to a waiter he just happens to meet in a restaurant."

"So, you think I should just forget about it?"

"What do you want? It's your call."

"Yeah, it's weird, but pretty exciting. I'm tired of serving meat to rich gringos. Being told I should convince the customers to order creamed spinach and dessert isn't what I dreamed about doing forever. I think I'll see where it goes. Or, do you think I'm nuts?"

"What's the worst that can happen? I guess the guy could be a crook and is looking for you to run drugs or endangered species. I hope that the country isn't Colombia or Bolivia."

"I hadn't thought of that. But no it's not one of those countries. You know, I'm going to call the guy and say yes. I can always back out. But first let me show you my bedroom." He took her hand. Both suppressed any disinclinations.

Compared to the house's one bedroom, the living room was kempt. The double bed was unmade, the polyester comforter laying on the floor and the sheets more off than on the unpadded mattress. Three pairs of shoes, all black, and three pairs of socks were scattered randomly over the floor that was covered in the same disgusting green shag. A 42-inch flat screen was mounted on one wall. Unlike the living room, there was a book in the bedroom – a travel guide to South America. A rickety recliner was strewn with work pants, lounge pants, underpants, and shirts of varied types and colors. Two of the four dresser drawers were open. On the top were another pair of socks, two empty Pepsi bottles, an old Philco clock radio, and a framed photograph of a beautiful Latina. Jen's long time supposition that her paramour was not monogamous seemed confirmed. But she was surprised that he hadn't hidden the picture before bringing her in for love. "Who's that?"

"It's my sister, Carmen. You haven't met her have you? You've got to meet her someday. She works in somebody's house in your part of town."

"That's good. Let's get to it." Jen's clothes were off in less than a minute after which she turned her attention to her lover's outfit, throwing the shoes, socks, pants, shirt and underwear with their mates on the recliner and the floor. She always supplied the condom as he claimed he was too embarrassed to purchase them himself; she had forgotten to bring one, but no worry, her period had finished just a few days earlier. She had not made love since the week before the hit and run. Neither she nor her husband had raised the subject. In spite of the extreme disorder of her lover's bed and its surroundings, it felt just right.

After showering in the disarray of the apartment's only bathroom, she returned to the bedroom to recover her clothing. Ernesto was finishing a phone call in the living room. "Yes, please tell Mr. Spencer that I will take the job." Jennifer prayed that the surname she just heard was merely a coincidence.

Word was getting around that Fred Klein was improving. Among the earliest recipients of the news were his poker-playing friends. As he had been a founding member of the game and a totally predictable participant, a little thing like a vehicular manslaughter charge would not be considered a reason for his being tossed from the list of contestants. Lawyer Schofield, personally closest to Klein, suggested to the others that Fred be invited to the next Friday night game. Recognizing that their friend would probably not be fully himself, Schofield suggested two major one-time changes. First, they would play only the simplest of games, five-card draw. Their usual evenings of dealer's choice involved a panoply of other forms of poker – Texas Hold-em, seven card high-low stud, Omaha and anaconda to name the most often chosen. They reckoned that Fred

Philanthropist

needed to have as few review subjects as possible. Secondly, for similar reasons, they limited the number of players to four. Six or seven were typical. Less than six players generally led to postponement of the game, but again Art and colleagues agreed that a full table might be more than Fred could handle. The elected players in addition to Lawyer Schofield were Optometrist Gettleman and Accountant Ross. Ross of Russian Hill offered to host the match.

Jennifer had been reluctant to give her imprimatur to Fred's venture outside the house without her at his side, but after discussing it with Art, she decided that the upsides of Fred's returning to normalcy were worth the risks. Art would be vigilant and call a halt if his friend became confused. Plus, it would be Jennifer's first evening without her spouse since his return from SF General. She'd hang out at home and read without distraction. She was titillated by the idea of a tête-à-tête with Ernesto, but dismissed it as too early and too risky – her husband might return much earlier than expected. Gettleman and Ross were OK with the plan, recognizing that it might be a very short night.

Schofield showed up at Fred's house half an hour before game time. Fred was dressed in his usual poker togs – black wool pants, white dress shirt, wing tips, and a black beret. He always reckoned that the dashing Fred was more likely to win big than the casual/slovenly one. He had no statistics to back up the premise. He was clearly nervous, knowing that he hadn't played in months and that his skills were likely to have waned. It wasn't the fear of losing significant cash. Theirs was not a high-stakes game. He had never lost $150 in his years of poker with the boys – nobody else had either. A big win or big loss was $75. But he was frightened of setting a precedent. "Art, promise to pull me out of there if I'm losing big, OK?"

"Sure, will do." It was going to take less than a losing streak for Schofield to bring his charge home early.

"Hurry, we got to stop at the 7-Eleven. I always bring Doritos and dip." Jennifer and Art looked straight at each other, conveying shared certainty that there was nothing to be gained by referencing the events of the last time the Klein family had anything to do with the convenience store on California St.

Fred was not going to drive to the poker game. He probably wasn't going to drive ever again. He disagreed with that, saying that he'd be back behind the wheel "pretty soon." He accepted the explanation that a temporary moratorium on driving was necessary according to both his cardiologist, keeper of the pacemaker, and his neurologist, the brain maven. The moratorium was also a good legal-political move. The most minor of fender-benders could stir the hornets' nest should it be reported on the news.

The two friends made the stop at the 7-Eleven. They went in together, chose their chips and dip, and paid the Indian lady at the register. "Nice to see you, Mr. Klein. We've missed you here. Hurry back."

They reached Ross' penthouse pad just before seven. Gettleman was already there. The stage was set in the game room of the 3000 square foot apartment with views in all directions – the full moon-dominated night was as clear as a freshly cleaned aquarium. The circular Chinese table was covered in brown chintz. There were no ashtrays. Smoking, even of cigars, had been outlawed by the players a decade before. Beer, usually exotic brews, always before a staple of the game, was nowhere to be seen. Four stacks of chips were laid out around the circle at 12, 3, 6, and 9, each made up of a bunch of white quarters, a smaller number of red halves and five blue dollars. As per tradition in the game, each player tossed four fresh ten dollar bills into a cherry wood bowl to pay for the initial chip buy-in of forty dollars. Ross was especially proud of his four matching black desk chairs, ergonomically engineered to gently support the backs of old men.

"High card deals," announced Ross after he did a Vegas-like demonstration of the two new decks of Bicycles, showing a full complement of 52 reds and 52 blues, no jokers. Gettleman's king outranked the others and he declared that the first hand would be five card draw, jacks or better to open. Each wealthy man tossed in twenty-five cents as an ante. The dealer distributed five cards to each, having shuffled the red deck while Ross did the same to the blues. Klein picked up his cards one at a time, being careful not to divulge their identity to his neighbors. He was the first bidder and he threw in fifty cents. Schofield matched the bet as did Ross. The dealer folded.

"How many cards do you want, Fred?" asked Gettleman.

"Huh?"

"Cards, Fred. How many?"

"Oh, yeah, cards. Give me two…no, three."

"Three says Klein." Dealer pulled three cards off the top and held them, waiting to give them to his friend. "Fred, you gotta give me three before I can give you these."

"Oh, yeah. Here." He took three cards from his hand and tossed them in the middle, face up. Usually, house rules would call for a miss-deal if discards were identified, but on this occasion Gettleman merely turned them over before handing Fred his replacements. Schofield took three also. Ross asked for four.

"You're the opener, Fred. Your bet."

"I'll bet a buck." He threw in a blue chip.

"Call," said Schofield, in turn.

"I'm out," said Ross who knew he couldn't beat a pair of jacks, the minimum for opening.

"It's just the two of us, Fred-baby. Whatcha got?"

"I've got a pair of eights."

"Huh-uh. I've got a pair of kings. My pot. But Fred, you have to have a pair of jacks or queens or more to have bet first. You didn't – you weren't allowed to open."

"Oh, yeah. I blew that one didn't I? Sorry."

"No problem. You didn't lose much, you rich SOB."

Three hands later, Klein having folded his cards in the previous two, opened the bidding once again, this time with five blue chips.

"Fred – you can't do that. You can't bet more than a dollar on the first round. Five is OK after the draw."

"Shoot, I knew that. You'd think I'd never played this game before." He withdrew all five of the blues and threw in a white one. The others all put in their quarters.

"How many cards, Fred?"

"None." Ross took one, Gettleman four, and Schofield three.

"I'm the opener. That'll be five dollars gentlemen." The opponents all tossed in their cards simultaneously.

"Show us your openers, winner." Fred turned over his cards. Five, nine, king, jack, jack.

"What's that all about, Fred?"

"I had a pair of jacks."

"So, why didn't you take any cards? Were you bluffing?"

"Hell no. Didn't think I needed to." He raked in his first legitimate pot of his post-pacemaker life.

"Let's eat," said Ross. Tradition had it that food was brought out at 10 PM. It was only 7:45. The Doritos, dip, popcorn and mixed nuts joined hot 'n spicy chicken wings on the sideboard. Klein ate a plateful. The dietary recommendations of Dr. Jameson were long forgotten.

Fred's three buddies communicated silently. Gettleman said, "My daughter and her family are flying in from Chicago this evening. I think I better be there to greet 'em. Sorry for finking out on you, but I should go."

"No sense in playing with only three guys. Fred, you and I should go home, too."

They redistributed the cash. Fred pocketed forty dollars and fifty cents. He had won half a dollar. In the car on the way home Art, keeping his eye on the road, not on his passenger said, "Fred, I think we tried this a little earlier than we should have. You weren't the Klein we know and love. Let's wait a few months 'til that Fred comes back."

Fred nodded slowly but said nothing. His first words were uttered as he came in the house, "Honey, I'm a winner.

The Philanthropist

Dear Mr. Klein,

………………………………..donation…………...whatever you feel you can afford…………………...children…………………

Sincerely,
Adrienne C
Children of the Planet

Dear Mr. and Mrs. Frederick Klein,

…………………...money………...beyond our present resources....
……………hunger…………...generous……………………………

Regards,
Ricardo M
Food Bank of California

Hello Frederick Klein

……………..drought………………………worsening poverty………….
microfinance……………help us…………………

Yours in Christ,
Amadou K
Africa Famine Relief

Averaging one or more per day, the pleas for donated funds came in. Fred's new status as alleged criminal seemed to have no influence one way or the other on their volume. Prior to his hematoma, he would make quick trash of the letters. After, he was a sitting duck for the appeals. Not one to trust electronic transfers of money, he'd write out checks, lick them into the enclosed envelopes and attach stamps, often those commemorative issues he had collected in his childhood, and which had experienced no meaningful increase in value; a decades-old five cent Eleanor Roosevelt was now worth a nickel. His checks were never written for less than $25 - never for more than $100. A little more if the appeals came from Jewish causes, sometimes zero if they included such comments as "Yours in Christ." He would always obey the request for personal information, including to the great displeasure of his wife, their phone number. He'd ask her what the number was each time until she decided to put a plasticized card on his desk with large, bold numerals, including the 415 area code. The potential downside of inclusion of phone numbers was, of course, an uptick in the number of phone calls from electronic voices and strangers seeking money. Fred did not see that as a downside. He loved to talk on the phone as long as one of his favorite shows wasn't on. He hadn't been able to get comfortable with the ons and offs of TiVo, although his sons had purchased it for him as a coming-home gift. While Jennifer would react with pique when the Firemen's Benevolent folks or the Committee to Save Endangered Reptiles called, and insist that their name be removed from the cold call list, Fred would spend at minimum a quarter hour chatting up his new friends, who would almost invariably come away with survey data or with a small pledge. Fred was, with his new-born impairment, no longer one of those seniors who give away big chunks of their fortune. Twenty-five, fifty, one hundred – those were his increments for most, although some, like Girl Scouts or the high school band would usually get five or ten.

 You don't gain fame as a philanthropist by giving away money in lots of a hundred dollars or less. Frederick was a noted philanthropist. He garnered that status after selling his TV station and hitting it richer with wise stock purchases and even wiser stock sales. He was never hurt by a bursting bubble. Fred knew when to fold 'em. His net worth, while not close to a billion, was well into the nine figure range.

His first big charitable gift went to the Jewish Federation Council. Klein did not know if he believed in God. He hadn't given it enough thought to put himself in either the agnostic or atheist box. Heaven and hell, not an issue of major concern to Jews, never entered his mind. He had been Bar Mitzvahed so knew some of the prayers, which he could recite fairly accurately in Hebrew. At one point, he knew what the Hebrew meant but that knowledge had long been lost. He had never felt that there was anything beneficial that might come to him by praying, so he, like his parents and children, never prayed for real. He'd read, or occasionally recited from memory the standard prayers at the Seder table, but to him they meant little more than a chapter in a novel or the listing in TV Guide. He didn't belong to a temple, although there were many in San Francisco who would gladly accept a request for inclusion in their congregation. He assumed that he'd be buried Jewish, marking one of only two moments (Bar Mitzvah and Death) in his existence, both sentient and non-sentient, where religion would play a part.

So, why the Jewish Federation Council? Like so many of those co-religionists with whom he was familiar, Fred was a non-religious Jew. A Jew, in his own mind, no less Jewish than one that went to synagogue every Friday night AND Saturday morning and donned the tallit and the phylacteries. He cared about the history of his people. He knew of and was emotional about the plight of the Jewish tribes of yore and the victims of twentieth-century horror. He cared about Israel. When a missile from Gaza hit a school near the Sea of Galilee, or a suicide bomber blew himself up in a bus in Jerusalem, it was as if the strike was directly on Pacific Heights. When a Jewish person anywhere in the world, be she from San Francisco, Brooklyn, Moscow, or Addis Ababa, was in trouble, Fred was there to help. Therefore, his and Barbara's first big charitable check was written to the Federation Council. He also gave to the Jewish Community Center not far from his home. Money went to Mt. Zion Hospital, even though it was now part of the University of California system. He was a major supporter of the Jewish Film Festival and the new downtown Contemporary Jewish Museum. His name, and that of his wife at the time, were etched into all the right walls.

The etching didn't stop at Jewish places. The Symphony, the Opera, and the Conservatory of Music (but not the Ballet) received Klein contributions. The art museums, the parks, the library, and the University of San Francisco, a Catholic school, benefitted. Boys' Club, Girls' Club, United Way, March of Dimes – look on their lists of significant supporters and you will not fail to find Mr. and Mrs. Frederick Klein.

Weeks before his accidents, Fred and Jennifer had been in intense discussions with the Institute of Aging in San Francisco. Fred was getting older; so were his few friends. He watched some of them become progressively less able to take care of themselves and unable to find affordable help. He knew that he'd never find anything unaffordable and wanted to create something to help less fortunate old people. Fred and Jen had asked that the Institute draw up an agreement that would involve five million of their dollars go toward a new housing project and skilled nursing facility. It was to be called the Jennifer and Frederick Klein Center. There'd be nothing in the title to mention age or aging. That agreement was on the desk of the Institute's CEO for her confirmation when Fred hit Teresa. Neither Klein had seen the document.

Big donations buy you, if you are in the market, seats on non-profit boards. Fred was usually in the market; he had little else to do in the years after he got to be very rich. He served on the SF Symphony Board, the SF Ballet Board, and the Boards of the Cancer Society, the Hospice of San Francisco, and the American Heart Association, San Francisco branch. He preferred to chair boards. A man of short attention span and relatively few words, he had a hard time tolerating meetings of more than 90 minutes. As chairman, he could wield a mean gavel and set the time limit.

Dementia diminishes one's boardsman skills. Fred was notified of meetings. Jennifer, with few exceptions, decided against his going to them. He put up no struggle, as he had when she showed reluctance at his desire to play poker. He was not willing to resign from any board. He, with the concurrence of his wife, was convinced that he'd regain his wits.

Jennifer had reactivated her status as a sexually active woman - not at home, as Fred's gradual improvement did not include libidinous awakening, but her visit to the disarray of Ernesto's place in the Excelsior had rekindled her longings for carnal love. She called her lover to arrange another Tuesday tryst.

"Not this week, *mi novia*. I'm going to school three days a week, Monday, Tuesday, and Thursday. And, I'm still working."

"School? What are you studying?"

"They are giving me a crash course in cattle raising and slaughtering. And, I'm getting some classes on politics in South America."

"Slaughtering? Are you actually killing steers? Gross!"

"No. I'm not killing them. I went to a slaughter house and watched, one time. Not pretty, but you want to eat a steak, somebody has to kill a cow."

"I guess. Can you tell me where you are going?"

"Sorry, I can't. They made me sign something that I'd keep everything a secret. I'm not sure that I was even allowed to say that it was about cattle."

"How about I come by on Wednesday? I've learned that abstinence doesn't work for me. I gotta get laid."

"Sorry Jen. I've got no time for that. They made me promise that I'd spend all my time outside of school and work reading about beef." Jennifer read into that a lot more than the words of the sentences, but her reading did not offer answers. No way that whoever had offered him the new job was going to organize surveillance of Ernesto's hovel. No way that he had fallen for some new woman in the brief time since their recent momentously satisfactory roll in the sack. She tried to put the rejection together with the fact that he had reported in to somebody named

Spencer; she couldn't. Whining wasn't going to help. Tears had never seemed to work with him. Nor pleading. She'd try again later.

Spencer, Bowman and Clark had suffered with the rest of Northern California's venture capitalists after the collapse of the dotcoms. Bowman and Clark were thankful for Spencer's expertise in agriculture. They didn't, for a second, understand why he thought that he could hit it big with Uruguayan Kobe beef, but they knew that their bread had been buttered in recent years by his successes in Ivorian cocoa, Moroccan fava beans, tilapia from the Russian steppes, and kudu meat from Botswana. The latter had dominated the exotic jerky market for years. Without Spencer's edible winners, the firm would surely have to move from the iconic Pyramid and likely cut back on company hybrids, I-Phones, and reclining seats in business class. Both partners were surprised by how quickly Mark had rebounded from the death of his wife. They had barely known Teresa, as there was no real socializing within the practice. But what they did know impressed them. She was a dream girl with a conquering smile and a hug for the ages. Mark had missed only five days at the office. At first there was a hint of gloom when he returned but he quickly morphed back into his same old back slapping, quick stepping, lunch skipping, partner berating, secretary firing, journal reading, two-finger typing, filthy-tongued self. "Let's get ass-kicking moving!"

One did not wait if he had an appointment with Mr. Spencer. Mr. Contreras had arrived at 9:40 for his 10 AM sit-down. He was seated in the office with the view by 9:45. He had not yet assumed the casual attire of his new employer, showing up in a camel hair jacket, blue striped button down and upscale khakis, too similar in hue to the jacket. Spencer could see by the lack of contrast in dress that his new hire had no significant other, be it Jennifer Klein, another woman or another man, in the house when he left for the financial district.

"*Como van las clases*, Ernesto?" He spoke a handful of words of Spanish, thanks to two years of the only language other than English taught at Hastings High. His accent was Nebraskan.

"*Muy bien, gracias*. I am learning very much about cattle and about Uruguay. And about Kobe beef."

"Tell me what you've learned about Kobe beef."

"I learned that we can't call it Kobe beef because the Japanese have trademarked the name. We can call it Kobe-style beef. The Japanese name is *Kobe bifu* – pretty easy language, no? Did you know that the basketball player Kobe Bryant is named after Kobe beef? I guess his parents had some when she was pregnant. The cattle don't get much exercise because they are raised on very small ranches. Some of them get massages in place of exercise. They all have beer in their diet – they say that increases their appetites and puts more fat, marbling, in the meat."

"Good work, Ernesto." He was not overwhelmed by the oral report; he wasn't seeking to be. "You ready to take a trip to Montevideo?"

"Sure, when?"

"Two weeks tomorrow. Let your bosses know that you'll be gone for a week."

Mark still did not have a great notion as to why he was going through the charade. So far, there was no way that his wife's killer was going to be affected by the shenanigans. The connection was tenuous at best – he employs, trains and sends south Klein's wife's illicit lover. And Klein's so out-to-lunch that, even if he learned about it, he wouldn't comprehend. Is that revenge? Do I need revenge? Jesus, I don't know. But there's money to be made in Kobe-style beef, raised in Uruguay and shipped to Chicago and the coasts. Why not confuse the matter and see what happens?

Jason Moves North

Emily Klein, wife of Jason and mother of two, kicked her husband out of the family home.

Jason had few friends, at least none that he figured would take him in. He had no interest whatever in living in a hotel or motel, even briefly. As much of his work at the time involved cases in the top half of the state, he decided to phone and ask his stepmother if he could spend a couple of weeks in the Pacific Heights house. There were plenty of unused bedrooms and full or half baths. Reluctantly, in view of the not infrequent enmity between her husband and her son-in-law, she accepted.

Hours after the call, Jason parked his rented convertible across the street and dragged two large suitcases, a back pack, a tennis racket, and his lizard skin briefcase filled with files, letters, and briefs up to the front door. Jennifer greeted him with a half-hearted hug before he rang or knocked. "Take the upstairs room on the left." That room featured an en suite bathroom with shower and tub. He was surprised at her generosity.

Showered and shaved for the first time since being tossed the previous afternoon, he came down to the family room dressed in gym pants and a baby-blue UCLA sweatshirt. His father, a Diet Coke in his hand, was watching something on the flat-screen that involved a panel of women. Jennifer sat with Fred on the leather couch, a nearly completed crossword puzzle on her lap. She placed the paper on the coffee table and asked her husband to toggle off the TV. The relationship between Jason and his stepmother had been testy since the day that Fred introduced her to his boys as his second bride-to-be. The nastiness had not long before been heightened by the discovery of her hand-holding with Ernesto at the Redwood Room. The Fred/Jason interactions were anything but smooth, but much of that, in the view of both the son and the father, was due to the mutual dislike between Fred and Emily.

"How are you, Jason?" asked Jennifer, softly and simply.

"Not so good."

"Do you want to talk about it?"

"Yes, please." A moment of silence followed. His brown eyes glistened but no tears flowed.

"What happened?" Fred nodded his head as Jen asked the question.

"Long story. Where to start? You probably know that Emily and I hadn't been doing very well lately – maybe ever since the second kid was born."

"No, we didn't know that. What do you mean, not doing well?"

"Everything. We'd fight all the time, about everything. Money. Sex. The kids. How much I was gone. Until the last few months, the kids never saw us battling, but that changed. Both of them made it real clear that they weren't happy with how their parents treated each other and treated them. I guess I was really short with both of them.

"We had a real blow up when Emily decided that our summer vacation was going to be on the Jersey Shore with her parents. I told her how much I didn't want to do that and that I wanted to go on a camping trip in the Sierras, that we had done Thanksgiving with her folks last year, and that they had come out to LA and stayed with us for a week in February. She said that I had told her that I was OK with a trip to New Jersey. I had no recollection whatever of that discussion. I don't think it happened. I really don't like being with the Parks, especially if it's in their house or they are paying the bill like they would on the Shore. It feels like a mausoleum. We all have to speak in hushed tones and the kids can't touch a thing without Mrs. Park warning them not to drop any of their valuable shit. There's no laughing – no joy at all – when they are around."

"I don't like them either," Fred said, his first words since Jason descended the staircase.

"Right, Dad. I knew that. So, a brouhaha ensued with Emily screaming and me yelling back and the kids hearing it. It wasn't a pretty sight."

"And what was the result?" asked Jennifer.

"The three of them are going to go for two weeks and I said I'd come for the second. That, of course, was before I left the house. All bets are off now – they'll probably take the trip and I'll hang out in the house and look after the dogs."

"So, is that the cause of the separation? It doesn't sound like such a big deal. It was just a fight. How'd that make you leave the house?"

"No, it wasn't. That fight happened about three weeks ago and we quieted down, mainly for the kids. But I was really pissed off. We hadn't made love in a very long time. I think she resented it as much as I did, but neither of us had any desire to be nice to the other. So, two weeks after the big fight, I called an escort service that a recently divorced client told me about. I told Emily that I was coming up to San Francisco on that big case. Instead, I spent a night with two hookers at the Holiday Inn off Sunset Boulevard. Big bucks. Can't say that I enjoyed it. All I could think of during the sex was how much better it was than being with Emily. I came home the next afternoon as if nothing had happened. She even kissed me as I came through the front door – probably because the kids were watching."

"So, what happened?"

"Yeah, what happened?" asked Fred as he fiddled with the remote.

"You can't believe what an idiot I was. I had cashed a check before I went to the hotel. I had been told what the women would cost, so I took out a bit more. When it was all over and I handed them the arranged fee, they asked for a tip. One of them said that half of the money goes to the escort service and that everybody gave them a tip – usually 20%. Twenty percent of a lot of money is a lot of money. In fact, it was just about as much as I had left over, so I gave it to them. I was afraid that they'd make a scene.

"So, no big deal? Wrong. I had no money to pay for the room. All I had was my American Express card, so I used it, knowing full well that Emily keeps tab on our credit cards. She's scared shitless that somebody is going to get our number and buy a fishing pole or shoes with it. The best

I could hope for is that she would see Holiday Inn on the list of charges and not check what city it was in. Wrong. The next day, she went on the internet site and there it was – Holiday Inn, Sunset Boulevard, Los Angeles, California. She assumed that her fears of a stolen credit card number were real and that somebody had stayed a night and charged it to us. She didn't say anything to me – just called AmEx and they told her that they have my signature on the charge. Well, you can imagine that shit hit fan when I got home from the office that afternoon. She had had AmEx fax her a copy of the billing slip and no sooner do I walk through the door and she sticks the piece of paper under my nose. 'What's this?' I took it from her and saw exactly what it was. "I thought you were in San Francisco!"

"It was obvious to me where this was going. No way could I explain it away. So, I suggested we go out back, get ourselves some wine and talk out of the hearing range of the kids. Surprisingly, she simmered down a bit and we went to the patio. So, I told her that I had paid for sex. I didn't mention that there were two women involved. I said something about how badly our sex life had been lately and how I had needs. She didn't show a great deal of sympathy. Usually, she's got a pretty foul mouth – everybody in entertainment law drops F bombs more than they say litigate or settlement or your honor – but none of her favorites came out. She, for just a second, looked like she'd cry. You know, I've never seen her cry, even when our daughter was going in for a spinal tap when they thought she had meningitis. But she was really pissed. She wondered whether I did that before. Actually, I hadn't – not once in all of our years together did I have sex with anybody other than her – can't say that I didn't want to from time to time. I don't know if she believed me when I said that. I tried to convince her that whoring was a lot better than having an affair with somebody at the office, or, worse, somebody that we both know. I think she always thought that I probably had somebody at the tennis club. There are tons of sexy young players there, who, by reputation, wouldn't look down on hooking up with a rich lawyer, especially one who they could talk to about movie stars. Nothing for me though. Fifteen love, thirty love, but no carnal love."

By this time, Fred had developed an interest in the story that his son was telling. As with his TV dramas, he could follow and remember, at least for a while, a story relayed by someone he knew. Jennifer had seen his memory skills improve gradually and significantly over the months since his injury. When asked, he could tell the story back pretty well. What he didn't do very often is question the story teller for more information. Or if he did, the questions would be two or three words and sought specific, usually insignificant information. To his son, he asked, "Were they blonds?"

"One was blond and the other redhead, Dad."

"Go ahead, Jason," said Jennifer.

"You won't believe it, but she asked me how much I paid the women. Emily is always worried that we spend too much. She could tell you the price of every item in her shopping cart before she checks out. I've never seen her look at any rack in a clothing store that doesn't say SALE on it. She makes sure I don't leave too big a tip when we eat out."

"Did you tell her?"

"Hell no, I didn't tell her. No reason to give her something like that to focus on as this plays out. Let me put it this way to you – sex isn't cheap, especially when you hire a pair. She didn't push the issue, thank God. I don't think she really wanted to know for fear that I had significantly diminished our net worth."

"How much did you pay, son?"

"Sorry Dad, I'm not saying."

"Oh, OK."

Jason continued, "So we talked and talked. Sometimes, she would yell – getting all excited – other times she would act hurt and sad. Never cried. I didn't say very much. She'd ask questions about the night and challenge me about other times. I tried to be as rational as possible – never raised my voice. I told her that there were no other times. She accused me of looking at some of her friends like I wanted to fuck them and I said something like "all men look." I didn't tell her that I didn't think much of her friends and that the last thing I'd want to do is fuck one of them.

"The way it was going, I thought she'd come around and recognize that it was a one-time thing and that we could deal with it. But out of nowhere, she said that I had to leave. She gave me the usual line about needing time to think things through, and that she needed space, and that as hard as it would be on the kids, we'd be better off apart for a while. I said that that would be crazy, that there'd be no reason for me not to stay – we could sleep in different rooms – heaven knows we have enough rooms. But she didn't buy into it. One of us had to leave and it wasn't going to be her. So, I packed the suitcases and called you. We both talked to the kids. Neither seemed very upset."

"I'm glad we can be of help," said Jennifer.

"That's really great to hear, Jen. I know that I've been a jerk with both of you. I haven't been much of a son... or step-son, in a long time.

"No problem, Jason. That's all in the past. So, where do you think it will go with your family from here?"

"I really don't know. I do know that one night stands usually don't cause a complete rift. I have a lot of friends who have gone through the same thing, or something a lot like it, and almost all of them end up back in the house, at least for a while. But frankly, I'm not sure that I want to go back. I don't know if I love her. Maybe I never loved her? God, I don't know. How do I say this? I'm not sure that I love the kids as much as a father should. She's programmed them to be just like her. Study, study, study, lessons, lessons, lessons. Violin lessons, golf lessons, tennis lessons, Korean classes. Gotta be class president, vice president isn't good enough. Gotta to be the best in everything. An A-minus is failure – reason for a visit with the teacher to find out why the minus."

Fred reentered the conversation. "Your children have never been very nice to me."

"I know that Dad. They're not nice to anyone very often."

"Are you going to go to a lawyer?"

"Not right now, Jen. I have to spend some time thinking about it myself. I don't know what's right and what's wrong."

"How about a counselor? I know a lady here who is a marriage and family therapist. A friend of mine swears by her."

"Thanks for the idea. You don't know this, but I spent a few years in the Scientology Church. They don't think much of mental health professionals. I left when they started hitting me up for money but I think that the no-psychiatry thing sank in pretty deep. Emily brought up the idea of marriage counseling but I told her that I had no time for that. So, while I am here, I'll be spending most of my time with my big case, do some reading, watch a few movies and hit some tennis balls."

"Jason."

"What Dad?"

"I love you. Hurry back."

"Thanks Dad. I'm not going anywhere. I'll be here with you for a while." Tears appeared in the already reddened eyes. He did not remember ever hearing his father mention love.

Fred leaned over and took the remote out of the basket.

More Twins

Jennifer had not seen Ernesto since her visit to his house six weeks earlier and not spoken to him since his rejection of her offer to visit him on a Wednesday. Fearing that he was losing interest in her because of his new jet-set job, and nervous that he'd not take the news she had for him well, she dialed his cell phone. Five rings later, his Latin-lover accented message told her that he couldn't answer his phone right now and that she should leave a message and give her number slowly so that he could call back. She told the electronic device that she had to talk with him; she had important information. Four hours later, he had not returned the call. She dialed again and within three rings, he answered.

"Why didn't you call me? I told you it was important."

"I didn't know you called."

"Didn't you check your phone?

"You know me better than that. I was in class and they make me turn off the phone. Then when I finish, I turn it on again."

She didn't believe him. She was sure that he wanted out of the affair. "How are you, Ernesto?"

"I'm fine, just fine. You know that I am going to South America on Friday, don't you?" It was Tuesday.

"No, how would I know that? We haven't talked in weeks.

"Sorry, guess that I didn't tell you before. Yes, I am off to Uruguay Friday morning."

"Uruguay, so that's where you are going. What are you doing there?"

"I still can't tell you. The boss is worried about somebody else finding out about his deal and stealing it from him.

"Who is the boss?"

"Can't tell you that either. All I can say is that he's a smart guy and very good at what he does. You told me you had something important to tell me."

"Yes, I do. I'm pregnant." No hesitation in the telling, long pause after.

"*Aye, carajo*! How can that happen? You are 42 years old."

"Actually my love, I am 44 years old. I am not the oldest pregnant woman in history, but I dare say that I am the oldest one married to a 75-year-old accused killer who has not done anything to impregnate me in a long time. And, as to how it happened - you, my friend, made it happen, with my help. As you recall, it had been a few months since we had had sex and I stopped taking my birth control pills when Fred was indicted. I started taking them again when I knew I was going to see you – like a day before we did it in that pig sty of yours. Really stupid of me, but my periods had been irregular so I thought I wasn't at any risk. Really dumb."

"Pig sty. What do you mean?"

"Jesus, is that what you just heard? Your room is a mess – you know that, but shit, man, we're going to have a baby!"

"Are you sure? Did you go to the doctor?"

"Come on. You're smarter than that. I missed a period – nothing unusual. But then I felt nauseated so I went to the drug store in Marin, not here in the city – I didn't want anybody that might have the slightest idea who I was seeing me buy a pregnancy test. Last night, I peed on the stick and the line turned blue – not a little bit blue, a lot blue. Positive. Unless I do something about it, I'm going to be a mom. Aren't we happy? ...Fuck it!" she yelled, loud enough for him to move the cell phone away from his ear.

"Calm down."

"Don't tell me to calm down! I am fucking pregnant by a Mexican and am married to a rich old Jew who might be headed to jail if he gets his memory back. Just picture this in the goddam *Chronicle*. What, dear God, am I going to do?"

"Don't call me a Mexican!"

"You are one. I'm sorry. I shouldn't have said that."

"Apologies accepted. So, what are you going to do?"

"I'm not going to have the kid. You know, as a teenager, I promised my parents that I'd never have an abortion. In fact, I think I promised that I'd never have sex before I got married. Amazing that my father, the big professor, didn't believe in abortions or sex before marriage. I kept that promise 'til I was about fifteen. But there was no way I'd need an abortion. I was always so careful about using protection – usually both pills and condoms. I should have gotten my tubes tied, but I was pretty sure that it would be impossible for me to get pregnant. You and I were so careful. So was I with my husbands – always used the pills religiously. But here I am with a fetus inside me that simply cannot see the light of day."

"How about Planned Parenthood?"

"I can't go there. The people who volunteer are people just like me – rich women from Pacific Heights and St. Francis Wood. Someone will recognize me and even though they are sworn to secrecy, the word would get out – Klein's wife has abortion! I like my gynecologist. I haven't seen him in a couple of years. He'd keep it quiet. But if he says abortion, and how can he not, it would have to be done outside of San Francisco – we're just too radioactive here."

"What do you want me to do? How can I help? I could pay half." To Contreras, a lapsed Catholic with deep-seated thoughts on such things, abortion was anathema. But he was not about to discuss it with his lover.

"Pay half? Don't be an idiot. Just get out of town. Maybe you should go to Uruguay." He could see her smiling over the phone. "I do love you, Ernesto, but you can't be around while this is going on. And, by the way, do you love me?"

He delayed a few milliseconds. "Of course I do." She didn't believe him.

"Hey Fred," she said in a loud enough voice so that he could hear over the auto chase, "I'm going to see my gynecologist. Haven't had a checkup in a while. No problems – just a routine exam."

He didn't turn his head toward her. "OK."

Her Ob/Gyn was headquartered on Sutter with all the other doctors-to-the-rich. Dr. Wachs was not the type that a woman getting a PAP could fantasize about. Old enough to qualify for Medicare, he was bald, frumpy, and dressed in khakis, a wrinkled shirt and threadbare white coat, the embroidered name almost illegible from thousands of wearings and hundreds of cleanings.

"How nice to see you, Jennifer. It's been a long time. I was afraid that you had changed offices."

"No, Dr. Wachs, I'm very happy here. I just haven't had any trouble and I read somewhere that every two years was enough for PAPs."

"I don't believe that. We've been doing yearly PAPs for as long as I've been a doctor – no reason to change. So, just a routine visit today?"

"No, not a routine visit. I'm pregnant."

Wachs had the face of a tournament-class poker player. "Pregnant, huh? Are we happy about this? I'm a little surprised. I've read about your husband and heard from others that he isn't his old self. What does he think about having another child at his age?"

"He doesn't know about it and probably couldn't understand it if I told him. But it's not his. We haven't slept together since his surgery. It's somebody else's."

"Oh. Don't I recall that you are taking birth control pills? Yes, your chart says that you've been getting regular refills, at least up to the beginning of the year."

"As you can tell, Doctor, I wasn't taking them very well."

"That's water under the bridge. How long since your last period?"

"As you might remember, I'm pretty irregular. But this time, it's been eight weeks. I had sex about seven weeks ago."

"I assume you've done a pregnancy test?"

"Of course." She was a bit irritated that he felt he had to ask the question.

"The first thing we need to do is confirm that you are pregnant with a repeat test and a pelvic exam. I've had cases where the woman says

Philanthropist

the test was positive but we find out that she did it wrong, or that the test was faulty. Not often, but not zero. While we're in there, we'll do a PAP."

Jennifer supplied a urine sample, disrobed, and put on the blue paper gown. The nurse, whose age had to be nearly identical to that of the doctor, helped her get into the position despised by almost all females. Jen had always thought that she'd suggest to the doctor that he find a way to at least make it so that the stirrups wouldn't hurt her feet, but never did. Wachs was gentle, making a potentially grossly unpleasant activity merely unpleasant.

"Your cervix does look bluish. That can be a sign of pregnancy. Not always. And, the uterus feels just a bit enlarged, again evidence toward pregnancy, early but still pregnancy." He took the brushing for the Pap smear and told her to sit up.

"Your cervix looks like you've never been pregnant before. True?"

"True. We've discussed that before. I never wanted to have a child and my first husband was so busy making money and trying to please God that he had no time for kids. Then, Fred had already had enough children, something that endeared him to me. The other men in my post-divorce life wanted me to produce heirs."

The nurse brought in the urine test results. Positive. No question. "Get dressed and come into my office." Wachs was abrupt but she was pleased that she wasn't going to have to make major decisions while attired in a now ripped and soiled paper gown.

The office was spartan. Diplomas and cheap reproductions of Impressionists on the walls, scattered patient files, blank prescription pads, and drug advertisements on the desk, and a reasonably new ecru wall to wall carpet on the floor. The chair to which she was directed was comfortable enough. The sofa looked more comfortable, but he wanted her where he could show her artist renderings of fetuses in wombs.

"Here are the facts, Jennifer, and you need to make a decision. Yes, you are pregnant. This isn't a false pregnancy test or some nasty uterine tumor that causes a pregnancy test to be positive. You are about five weeks along. That's very early. The fetus is about the size of an apple seed. The child is not viable and won't be for about five months. So, you've got three options. One is to have the child. Two is to have a traditional abortion – minor surgery. Three is to have a chemical abortion – using medicines."

"You mean no surgery? You can just give me some pills and the pregnancy will end?" asked Jennifer, incredulously.

"That's correct. The pills work more than 90 per cent of the time and they are no more dangerous than the surgery. You've heard of RU-486 haven't you?"

"Yeah, I guess I remember a lot of ruckus from the right-to-life people a few years ago. You can get rid of option one. I am not going to have this child. My apologies to all those people in America who think that's murder. Give me murder any day rather than having another man's child in my situation. As to the other two options, can you give me any reasons that I shouldn't take the pills?"

"I really can't. There are still a lot more surgical abortions in the US than medical ones, but the research says that the two have about the same results and about the same low risks. The pills cost a little bit more than the surgery – not significant for you, I'd assume. Insurance won't pay, but we're not talking about a whole lot of money."

"Doctor Wachs, you are my hero! You have saved my life, or at least you've saved my marriage. Give me the pills."

"Not quite so fast, Jennifer. We've got to do an ultrasound and get a couple of blood tests to make sure you are OK. We can do the ultrasound here in the office and we can draw the blood and send it to the lab and we'll get the results by tomorrow morning. Make an appointment and I'll see you tomorrow before noon."

"I've got my reading group in the morning. How about the afternoon?"

"Sorry, it's Wednesday. I'm playing golf."

The next morning, she learned that the ultrasound showed not one but two fetuses while the blood tests revealed nothing else disturbing. She was given two kinds of pills - one, the RU-486, to swallow in the doctor's

Philanthropist

office, the other to put between gum and cheek like dipping tobacco 24 hours later. Half an hour after the second medicine she began bleeding, more heavily than she would in a period. The cramps were severe but passed in a few hours, as the bleeding stopped. She never saw anything other than blood. Two weeks later, the ultrasound was repeated. There were no fetuses in the uterus. Everything looked perfectly normal for a 44-year-old woman.

For those two weeks, she basically isolated herself. Fred noticed nothing different about her; he was too busy watching shows. Jason, who spent most of his time elsewhere, knew something was different but he was so preoccupied with his own concerns that he made little of it. The twins made their weekly visit but paid no real attention to their stepmother except to get her take on their father's progress. Ernesto never called. She never called him. She wasn't sure what continent he was on. She cried every day, slept poorly, ate little, and lost ten pounds. She had never felt so alone. She talked to the doctor. Ernesto knew. Not another of the six billion on earth was there for her to tell that she had just put an end to two humans-to-be. Her ex-husband? He was too busy trying to find a state where he and his live-in same sex golf professional could legally marry. Her sister? She had become a spokesperson for a New Jersey right-to-life non-profit. Her parents? Dad had died and mother was another anti-abortionist. Jason. No. Robert, Phillip. No. No.

Ernesto was on the North American continent – San Francisco, to be specific. The travel section of Spencer, Bowman and Clark had made him reservations, first class to Montevideo, on a combination of United and Argentine Airlines. His only previous experience in the air was a round trip from SFO to LAX for a cousin's wedding two years before. He was outfitted with a passport, his first brief case, his first business cards, and his first laptop. His only suit had been the tuxedo, obligatory attire at Beef, Ltd., that he bought off the rack when he was first employed at the steakhouse. All his earlier jobs had required nothing more than smart casual; he had purchased the beige sport coat and wool pants for a wedding.

For his Kobe Beef trip, he chose something dark gray at Macy's and accessorized with shirts and ties picked out for him by the salesman. He was rather taken by his new look. He spent hours in his house dressed to kill, walking by and standing erect in front of his bathroom mirror. He thought about calling Jennifer to show off but did not follow through as he wasn't sure where their affair was going. He was about to be rich, or at least richer, and thought that it might be time to take a different tack with his life. Marriage? Children? Maybe it was time to settle down. He had been a US citizen for eight years. He knew that a return to Mexico was no longer in the cards. He was here to stay. But Jennifer?

The night before his 2:25 PM flight to Houston his phone rang. He guessed it was from the restaurant. It was the first night of his two week leave of absence from Beef. He knew that the boss wasn't happy, but Ernesto was his best waiter. He wasn't about to threaten his job.

"Ernesto, this is Mr. Spencer."

"Yes, sir. Nice to hear from you." He was expecting last minute instructions like a trainer offers a jockey. He felt prepared for all eventualities – they had trained him well.

"Ernesto, you aren't going. Sorry to break the news this late, but your trip is off."

"Oh...Why?"

"Got a call from Senor Gomez, our man in Montevideo. He said that he didn't want to talk to anybody but one of the big bosses. Said he was going to back out if I didn't come. I can't go, but I'm sending my partner, Mr. Bowman. Gomez is OK with a partner. Bowman speaks Spanish."

"But I don't understand. I did all this training and bought new clothes, and..."

"Sorry, Ernesto. Call me sometime next week and we'll see if we can find something else for you." Spencer hung up the phone.

The explanation offered Contreras was not the way it happened. Bowman and Clark had insisted on a partnership meeting. All was not well in the firm with the loss of so much tech. They had plenty of cash but venture

Philanthropist

capitalists don't make their money by letting principle sit in the bank or in publically traded equities.

"Mark, we don't understand why you are handling Kobe the way you are," said Clark, using the codename for the Uruguayan venture. "We can't figure out why you are sending this rookie Mexican guy down there. Yeah, this is no Google-to-be, but it can be a real winner for us, at least according to the charts that you showed us."

"Contreras is a good man. He trained up real good. He knows his stuff now and it doesn't hurt that Spanish is his first language." Spencer was on defense.

"Don't forget, Mark, I speak Spanish pretty well – Peace Corps in Honduras, remember?" responded Bowman. "I'd love to go down there myself – I've never been in that part of South America. I know it's your file – you came up with the idea, but I also know that you don't want to leave the City."

"We've spent a lot of money on Contreras."

"What do they say about good money after bad?"

"Come on guys, gimme a break. This guy is OK. It's just a first meeting. He isn't going to screw it up."

"Sorry, Mark," said Clark. "The two of us have real reservations about this and we either want you or one of us to go." As only full partners vote, the electorate numbered 3 and 2 voted no on Ernesto.

"Jesus. He's going tonight. How are we going to handle this one?"

"I'm sure you can work that one out, friend. You got Mr. Contreras on board. Now, get him off that flight."

"OK. It isn't going to be pretty, but I'll call him. Then, I'll have to call Uruguay and let them know that we won't have our man in town tomorrow after all."

"So, are you going to go in his place?" asked Bowman

"I can't. You know that. I can't leave Meagan with the nanny yet. Neither Bowman nor Clark had the slightest idea that the nanny was Ernesto's sister.

"I take it that means that you want me to go?" asked Bowman.

"If you can, yes."

"You owe me one, Mr. Senior Partner. I can't get ready tonight but I'll shoot for the end of the week."

Ernesto was devastated. He had counted on his life changing very much for the better. He was not going to have to survive on taking orders for meat and creamed spinach plus the contributions of Jennifer Klein and assorted other females. High finance beckoned. He had envisioned the door on the 14th floor of the Transamerica Pyramid announcing the firm of Spencer, Bowman, Clark, and Contreras. That vision had instantly blurred. Spencer hadn't even said what was to happen next. Was he fired? Had he had a job in the first place? During training, he had received generous but not overwhelming checks. The big paydays were to have started tomorrow. He wouldn't let anybody know – no call to Jennifer, no call to Carmen. His fellow servers at Beef were only to know that the Uruguayan adventure had been postponed. Embarrassed. Devastated. Surely he was offered a complete explanation. He wasn't going to call Spencer. Spencer had to call him.

The mega-million dollar case that brought Jason to the Bay Area, an intellectual property matter involving big names in Silicon Valley, Hollywood, China, and Israel, was heating up, but heating up of the case meant cooling down for Jason Klein. His tasks, while important, did not involve his speaking to judges and juries in courtrooms. He deposed the big names, and read, then summarized documents. He'd occasionally have to be at the trial to whisper in the ear of the litigators. His reasons for staying in San Francisco were diminishing with his role in the legal matter. Emily showed no signs of welcoming him back in the family home. He had talked to his kids every day, when they were not at lessons or in the middle of practice, but his wife would say no more to him than hello when she answered his calls. If he asked a child to get his mother on the phone, he'd be told that she was busy. Neither child said anything about missing their father. He longed for, but never heard the plea, "Come home, Daddy." After Emily and the kids returned from their visit to the Parks, he'd go to LA on weekends and have a few hours with the kids, taking them to the beach, the movies, or the zoo, receiving no thanks for his efforts or expressions of sadness that he'd not be in their lives for the next several days. He was losing his family.

Concurrently, Jennifer was losing her lover. She learned that he was still in town, by the subterfuge of calling his workplace and asking if he was working that night. He had not gone to Uruguay. But he had not called her and he did not respond to the several calls she made to his cell phone. He had no land line at home. She'd let the mobile ring a dozen times. She had been told, in no uncertain terms, not to interrupt him at work. How could he do this to her? They'd been as close as two people could get, or at least as close as she could get with anybody, for fifteen years and now, nothing. He'd created life inside of her womb. He'd been there when she thought her husband had killed himself. Now, nothing.

Jennifer Klein was in love with two men. Jennifer loved Fred. She very much loved Fred, a man who no longer could express his love for her, in words or deeds. He could lie with her in bed, even respond to her request for a pre-sleep kiss. But he could go no further. To her question as to whether he loved her, he'd unhesitatingly say yes, but he would not offer the same sentiment unsolicited. His request for Viagra when he left the hospital masked a total lack of interest in physical love. She would not ask him, assuming that he didn't have the cognitive skills to give a logical answer. She feared that aggressiveness on her part might lead to physical and chemical responses in her partner that would jeopardize his heart, undoing the effectiveness of the pacemaker. She could kill him. She fought with the image of a dead old man next to her, a victim of her lust. She regretted that she had been too embarrassed to bring up intercourse during his many medical appointments. Maybe she should call Dr. Jameson. After all, Jameson was her doctor too. No, we'll wait 'til the next visit. Jennifer was buoyed by his slow but sure improvement over the months since his discharge. Surely, he would once again become a husband in the deepest sense of the word.

Why did Jennifer love Fred? It was a question she asked herself, but more often, the question was asked by others. No one, except her sister who asked it before Fred and she tied the knot eight years ago ("I don't know, I just do."), ever asked it directly of Jennifer. After all, he was an old man and she was not an old woman. He was rich, but so was she. He was richer than she, but there was nothing she could not have or do for lack of resources. Her first husband, when he moved out to be with the golf pro, left her very well heeled. Fred was pleasant, funny, interested in interesting things, and reasonably sexy. She didn't need great sex - that she got with Ernesto and she saw no reason that she'd have to give that up. While the ex embarrassed her when they went out, she was proud to be seen with Fred. She basked in the glow of being a famous philanthropist's wife. She was thrilled any time she went to a fancy dress ball or dedication of a new hospital or building, knowing that Mr. and Mrs. Klein were going to be a center of attention. She secretly kept a scrap book of articles dealing with their efforts to improve the community. She felt important and had Fred Klein to thank for it. The felony, which she had believed would lead to his imprisonment, and the heart and brain calamities, which she now assumed would keep him out of prison, were no reason to stop loving him. She would continue to be very proud of the title, Mrs. Frederick Klein.

Jennifer loved Ernesto. She had loved him for longer than she had known her husband. Ernesto was easy. He made no demands on her, other than for love at its most biological. That was a demand that had no downside. She demanded it of him and he demanded it back. It didn't have to be a demand frequently fulfilled. A couple times a month was the average for the decade prior to the Event. Only once since and that produced an embryo, but that was OK, until now. Plus, Ernesto was her buddy. She had few women friends – none with whom she could share the deep stuff.

But now, nothing. She was losing her best friend. She was losing her helper, the man who was there in the middle of the night when her husband was missing, feared dead. She was losing the only person with whom she could belly laugh. She was losing her fuck-buddy.

But surely he'd be back. He didn't go to Uruguay. She had no idea why he didn't go, but she never knew why he was going to go in the first place. He's obviously upset by what happened to stop him from going, but he'll get over it. He's such an easy going guy. And he loves her, doesn't he? Yes, there are other women in his life, but none that matter, at least he says that none matter. He'd never lie to her, or would he? Isn't his not calling to say that he didn't go a lie? Isn't his not answering her calls a lie? Surely, he'll return to her. Maybe.

Irving Greenberg had not been in touch with his client, Klein, in weeks. There had been no reason to call or have him visit the office as neither Judge Gasparini nor the DA had made any contact. The newspapers had been void of relevant information and no one from the Klein contingent had spoken up. Greenberg saw no reason to push the matter. The longer it went, the less the emotional need for revenge, at least in the community at large. Should the case go to trial, it would be heard in San Francisco. A call for it to be moved to another venue where the facts were not as widely known would, with little doubt, be rejected on the basis of cost savings. Therefore, the longer the time between the alleged crime and the trial, the better the odds on a good verdict.

The lull was not to last. Greenberg received an email from the Judge's clerk asking him to set up an appointment with a court designated psychiatrist. It was time to determine whether the alleged perpetrator was fit to stand trial.

Roger Stern, MD, PhD, was a product of University of California campuses in Berkeley and San Francisco. His doctoral thesis in Neurosciences at Berkeley concerned the criminal mind and the effect of prescription drugs on it. As a forensic psychiatrist, he had become a good, and therefore wealthy, friend of the court, regularly called to testify by plaintiffs or defendants and by judges to render unbiased opinions.

Jason and Jennifer entered the TV room together, dressed to go out. Fred was watching Oprah. "Dad, it's time to go to the doctor. You are going to be seeing a new one – his name is Dr. Stern. He's a psychiatrist."

"I am not crazy! I'm just fine. I'm not depressed and I sure as hell am not hearing voices. I don't need to see a shrink.

"Nobody thinks you are crazy, honey," said Jennifer.

"So, why am I seeing this guy?"

"The Judge has insisted. They want to know if you are OK to go to trial."

"Ah ha. I guess that I better sound like I'm crazy."

"I wish it were that easy, Dad. Psychiatrists are pretty good seeing through that. Just be yourself. If you can remember something, say so, but don't be afraid to say that you don't remember."

On entering the office of Dr. Stern, father, stepmother and son encountered only one other person in the waiting room, Mr. Greenberg.

"Hello, Fred," he said sprightly.

"Hello, Steve.

"It's Irv Greenberg. Not Steve."

"Oh, sorry Irv. I had a friend named..."

"Yes, you told me that before. You do know who I am, don't you?"

"You're a lawyer aren't you? But I thought Artie Schofield was my lawyer?"

"He is, but I'm helping you in your criminal case. Do you know why you are here today?"

"To show the doctor that I'm not crazy anymore and that I can go to court so that they can throw me in jail?"

"Not exactly. You are here so that Dr. Stern can interview you to see how your mind is working. It wasn't working so well after your surgery and we all know that it's working better now. But it's up to the doctor to recommend to the judge whether or not you are able to understand well enough to help in your own defense."

"I don't know. Am I?"

"I don't have an opinion. Maybe yes, maybe no. But I don't make the call. Obviously, I'd like to put a trial off as long as possible. The longer we wait, the better your chances are. Judge Gasparini will make the final call, but he'll base it on the opinion of this doctor. Just be yourself, Fred." Klein was called into the doctor's office. Greenberg, Jason and Jennifer remained in the waiting room.

Fred expected to be asked to lie down on a couch. He liked the idea, but when the nurse took him in, she led him to a chair, albeit a comfortable one, across the large desk from the pony-tailed and single ear-ringed Doctor Stern. In conflict with the jewelry and hair style, he was dressed in a gray suit of distinction, a professionally pressed white shirt and green, orange, and black striped bow tie. He offered, and Fred accepted his hand in greeting.

"Welcome, Mr. Klein, I am Doctor Stern."

"I know that. Your name is on your office door."

"Yes, so it is. Let me tell you a little about what we are doing here today. Usually, my job is to determine whether a patient was sane when he or she allegedly committed a crime. Tell me if you don't understand something I say."

"I understand. Don't worry about that. I'm in MENSA."

"Aha. Sometimes we doctors say things that even the smartest people don't understand. Just tell me if that happens."

"OK."

"Nobody questions whether your mental health was normal when the episode happened."

"What episode?"

"I understand that you were involved in a traffic accident in which a woman died."

"Oh, yeah. They told me about that, but I can't remember a thing about it."

"Our purpose is to determine whether you are mentally competent now, not then, to stand trial."

"Go for it, Doc."

From his desk drawer, Stern pulled out a foolscap pad and a Mont Blanc pen. "Shall I call you Fred or Mr. Klein?"

"I don't care. Just don't call me Freddy. I hate it when people call me Freddy, even my wife."

"Fred it is. I am going to administer what is called a Mini-Mental Status examination to you. There will be a number of questions, some of which may seem terribly simple. To start, Fred, I am going to name three items for you to remember and later on I'll ask you what they are. A book, a fish and a tree. Please repeat those things."

"Book, fish, tree."

"Good." He wrote a note on his pad. "Do you know what day it is."

"Uh, Wednesday?"

"No, it's Thursday. Close. What is the date?"

"Come on Doc. I'm retired. Some day you will be too. All the days feel the same. I don't know, the 15th?"

"It's the 3rd. And the month?"

"February?"

"Right. Year?" Fred scored on that one. He could not identify the season; many San Franciscans get that wrong.

"Now, who is the President?" Fred nailed it. "Who was the last President?" Again right on, with a snide comment on the politics of modern day Republicans.

Fred was able to say that he was in a doctor's office in San Francisco, California. He couldn't specify the county's name. Again, most San Franciscans don't understand that their city and county are one and the same, unless of course they had run for the job of County Supervisor.

"Now, Fred, a little math. Start with 100. Now subtract 7 from that and keep subtracting from the answer."

"Uh, 93?"

"Well done. Seven from that?"

"From what?"

"93."

"I don't know. Arithmetic was never my strong point."

"OK, got it. Now I want you to spell backwards the word WORLD."

"D. O. R. W. L."

"OK, Fred. Now, can you tell me what those three things are that I asked you to remember?" It had been about ten minutes since the list was given.

"Uh…book?"

"That's right. What else?"

"A pen?"

"No, pen is not one of them. Can you remember the other two?"

"A car? I remember that they were easy things. Yeah, a car."

"No, not a car. They were a fish and a tree."

"Oh, yeah. Now I remember. Book, fish and tree."

"We'll ask you those again. Try to remember."

"What's this?" Stern pointed to his watch and then a pencil. Fred was two for two.

"Repeat after me, No ifs, ands or buts." Fred repeated the aphorism flawlessly.

The doctor handed Klein a piece of paper that said, "Take the paper in your hand, fold it in half and put it on the floor." He folded the paper once and laid it on the desk.

Stern held up a card reading, "Close your eyes." Fred closed them after reading the order aloud.

When asked to write a sentence, Fred, his penmanship barely legible wrote, "I am an old man."

He was handed another card with a picture of two intersecting pentagons and asked to copy it. He drew two rectangles that did not intersect.

"Now let's talk about you and your family." Stern asked him questions about his parents, his education and occupation, his wives, his children and grandchildren. Klein did well, getting all the names and most of the dates. He teared up when asked about his first wife and the reason they were no longer together. He saw fit to tell the doctor how much money he made in the sale of the TV station and the expertise with which he embellished his net worth buying low and selling high.

"Now, tell me what you remember about the accident."

"You mean the one where the mother was killed?"

"Yes, that one."

"I can tell you what they told me."

"What who told you?"

"My wife and my son Jason, the lawyer, and my criminal lawyer, Steve Greenberg."

"You mean Irving Greenberg?" Stern and Greenberg had crossed legal paths often.

"Right, Irv Greenberg. I had a high school buddy named Steve Greenberg."

"Tell me what you were told by your wife and son and attorney."

"They said that I was driving my Lexus to a poker game and that I hit this lady when she got out of her car but that I didn't stop and just kept driving and went to the poker game."

"Do you remember what time of day it was that that happened?"

"Doc, I don't remember that it happened, let alone what time of day. It must have happened in the early evening 'cause that's when I play poker."

"Do you remember the poker game? Did you win or lose?"

"No clue. I usually win. Those guys aren't very good at cards. You know, I could have been a big winner on all those TV poker shows. Some guy just won over a million bucks last week – lucky bastard."

"OK. What can you tell me about the time between the accident and the time you ended up in the hospital because of your heart attack and head injury?"

"Not a goddam thing. I hear that I was arrested and then bailed out for a shitload of money. No way was that necessary. I'm not running away. And, by the way, Doc, I wasn't drunk. I hear that they think I was but I never drive if I've drunk too much. Couple of glasses of wine, that's it."

"OK. And, I'm sure you wouldn't run away, Fred. What about your heart and brain?"

"They tell me I was in the hospital for more than a month but I don't remember anything about it. Actually, I do remember one thing. The man who wheeled me out was a big fat guy with one arm who told me that he had been a surgeon in Africa."

"Interesting. That's all you remember about a month in the hospital?"

"Yep. That's all."

"So, what are the first things you remember after getting home from the hospital?"

"I do remember that I started watching a lot of television. Before, I know that if it wasn't news or sports, I wouldn't turn it on. Believe it or not, I used to own a TV station, but I never watched. My second wife, Jennifer – she'd watch shows at night, especially when I went to meetings. But not me. Sports, especially the World Series, Super Bowl, Final Four, news and presidential debates – that's about it…actually, I do remember that I watched a lot when Kennedy was killed and when the Challenger spacecraft went down and when the Arabs hit the towers. But now I'm glued to the set all day."

"Why do you think that is?"

"Can't tell you, Doc. I just like it. Hell, I'll even spend time watching the channel where they sell stuff like necklaces. Never bought a thing but for some reason, I watch that shit."

"No harm in that. What else do you remember about the time since you got out of the hospital?"

"Going to doctors. I must go to two doctors every week. Before all this happened, I never went to them. In fact, my wife made me go and that's what led to all of this?"

"What do you mean, that's what led to all of this?"

"She sent me to her doctor, a woman – can't remember her name now. She made me have blood tests and my cholesterol was too high. Told me that I'd have to change my diet. Can you imagine? Seventy-five years old, in great health and I've got to give up everything that I like. The cunt! Oops, pardon my French."

"No worry about language. You really are angry about that, aren't you?"

"I was angry then and I'm still angry."

"Are you still on a diet for cholesterol?"

"Not anymore, but the horse is out of the barn. I've had a heart attack. Can't get any worse." Stern was impressed by the horse and barn comment.

"So why are you still angry?"

"Because I wouldn't be here if I hadn't gone to that bitch."

"What do you mean?"

"I was so pissed off that day that I couldn't think about anything else. That's got to be the reason that I hit that woman and didn't stop."

"So you do remember something about it?"

"Yes, doc. I remember leaving the house in a huff and I'm guessing that it's what led to the accident."

"Do you remember the accident itself now?"

"No."

"How does this make you feel?"

"How do you think it makes me feel? Bad. Really bad. A kid lost her mother because I was upset about having to eat vegetables. What an asshole!"

"Let's take a little break, Fred." Both doctor and patient went to their separate toilets in separate bathrooms. Fred was offered coffee, tea or water. He asked for Diet Coke and one was found. He went into the waiting room, finding none of his entourage. They, according to the receptionist, were told that it would be at least an hour and that they need not wait in the office.

Five minutes later, the two returned to their chairs. "How about those three items?"

Fred smiled. "This time I remember them. Book, car and fish."

"You're getting closer. It's book, fish and tree."

"Oh, yeah. Book, fish and tree. Ask me again."

"I will. Now let's talk a little about your family life. Tell me about your wife...Jennifer, no?"

"Yes, Jennifer. She's my second wife. Barbara was my first wife – God, was she wonderful. A perfect woman that…"

"I want to talk about Jennifer. I saw her in the waiting room. She's much younger than you, isn't she?"

"Yeah, 30 years. Isn't she a knockout?" Stern, also 30 years younger than his patient, had never heard a woman referred to that way.

"Fred, I can understand your attraction for her. Most men covet younger, attractive women at some time in their lives. Only a few succeed in setting up house with one. I don't mean this as an insult, but why do you think that she had interest in you?"

"Come on. I'm a pretty good catch. Rich, good looking and, if I might brag a bit, well hung and mighty good in the sack. And, I'm a good guy. Everybody likes me. Well not everybody or I'd be a Supervisor or Mayor by now, but I'm funny and have lots of interests like sports and movies and hiking and art."

Dr. Stern sat up straighter in his chair. "Let's look at that list. You are rich, but I've heard that her first husband left her very well off, that she could live just fine without your money. Good looking, for sure, but that doesn't get around the fact that you are 76 years old. Surely, she'd have no trouble rounding up a younger guy just as good looking. And, tell me more about the sex. How often do you make love?"

"At least once a week. Gotta admit that I've been using Viagra for a few years," answered Fred, taking his eye off the questioner.

"Is it still once a week since the surgery?"

"Well, no. I don't think she wants to screw – probably thinks that it will kill me."

"Do you ask?"

"I used to, but not now."

"So, getting back to my question, why is she with you?"

"I guess I don't know. I guess it's 'cause I'm such a good guy. Plus she likes the fact that we're in the paper a lot at fundraisers and conventions. She's become quite the big shot since she married me. Goes to almost as many meetings as I do."

"Fred, you are a great catch. Jennifer's lucky to have caught you."

"One other thing about her, Doc. I think she probably has something on the side."

"Do you mean another man in her life?"

"Right."

"Why do you think that?"

"She's too content. I know that once a week isn't enough for her. There were days, way back just after we were married, when things were nothing out of the ordinary when she'd come home from meetings or lunches smiling like a cat who had just done in a rat. She acts like she'd just had a dozen cups of coffee – jittery, talkative."

"Have you ever asked her if there's someone else?"

"Huh uh. I don't want to know."

"So, would it be OK if you found out that you were right?"

"Hell, no, it wouldn't be OK."

"Then, what would you do if you did find out?"

"Nothing."

Stern jotted a note. "Let's change subjects, Fred. My main job is to report to the judge my opinion on whether or not you should go to trial. The major issue there is not whether you are sane or insane or whether you know right from wrong, but whether you can help the lawyer, Mr. Greenberg, in defending you."

"Why not?"

"First, your memory for the events is pretty bad, no?"

"Right, I don't remember anything."

"That's not exactly true. You told me that you were angry as you went to the poker game."

"OK, but I don't remember hitting anybody."

"I understand. That's evidence that your memory is not good. Here's a question for you. How should your lawyer defend you? What should he say to the jury to convince them that you shouldn't be declared guilty?"

"I'm not a lawyer – that's his job!"

"But you've got to help him."

"If he can't convince them, I need a different lawyer. I can't go to jail. It would kill me!"

Stern wrote a longer note than usual. "Well, Fred. That ought to do it for this meeting. I'll write my report for the judge. Thanks for coming in."

"No problem. How did I do?"

"You did fine. Oh, by the way, what were those three things?"

"A book, a fish and…I forget the third one."

After the Kleins left the office, Greenberg and Dr. Stern met briefly. The doctor told the lawyer that he'd be sending the official report to Judge Gasparini but that there was no doubt in his mind that the patient was not ready to go to trial. Maybe in another couple of months – not now.

The Pyramid

Three weeks had elapsed since Spencer called Contreras telling him that he wouldn't be going to Montevideo. Ernesto assumed that he'd hear from him with further explanation of the change of plans. As far as Ernesto knew, Spencer himself had taken the trip. He was unaware of the option of one of the other partners doing so. He expected that Spencer would call when he returned to San Francisco, but as two weeks lengthened into three, he recognized that all may not be quite as simple as Spencer had made it out to be. He called the offices of Spencer, Bowman and Clark and spoke to the male secretary, with whom he thought he had hit it off well on the handful of previous visits to the home office. The secretary treated him like he was a cold caller seeking a job. "Please have Mr. Spencer call me," he said, knowing that the odds of that happening were low. He hand wrote a letter asking for an explanation but knew that his mediocre written English skills and doctor-like penmanship were unlikely to produce the desired response. An envelope from the firm finally arrived at his home; he thought it would be an answer to his queries. It was nothing more than a modest check to cover the time he had spent in training and a request for return of the unused tickets.

Additional calls to the office were no more productive. He chose to confront Spencer directly. He bused to the Pyramid at the corner of Clay and Montgomery and proceeded to the welcome desk in the lobby manned by an imposing fellow Latino. "Name is Ernesto Contreras. I'm here to visit Mr. Mark Spencer at Spencer, Bowman and Clark."

"Do you have an appointment?"

"No, but I know he will see me. You remember me. I came here a bunch of times a few weeks ago when I was in training."

"Sorry, I'm new here. Let me call upstairs." He mumbled into a handset such that Ernesto couldn't decipher the discussion. "I'm sorry Mr. Contreras. Mr. Spencer is not in his office."

"Can I just go up and talk to his secretary. He and I are good friends."

"No, sir, you can't. Security, you know. You remember when that law office got shot up a couple of blocks from here? We don't want that happening here."

Ernesto turned his coat pockets inside out. "You can check me. No guns. No knives."

"Sorry. Unless I get an OK from the office, I can't send anybody up. Why don't you get an appointment and come back tomorrow?"

"Yeah, right. I've tried that."

"Try again."

"I'm going to sit on your couch over there and wait for him. If he's in, he's gotta come out sometime. And, if he's out, he's going to go back to his office, if not today, tomorrow."

"I'm very sorry, Mr. Contreras. That sofa is for people who have appointments and are waiting for somebody from the office to come get them. You'll have to wait outside."

"And what if I do sit there?"

"I'll have to call security."

"OK. I'll wait out there. At least it's not raining. Thanks for nothing."

"You are welcome, sir."

Ernesto left the lobby wishing there was a door to slam. Where to wait? Obviously, Spencer had to come through the same door; it's the way to the elevators that he could see. Hundreds of people go through the entrance every day, either to conduct business on one of the 48 floors or to use the virtual lookouts on the ground floor that replaced the actual lookout after September 11, 2001. There's no bench with a view of the entrance, so Ernesto would have to stand. Should be no problem for a waiter who is on his feet every working day from six to midnight. He had come with his dress shoes, not the black sneakers he wore at work with his tuxedo. His feet would hurt if Spencer didn't show up soon – small price to pay.

    He paced. Up Montgomery to Washington, down Montgomery to Clay. He calculated that at his slow pace it took almost a full minute to go from the northeast corner to the southeast one and he'd always have direct site of people streaming in and out of the tower. One of the skills he was taught in his training program was to observe people in his vicinity to get an idea of the local population. The parade into, out of, and passing by Transamerica he guessed was unlike that in the centers of most of the world's cities. More men than women, but not by much. Asians outnumbered Caucasians, again by a small percentage. There were plenty of African Americans and Latinos, maybe ten percent of each. He noticed that while the African Americans were dressed as well as or better than the Asians and Caucasians, the Latinos mostly looked like they did the dirty work. Jeans, T-shirts, ratty sweaters and well-worn tennis shoes or work boots were more common than well-tailored skirts and blouses, suits, ties and wingtips. He felt pretty good about himself as a Mexican who looked like he belonged to the *primera clase*. Almost nobody strolled. They walked with a purpose; they were going somewhere, having come from somewhere, and they had to get there quickly. More than anything, he was impressed by how young everybody looked. At 40, he was a veritable senior citizen on Montgomery Street. He estimated thirty to be the median age. He had learned about median versus average in his course, too. He was amazed by how often two people walking in opposite directions seemed to know one another. They'd shake hands or hug or buzz kiss, speak no more than a dozen words and be on their way. Sometimes, two walkers would nod without speaking. Contreras assumed that they were either pairs who thought they knew each other but weren't sure, pairs who weren't fond of each other or pairs of vastly differing levels on the totem that was high finance by the Bay.

    Ernesto was not there to study demography. He was on the lookout for someone who screwed him over. He kept thinking that there must be something that he wasn't getting. Mark Spencer was such a nice fellow.

He hadn't spent much time with him, but when he did, they hit if off well. Was it a report he got from the trainers at the firm or at UC Davis where he learned about cattle? He'd be surprised as they kept telling him how quickly he learned. Could it have been an issue with his partners? Who knows? Ernesto never laid eyes on either Bowman or Clark. Was it his English – did he sound like an immigrant? Nobody ever told him that. The women in his life, especially Jennifer Klein, frequently complimented him on his vocabulary and lack of an accent. Yes, it was strange that Spencer should have picked him for an important position after ninety minutes as his waiter in a restaurant, but he could think of nothing that could have made that happen other than what was on the surface. He was a very good waiter, a very smart man who spoke Spanish and knew beef. There's got to be something else.

Another thought hit him, out of the blue. There's a parking lot under the building. Spencer's going to come and go to his office and never step through these doors. There's no way to provoke an encounter. But didn't he say once that he took a bus from his house to work? Yeah, he bragged about how he saved so much energy. Contreras opted to continue his stakeout.

He first started looking about ten in the morning. He was not concerned about not recognizing the man. Spencer was taller than 90% of those walking in and out of the building. Plus, as Ernesto had him pegged as being in his mid-40's, he was older than most. They had spent at least two hours face to face over the weeks, even though their last meeting was well over a month earlier. He calculated that the two most likely times to see him were the lunch hour and quitting time. He wasn't sure when Spencer ate or when he quit, but thought that he likely ate at his desk and worked late. He pictured a Mrs. Spencer dutifully waiting for her hard working husband to come home and two or three kids whose bedtimes were dictated by the work schedule of their father. During their time together, Spencer asked several questions about Ernesto's personal life, but offered no insight into his own. Surely, Spencer wouldn't leave right at noon for lunch, so Ernesto, not one to skip a meal nor one with an unusually efficient bladder, decided to duck across the street to a Starbucks for a pastry and a pee. He was gone no more than a quarter hour, returning to his movable lookout in front of the Pyramid.

Three times in the afternoon, he saw a man fitting his image of his new nemesis, all approaching on the street rather than exiting from the tower. His pulse accelerated, only to quickly decelerate when he saw the men up close. He hoped that Spencer would be one of the rush of workers exiting between five and six. Hopes were dashed. He'd stay until eight; he wasn't scheduled to wait tables that evening. The odds of a meeting on the sidewalk after eight were slim. He wasn't going to stay all night. Unsuccessful, he rode the two buses, packed with a Babel's Tower of riders, back to the Excelsior, took a hot shower to spray some of the aches out of his legs and feet, and fell into the disarray of his unmade bed where he could not fall asleep. How long would he keep this up? Was there any other way to find Spencer? There were dozens of Spencers in the phone book. He wasn't going to call all of them and he guessed that his prey wasn't one of them, anyway. No one that rich was going to have a listed number. Ernesto didn't have a computer at home so he couldn't do a search. He knew there was such a thing as Google for finding people, but had no idea how that was done. Maybe he could have somebody at work help him when he went the next night. He decided to give his stakeout another try in the morning and with the aid of something he bought in the drug store, he drifted into an agitated slumber.

He wanted to make sure that he would get to the Pyramid before Spencer arrived, so he mapped out a trip involving not two slow buses but one bus and BART, lessening the chance of being delayed by traffic. He boarded Muni Bus 14 and hadn't gone a block from his stop when an altercation broke out between a disheveled forty-something Caucasian man dressed in a beat-up bomber jacket, holey jeans, and worn out tennis shoes through which both great toes saw the light of day, and a young Central American woman with her cell phone pressed tightly to her ear. She was arguing, in Spanish with someone, almost surely someone with whom she was sleeping or had been sleeping, in a voice that could be

Philanthropist

easily heard by all riders on the double-length bus. The female protagonist, clearly on her way to work at a workplace where tidy, upscale clothing was required, ran through all of the Spanish expletives that Ernesto knew and one or two that he didn't. City bus riders tend to keep their mouths shut and that was true for most of the polyglot load of passengers that morning. The male protagonist, who had been unsuccessfully attempting to strike up conversations with several of those in nearby seats, decided to attempt to restore order and get her off the phone. "Shut the fuck up!" he screeched, easily surpassing her voice level. The young woman showed no evidence of having heard his command and continued to lambast the poor person, probably male, on the other end of the line. Two late-middle aged Filipinos, obviously married to each other, sitting one seat in front of the loud lady, turned around to add their approval to the idea of silence. A black man in a three piece suit and three Latinos, two men, one woman, all in smart-casual, spoke up. One of the Latino men gently placed his hand on the shoulder of the so-far oblivious conversationalist, trying to act as peacemaker. The angry woman reacted badly. She spun about and belted the self-appointed mediator in the side of the face with the hand that held the cell phone like a mugger with brass knuckles. A laceration immediately opened on the cheek of the handsome victim. Blood flowed onto his white, button-down collar. The melee intensified with the injured party's male colleague subduing the belligerent with a bear hug, the female yelling for the driver to stop the bus and the original male of shut-the-fuck-up fame going from rider to rider to sign them up as witnesses.

Ernesto's concern was not the blood and not the embarrassment he felt as a result of the behavior of a fellow Mexican-American, but the fact that the brawl was going to cause him to get to Montgomery and Clay after Spencer. The double carriage bus was so long that it required a relay of calls before the driver, a good natured gray-bearded black man, knew that there was trouble in the back. He found a spot to stop the vehicle, kept the doors closed, and made his way to the rear. Many of his customers yelled of their immediate need to get off. They were ignored in spite of the hail of fucks and shits and goddamns, assorted non-English epithets and threats of lawsuits. Two or three passengers had already called 911 and it was less than three minutes before a squad car pulled up and two officers boarded the bus. An ambulance arrived a minute later; one 911-caller thought that the laceration required emergency care. Ernesto's sole concern was to get out and find another means of conveyance. The police, having plenty of willing witnesses thanks to the work of the man with holes in his shoes, allowed the rest of the people to get off. Ernesto, not close to his BART transfer spot and knowing that hailing a cab in the Excelsior would be fruitless, waited five minutes for the next bus destined for the financial district. During the short interlude, he watched the ambulance load up the lacerated Latino and the cops cuff the disgruntled cell-phone user and force her into the black and white. The follow-up bus, while more crowded than its predecessor, was a slowly moving electrified island of peace. Ernesto arrived at the Transamerica tower 45 minute later than he had planned. Feeling famished, he stopped in at the Starbucks, waiting longer than was comfortable in the queue, swiping his debit card in payment for his Americano and his apple fritter to go, crossed the street and began the pacing ritual once again. His great fear was that, because of the battle of the bus, Spencer had beaten him to the corner. But it was still ten minutes shy of seven thirty, the time he predicted for Spencer's arrival.

He noticed that the early-morning camaraderie between walkers was less intense than that of the afternoon; people were too hurried for hugs, handshakes or high-fives. Lots of nodding. An occasional toothy smile. A few one-word greetings – "Hey," "Yo," "Howzitgoing?" and even "Hi," and "Hello." Minutes after he took up his mobile post, he spotted Spencer. This time there was no doubt as to identity. Mark Spencer was walking at a thoroughbred pace, decked out in designer jeans, running shoes, an orange and black Giants jacket zipped to the neck to ward off the San Francisco morning chill, and a matching cap. Ernesto had to nearly sprint to place himself between Spencer and the front door of the Pyramid. "Mr. Spencer, I have to talk with you."

Spencer always listened to music or podcasts on his way to work, the volume high enough to drown out the disruption of the talk of his fellow bus riders and the cacophony of street sound of early morning city life. He did not hear Contreras through his noise-canceling earphones.

Ernesto saw that he wasn't being heard so he stepped immediately in front of the man who he had been seeking for hours. Paying no specific attention to whoever had just intruded into his space, Spencer tried to step around, but Contreras parried, moving right to counter Spencer's shift to the left. Spencer stopped dead in his tracks. "Excuse me," he said calmly but brusquely, without taking off his earphones or looking the other man in the face.

Ernesto raised his voice to overcome the MP3 player, "Mr. Spencer, we have to talk."

Spencer focused, recognized Ernesto and removed the phones. "How can I help you, Mr. Contreras?"

"We need to have a discussion, Sir."

"I'm sorry. I am very busy right now. There's a client waiting for me upstairs. Why don't you call my secretary and set up an appointment? Next week should be fairly open."

"No. Next week is not soon enough. I've been calling your secretary for days and he won't do anything for me. We've got to talk, now."

"Sorry, no can do." He again tried to go around his ex-employee but Contreras deftly blocked his way. Spencer, much the larger of the two, put both hands on Contreras's right shoulder attempting to push him aside. Contreras held his ground like an offensive tackle.

"Mr. Contreras, you are blocking my way. Please let me through, now."

"Not until you tell me what really happened."

Neither potential combatant had been involved in fisticuffs since childhood, but both clenched fists as an involuntary response. Spencer saw someone from his floor entering the building. He did not know the woman's name. "Hey, would you get the guard out here...right away?" She nodded and walked quickly to the security desk. Spencer, who was facing in toward the entrance, saw the guard, firearm in its holster at his side, come toward the site of the altercation. Contreras, faced the other way, did not.

"Mr. Spencer, how can I help you?" Contreras turned toward the man, recognizing him as the uniformed Latino who had rejected his requests the previous day.

"Thanks, Pedro. Tell this man to leave me alone. I am trying to get to my office and he's making it difficult."

"Certainly, Sir." He altered his gaze toward Ernesto. "Aren't you the man that gave me so much trouble yesterday?"

"I gave you no trouble. I only asked you if I could go up to Mr. Spencer's office to talk to him."

"I don't really care what happened yesterday. Let Mr. Spencer get by. If not, I'll have to call the SFPD."

Ernesto moved enough to let Spencer go toward the entry door.

"You have to talk to me! You screwed me!" he yelled, catching the attention of a handful of others in the area.

"I don't have to do anything, Mr. Contreras. Once you cool down a little, like tomorrow, call my office and if you are prepared to be civil, I'll have my secretary set up an appointment."

"To hell with you! You know goddam well that your secretary is not going to even talk to me." He shuffled away slowly, as did the small crowd of onlookers who had collected, expecting to see fireworks.

The next morning, he had simmered down and thought that maybe Spencer had been sincere in his offer of a meeting. After all, he had been sincere at the restaurant and sincere in his office the next day, and sincere during the several meetings they had had before he pulled the rug out from under his feet. "Hello, this is Ernesto Contreras again. Mr. Spencer told me that if I called today he would set up an appointment with me."

"He didn't say anything to me, sir. I'll check with him after he gets out of a meeting he's in right now. I'll call you back as soon as possible."

At four o'clock, he had heard nothing. He put on his tuxedo and went to work. He received no calls that night or the following day. A reminder message on the secretary's voice mail produced no response.

We Don't Want to be Mormons

For the first time since the hospitalization, Fred and Jennifer went to the movies. Before, they were huge fans. They preferred avant-garde and foreign films, but would sample mainstream ones if the *Chronicle* and *New Yorker* both rated them highly. They usually attended matinees. The crowds were smaller, older, and quieter, plus the tickets were cheaper. Fred would get senior rates and Jen bought discounted tickets for early birds. When his mind was at full strength, they'd debate the acting, the directing, the cinematography, and the screen play. The shared interest in movies was one of the strong attractions bringing the two together. Neither of their previous spouses felt as strongly about the cinema as they did. Barbara Klein never had the time or interest and Mr. Taylor was happy to go with Jennifer to a movie as long as it was showing in one of his two theaters. He refused to enrich his competition by buying their tickets. At Taylor's multiplexes there were plenty of blockbusters, but very few low budget films that would appeal to anybody older than 30.

Jennifer did not want to stress her husband's cognitive skills, so she chose a documentary about an architect for Fred's first post-operative cinematic foray. They were two of an audience of five at the 3 PM show. The film was interesting enough to keep her attention and it appeared to her that Fred was captivated as well; he didn't fall asleep. As it concluded, she asked him how he liked it.

"Good movie. I liked it a lot. How about you?"

"It was OK," she answered. Pretty slow, I thought. I didn't like the narrator's voice."

Philanthropist

"Yeah, slow. But don't you think that the museum he did in Chicago was great?" Jennifer was impressed; her husband had an opinion about something other than himself, his family, and his doctors. The improvement was moving right along.

Jennifer asked Fred to wait in front of the theater while she walked the four blocks to get the car. When she got in the driver's seat, she checked her cell for missed calls, having dutifully turned it off in the theater. There were two voice mails - one from the salon reminding her of her appointment the following morning and the other from Ernesto. "Call me when you have a minute."

It hit her with an impact somewhere between those of 'You are pregnant' and 'Your biopsy was benign.' She played it twice more to see if she could learn anything about why he called. She couldn't. She couldn't make Fred wait on the sidewalk any longer, not being absolutely certain that he wouldn't walk away and get lost. He hadn't gotten lost ever, but the discharge lady at the hospital had warned her about the possibility. She didn't remember the ride home. Her pulse ran a mile a minute. She started getting dizzy from hyperventilation. She pulled into the garage, relieved that she hadn't collided with anything or anybody.

"I'm glad we did that Jen. Let's go to lots of movies. I'm getting sick of cop shows."

"Yes, dear. We'll do that."

"Thanks for the movie, dear. I love you."

"I love you, too."

She couldn't just go and make a call at home. "Fred, I'm going to go for a walk. Sitting in that theater made me stiff."

"No problem. I'll watch a little TV."

Jennifer was not in class A physical condition. The last time she had used her gym membership was the week before the hit and run. She'd continue to pay fees, certain that the inactivity was temporary. Walks around the block were about as much as she could comfortably do. Anything more than a block from her Pacific Heights home meant dealing

Larry Hill

with heights, not insignificant ones, on or adjacent to Pacific Avenue. She wished that they had a dog that would make her walk. They had met as a result of the two dogs, now deceased. They decided against replacement dog or dogs to keep a level of freedom for the traveling that they never really got into. Maybe, now that extensive travel was probably not a logical goal, it was time to dog shop. Fred could use companionship and Jennifer needed a reason to exercise.

With more than minimal effort, Jen reached a city park three blocks from home. She found an available bench and took out her cell. Ernesto was listed under Con on her contact list. She could invent a Connie should Fred find Con and inquire. Con had no speed dial designation so she called up the number and pushed Send. Two rings, three, four. "I can't come to the phone right now…"

"Ernesto, it's me. God, am I happy that you called. I thought I'd never hear from you or see you again. Please call me in the next few minutes if you get this. I'm out of the house and you know I can't talk to you at home."

It was a typical fall day in the Heights. Sunny and in the mid-60s – a hint of breeze, just enough to offer a barely audible rustle of leaves. San Francisco was not a birdwatchers' paradise. A few rowdy crows, demanding house sparrows, and sing-songy yellow warblers were all she could see or hear. Strolling around the park were a dozen or more nanny/child teams, the nannies Filipino, Mexican, or Salvadorian and the children Asian or Caucasian. Most of the children were pushed in strollers or prams that would have cost as much as a reasonable used car; some kids were big enough to run around noisily. Committees of nannies chatted with each other, one group in Tagalog, the other in Spanish, while keeping close eyes on their charges. The older kids frolicked. Laughs intermingled with cries of joy and shorter cries of pain. Jennifer, as she had so many times in the past score of years, asked herself why she had made that decision not to be a mother. Or did she make that decision? Mr. Taylor didn't want children. He wanted to make money and serve Jesus. That was OK with her, wasn't it? Her mother was a dour, unsmiling, unhappy woman. Her sister, older by seven years, had married young but unsatisfactorily. She became dour, unsmiling, and unhappy. Her two daughters were destined for the same, especially after their father dropped into a life of alcohol and adultery. Why would I, Jennifer, do the same to myself and to any kids I might have? But what's happening in the park really looks like fun. But those aren't mothers. Those are baby sitters. What are the mothers doing right now? Working, eating, drinking, shopping, fucking? Fucking sounds nice, but with whom?

Her ring tone interrupted the day dream. The LED lit up, CON.

"Ernesto. Oh Ernesto. Where have you been all my life?"

"Hello Jennifer," he responded with no obvious emotion. "I'm very sorry that I haven't answered your calls. I just couldn't."

"What do you mean, 'couldn't?' Of course you could have. I left a hundred calls."

"Jennifer, I can't talk on the phone right now. But we need to talk, soon. Do you have any time tomorrow?"

"In fact, I do. I have a hair appointment tomorrow morning at 10. Fred doesn't have any idea how long things like that take, so we could get together after. How about getting a room at one of those motels on Lombard?" She was leery about meeting at the Clift. "God, I miss you!"

"No, no room. But I've got to talk to you. Let's meet in Golden Gate Park."

Jennifer's sails deflated. "Oh, OK. Where?"

"I'll meet you in front of the DeYoung Museum, say at noon. We'll walk through the Botanical Garden and find a bench. OK?"

"I'd rather find a bed than a bench, but OK."

The return to home from the little park was usually physically easier than that from home to park, but this time, it was harder. Her excitement at having seen on "Missed Calls" that he had attempted to reach her was obliterated by the call itself. Something that she could not begin to fathom was up.

On returning, she found her husband transfixed by a college basketball game. He'd clap and cheer when one team scored and yell expletives when their opponents made a basket. "Who's playing, dear?"

"Duke and North Carolina."

"So what's the big deal? You didn't go to either of those schools."

"I hate Duke. Everybody hates Duke. I don't like UNC any better, but they're not as evil as Duke, so in this game, I love 'em."

"I don't hate Duke, so if everybody else does, I better root for them. Go Duke!" Jennifer loved to love things that others loved to hate – undocumented aliens, movies about asteroids destined to hit Earth, sweet wine, all-you-can-eat restaurants, and the New York Yankees.

Jason, having changed from his day of discovery, came into the room, looked at the TV, recognized the uniforms, and said matter-of-factly, "I hate Duke."

Changing subjects from tall young men playing ball, Jennifer pointed out that she hadn't taken anything out for dinner and suggested that they go out, maybe Thai or Vietnamese.

"Great idea," said Jason. "This time it's on me. You guys have been too good to me. You make the call and I'll pay the bill."

"OK, Kid. We'll find the most expensive Vietnamese place in three counties," responded Fred. Jennifer was thrilled by the change in the father and son relationship in the few weeks that Jason had boarded in their home. And, what better sign that Fred was on his way back than the fact his sense of humor had returned? For a moment, she had forgotten about the call in the park.

The salon was located on Sacramento St., not far from Pacific Heights. Jennifer drove even though she'd probably end up in a parking space as close to home as to the shop. She did not tell her husband that she was driving; to him, that was not an important piece of information. The cut and coloring took almost two hours. She didn't call home when she left. Fred was now quite capable of taking care of himself in the friendly confines of his house. He expertly crafted a tuna sandwich with just enough mayo not to upset his internist, garnished with a reasonable handful of chips and half a dill pickle.

As the fog had not cleared in the western part of the city, Golden Gate Park was chilly. Parking was not a problem in the park on a week day. As it was a few minutes before the noon horn blew, she expected to get to the museum before Ernesto. She was wrong. He was leaning on the wall just in front of the visitors' entrance. He had seen her before she picked him out of the dozen or so people in the area. She hoped for, but doubted she would get, something akin to a fifties cinematic greeting. Her doubts were well founded; his hug was feeble, his smile, forced. She went from hopeful to infuriated in an instant. They walked without handholding the several hundred feet from the museum to the Garden and quickly found a bench amongst the South African fynbos.

"Good to see you, Jen."

"Yes. Good to see you, too."

Silence. Thirty seconds, maybe forty-five. Jennifer looked at Ernesto. Ernesto looked at plants.

"I think you owe me an explanation," she said.

"Right. I do. I don't know where to start."

"How about why I didn't hear from you after I told you I was pregnant. Didn't you want to know what I did about it? How about why I didn't know that you hadn't gone to South America. How about why you didn't answer any of my phone calls. Hell, I even wrote you a letter – I hadn't written any letters in years. You know something, Mr. Contreras – you are a bastard, a son of a bitch, an *hijo de puta*." In anticipation, she had Googled for the worst Spanish invective she could find. She felt better having used it.

"You are very right. I am all those, and worse. I'm sorry. I'm sorry. I'm sorry. But I love you. I really love you."

"Cut the crap. If you love someone, you don't treat them like dirt. And, my friend, I feel very dirty right now."

"I know how you feel. I understand. I'm sorry."

"No, you don't have a fucking clue how I feel. You don't understand a damn thing."

"OK. OK. You're right. I don't understand how you feel. I know how I feel though. Let me explain."

"Go for it, buster."

"All right. Give me a minute." He wished that he'd be able to make his presentation in Spanish, but obviously couldn't. He ran his fingers through his black hair and retied a loose shoestring.

"No minutes. Just give it to me."

"OK. Here I go. About the pregnancy. Remember what you told me? Something like, 'Get out of town.' You didn't want me involved. You told me you'd go to your doctor and he'd help you. I really felt you meant what you said, that I should stay out of it."

"You're right. I did say that. But look. This was a big deal. You should have called. You were the goddam father."

"Sorry, Jen. With this one I was just following orders."

"All right. I guess I got carried away. It would have been really nice to hear from you, but it's probably my fault."

"So what happened? Did you have an abortion?"

She told him about the pills and the bleeding and how depressed she was when she didn't have anybody to talk to. He sympathized.

"Now, Uruguay." He filled in the holes regarding Kobe beef and South America, but did not immediately identify the capitalist who had done him wrong.

"You aren't going to believe this but here goes. I prepared my ass off for the trip. I spent all that time at Davis and then in the firm's office. I knew beef and I knew business. Actually, I was proud of myself. I hadn't studied anything since college, but I'm still a pretty good student. Ask me any question about Uruguay and I can give you the answer – who is the President? When is Independence Day? What do they import from the US? I knew all that shit. I even bought a new suit – three hundred bucks at Macy's. I had tickets, first class, and a room at the Sheraton – they say it's the best place in town. I'm ready to leave the next afternoon and the boss calls telling me that I'm not going. Something about the guy they work for in Montevideo – that's the capital of Uruguay."

"Duh. What do you think I am - an idiot?"

"Sorry. The boss says that one of the partners will have to go or the cattleman will pull out of the deal. He just shines me on – tells me I'm not going, nothing more. And I've tried to get an answer in a hundred ways, but all I hear is that Spencer will call me back. Never does."

"Wait a second! Spencer? What's his first name?"

"Mark. Mark Spencer."

Jennifer well remembered having heard the name Spencer at Ernesto's house, but she'd spent no time thinking about it since, dismissing it as a coincidence.

"Well, I'll be a son of a bitch. Don't you know who that is?"

"I guess I don't. All I know is that he is a big roller and is the first name on a firm in the Transamerica building. And, until all of this happened, I thought he was a nice guy."

"He may be that, my friend, but Mark Spencer is also the husband, no, the widower of the woman who was killed in the hit and run that they say my husband committed."

"Jesus. I thought it was strange that he picked me out of a restaurant to send me to Uruguay to work on a big deal. Then, even stranger when he tells me at the last minute that I'm not going. But I don't understand it. Why would he do this to me? I didn't kill his wife."

"No you didn't, Ernesto, and neither did I. It doesn't make any sense, does it? Think about it. A man loses his wife when some old guy hits her with his car and runs away. The guy is arrested and becomes big news all over town, then gets out on bail but will eventually come to trial in an open and shut case. And then the old guy has his own accident and may not go to trial after all. What could be motivating him? What's to gain by playing with the emotions not of the killer, not of the killer's family, but of the lover of the killer's second wife? And how the hell did he ever get to know about you and me? We've been pretty damn good about keeping this quiet- until that time in the Redwood Room."

"You don't think that your stepson... what's his name...put Spencer up to this, do you?"

"Jason's his name. And, no, I can't imagine any reason whatsoever for Jason to contact Mark Spencer, tell him about our affair, and suggest that there might be something gained by messing with you. And then Spencer saying, 'What a good idea. I think I'll drum up some big role for him to play in my business and then pull the rug out from under him. That'll really help me get over losing my wife.' That's idiotic, but give me another explanation for all this."

"I can't. But look what it's done to you and me. Before Spencer came into the restaurant, we were fine. More than fine – you were the only person I could talk to about anything serious."

Jen nodded. "Yeah, same for me, but what the hell happened to you? You get this big offer and suddenly I'm out of your life. No calls, no answers to my calls."

"I'm really sorry, *mi amor*. You're right. I thought I was pretty hot shit. I started thinking different about my life. I thought it was time to start thinking about a family, kids, a full-time wife, a nice house, not that piece of junk that I live in now. And that meant that I'd have to give you up."

"You could have told me that. I'm a big girl. We've had fifteen years of something pretty goddam important, and you just stop all contact because you have a new suit and a first class ticket to Montevideo. You're a coward, aren't you?"

"Yes, I was a coward."

"I didn't say you were one. You ARE one."

"OK. But I'm gonna change. Let me show you how much I love you. Let's get a room."

"Oh, come on, Ernie. That's really horse shit. Yesterday, a room with you was what I longed for, but not today. You go figure out what you are going to do with your life. Once you do that, let me know, by telephone, or better, since you're such a good student, study up on how to use email. You know, we've been more than lovers for all these years – we've been best friends. I wouldn't mind getting back to that, but get your own act together and maybe try again."

Two teen-aged boys in short sleeve white shirts, skimpier than appropriate for the windy cloud-covered park, and dark, narrow ties walked up to the morose looking couple on the bench. "Hi, how are you folks doing today?" asked one, a wide smile showing bright white adult teeth.

"We're just fine," said Ernesto, grumpily.

"Yes, we are fine," said Jennifer, "but I don't think we want to become Mormons today. Maybe later. Thanks for stopping by and have a great afternoon."

Stepmom

Jason had been a guest in his father's and stepmother's house for several weeks. He was not likely to be returning to Los Angeles any time soon, having recently received notification from Emily that, not only was she going to be filing for divorce, but that she was leaving her high-flying practice in Beverly Hills to take an even more lucrative position as a partner with a mergers and acquisitions specialty firm in Manhattan. In addition to being involved in the great mergers of the day, she'd be close to her parents, whom the children would get to see weekly rather than seasonally.

Jason was, to his surprise and the surprise of Jen and even Fred, not terribly upset by the news. His work had been going very well in San Francisco. His big case had settled, not for the thirty-million the plaintiff wanted but for just a few million short of that. His LA firm had been giving thought to setting up an office in the Bay Area. Jason, a partner for four years, would be an ideal helmsman to get the office moving.

He liked the part that he wouldn't have anything to do with his in-laws. Mr. and Mrs. Park were not among his favorites. Moreover, he was not overly troubled by the prospect of his two offspring living on the opposite coast. Not one to say that the most important defining aspect of his life was being a "Good Dad," he calculated that seeing his kids in the summers and occasional holidays would be just about right. He had grown weary of squiring them to classes, lessons, games, and meets. He hadn't heard many '"Thanks Dads" and rarely learned of the outcomes of the meets or the progress of the lessons. He hoped that the children would grow up to be successful adults and perhaps show a little gratitude if and when they developed wisdom with the success.

Jason initially did not worry about the financial aspects of divorce. Both he and she took in handsome salaries, hers about to be more handsome than before. Plus their LA home, while not as valuable as it was prior to the housing crisis, was still worth much more than was owned on it. He'd put his foot down regarding schooling. The public school in West Los Angeles had been more than good enough. He'd leave it to Emily to find an equivalent in New York. If she thought that only a private school would suffice, she'd come up with the tuition. Alimony, thank goodness, would not be an issue. While he reckoned that they could make the split without hiring lawyers, she employed a woman known for making rich LA working-wives even richer. He was therefore forced to counter, signing on with one of San Francisco's finest. He didn't know what issues had to be negotiated but based on his years in the profession, knew that he'd be screwed if he didn't have a powerhouse attorney on his side.

He was sitting in the downstairs den, scotch on the rocks in hand, reading the *New York Times* on the computer when his stepmother walked in. Often, on seeing her after a bit of time, his immediate reaction was one of envy of his father. Jennifer turned heads and Jason's head was one that turned. Her auburn hair, azure eyes, tiny nose, and thin, barely colored lips conveyed a classic 40s and 50s motion picture beauty. Her figure was full but not at all excessive. Her slight but shapely legs would have been just right for silk stockings forty years earlier. As a single man to be, one who assumed he wouldn't stay that way too long, he hoped that he could do half as well as his Dad. It was clear at this time, however, that his stepmother was not her usual self. Her beauty was capped by an expression of intense discomfort.

"Jennifer, what's up? You don't look good."

She shut the door although it was unlikely that Fred, a floor above with TV volume at high decibels, could hear anything they would be saying.

"Jason, it's time that we laid all our cards on the table. You've been here over a month and neither of us has said a word about the meeting at the Clift."

"Right. I didn't think that I was the one who should bring it up."

"Yeah, true. I've got a question. Did you say anything about what you saw to anybody else?"

He hesitated but wasn't about to lie at this point. "Yeah, I met with the twins a few days after the meeting and told them. And then, assuming that it might have impact on his legal situation, we talked it over with Irving Greenberg."

"What do you mean impact on the legal situation?"

"We didn't know. But in today's world, surprising releases about who's sleeping with whom become big news and we didn't want either Dad or his lawyer to be hit with something."

"What did Greenberg say?"

"He didn't think much of it. Said that it would have no bearing on a trial. Might be a middle of the Bay Area section headline in the *Chronicle*, but it wouldn't have legs."

"I guess that's good to hear," said Jennifer. "Now, let me tell you what I learned today. Remember the guy I was with?"

"Ernie?"

"Ernesto. Doesn't like to be called Ernie. He and I have been together for a long time. Long before your father and I even met. When Fred and I got married, we stopped seeing each other for a while, but got back together, maybe once a month, after about a year."

"Does Dad know anything about this?"

"We've never talked about it, he says things from time to time that make me think that he knows, and even that it's OK with him. Remember, there are 30 years between us."

"You don't need to remind me of that. Was there…is there, any chance that you are going to leave my father for this guy?"

"Jesus, no! I'm sorry for saying this to you, his son, but the main reason Ernesto and I get together is for sex."

"You mean that my father cannot perform? Can't he get it up?"

"I don't want to talk about your father that way. Actually saying it's only for sex is not exactly correct. Ernesto has been helpful to me a lot and serves as a confidant. Remember when your father was missing- when he was in Emergency at the General? It was Ernesto I asked to find him. He called all the hospitals and the morgue. He didn't find him but he was a godsend.

"OK. I think I got the picture. But you look like something bad has just happened. I take it that it has something to do with your boyfriend."

"Come on Jason. Cut the boyfriend crap. You're more mature than that."

"Sorry. So, what happened?"

Jennifer relayed the story, starting with her call from Ernesto asking her whether he should pursue this job opportunity presented by a man who had eaten in his restaurant, following with the story of his taking the job to do something with cattle in Uruguay and then, at the last minute, being told not to go, for no reason. She showed no emotion when she relayed the part in which Ernesto seems to break off with her – no calls, no responses to her calls.

"And then yesterday, I'm at the movies with Fred and find on my cell a call from Ernesto. I dropped your Dad off at home and went to the park to return his call and, all of a sudden, he has to meet me the next day, like today. So we meet at Golden Gate Park and guess who he tells me was the man who offered him the job and then took it away?"

"Donald Trump?"

"Funny. Real funny. It was none other than Mark Spencer."

"Oh my God. Why? Why did he do something like that?"

"I have absolutely no idea. Ernesto doesn't either. By the way, he's a very smart man, in spite of his performance when he was trying to explain who he was and what he did when you met him at the Clift. We still laugh about the EF Hutton comment."

"Yeah, that was hilarious. But how does Spencer gain anything from doing this. Is he just a malicious son-of-a-bitch?"

"He did just lose his wife and the mother of his daughter. He's got a right to be angry and there's no easy way to take it out on Fred. He's not going to sneak into our house and shoot him. So, I guess he was just striking out and found an easy target."

"Probably right. So, what's our next step?" asked Jason.

Larry Hill

"No next step. Spencer's probably stewing in his juices now. He's not dumb but he probably is thinking that he was awfully dumb with that act. My guess is we hear nothing more from him until the criminal case is finished and a civil one is filed."

"Are you going to tell Phillip and Robert about this?"

"I don't want to go over it again. You go ahead and tell them the gruesome details. But do let them know that I'm sticking with their father. No more extracurricular fucking for me."

The bachelor-to-be was jolted by the comment but had recovered when, a few seconds later, his father came into the room. Both Jason and Jennifer noticed how much better he was looking. The limp which they had first noticed when he left the hospital was totally absent. He walked more assuredly, almost jauntily. He seemed to care about what he wore – never, even in the immediate post-hospital period, had he relied on anybody else to choose his daily garb, but for months he cared little whether his clothes were wrinkled or colors were mismatched. He was now wearing fashionable polos, pressed trousers, and either shoes that shined or high priced athletic footwear. His thick head of white hair was neatly coiffed. It had been six months since he cracked his skull in the Eddy Street bar. There had been no mention of him or of Teresa Spencer in the papers in a long time. Their names hadn't even appeared when Judge Gasparini issued a two month delay of proceedings after Fred's visit to the psychiatrist. It was clear to his family, however, that Fred had made meaningful progress since he had seen Dr. Stern.

"What have you two been talking about?" he asked as he sat on the antique oak rocking chair that Barbara had bought him for their 15th anniversary.

"Oh, nothing, Dad. Forty Niners stuff mainly. I can't believe how much Jen knows about football."

"Don't forget that I was a cheerleader in high school. What were you watching, honey?"

"Something on the History Channel – a show about Oliver Cromwell. I'd seen it before. What a bastard that guy was. First, he has the king

190

killed and then screws up England so badly that they have to bring back the monarchy."

"You're sounding pretty savvy, Dad. That brain of yours is making a hell of a comeback. What do you think, Jen?"

"No doubt about it. You aren't quite your old self yet Fred, but you're getting there."

"What do you mean, not my old self? Why don't we go upstairs and let me show you."

"Cut that out, honey. Jason's here. Maybe tonight."

Jason, blushing, suggested that he could go for a long walk. He had never heard his father talk like that, but was not about to get in the way of progress.

"Maybe tonight," Jennifer repeated. "Why don't we go for a drive to Marin? We haven't been to the Headlands in years and the weather's perfect."

"Good idea. I'm getting sick of television. You wanna go with us, Jase?"

"No, Dad. You guys go. I've got some work to do."

Fred got out of the rocker and headed to the closet for his leather jacket. "Why don't I drive?"

"Are you out of your mind?" Jennifer responded instantaneously. "We've talked about this over and over. Your driving days are behind you. The last time you drove, somebody's mother was killed. And that was on the straight streets of San Francisco, not the curves and hills of West Marin. I'll drive."

"Yes, dear."

The Trial is Set

Irving Greenberg phoned the house. It had been two months since the first visit to Dr. Stern. The Judge wanted another evaluation; he had heard talk that Klein was improving. Gasparini had not drawn any sexy cases in the interim and was anxious to get the City and County of San Francisco vs. Frederick Klein underway. He had high hopes for advancement. There was a Republican in the Governor's mansion and talk of an impending vacancy on the appellate court, sure to go to a Northern Californian as the South dominated that bench beyond its statistics. A well-publicized successful adjudication of Klein was sure to garner him points toward an appointment.

Fred had scored a 14 on his Mini-Mental Status examination the first time around. Anything under 20 was considered evidence for cognitive impairment. When Dr. Roger Stern saw him a second time, he posed the same questions. This time Fred spelled it DLROW and knew that 7 from 93 was 86 and 7 from that was 79. He scored 24 out of 30, a normal value. Stern, recognizing the great political importance of his evaluation, referred Fred to a neuropsychologist who administered eight hours of testing for memory, perception, language, and attention. Both professionals deemed the accused able to stand trial and aid in his own defense. Judge Gasparini set a trial date for ten weeks later. He ordered that his staff put aside four weeks for jury selection, testimony and deliberation.

Jennifer, Jason, and Fred arrived at Greenberg's Spear Street office ten minutes before their 10 AM appointment. Phillip had asked to be included but the lawyer denied the request simply because his office was small.

"Good morning, Fred," welcomed Greenberg.

"Good morning, Irv." It was the first time he had called his criminal defense something other than Steve.

"I presume that you've heard the news that there is a trial set for the middle of May?"

"Hard not to hear the news. Jason told me about it yesterday. Half an hour later, I saw it on TV. They showed those pictures of me leaving jail when I got bailed out. And, they showed the photos of the woman I hit, plus her child. Beautiful little girl."

"Here's the story. Right now you are scheduled to go on trial on May 14 and they expect the trial to last at least two weeks and maybe as much as a month. I opted for a jury – hope that's OK with you. You are charged with vehicular manslaughter. Your situation is, of course, bad because of the fact you left the scene. There is a presumption that you may have done that because you were drunk. You've got no way to prove that you weren't. They've got no way to prove that you were. Worst case scenario, Fred, is they find you guilty and you are sentenced to spend as many as ten years in prison."

"Ten years! Jesus, I'm not going to live that long. I'm an old man – a sick old man. They can't do that."

"I'm sorry to say that they very well can do that. You are one famous alleged criminal. You heard about the turnout at the victim's funeral – major politicos. The paper was full of letters to the editor calling for your hide. If you get off with a slap on the wrist, the city will be up in arms."

"So, what do I do?"

"That remains to be seen. I talked with the DA yesterday and he said that they aren't in any mood to let you off lightly. They are ready to go to trial and have assigned what he refers to as his best prosecutor, a woman named Burleson, a Yale Law grad, to the case. Plus, he tells me that the word is that the Judge wants this to go to trial. He's looking to be on TV and in the paper as much as possible – thinks that he might get a seat on the appellate bench.

"What are the options, Irv?" asked Jennifer.

"Obviously, we can try to make a deal with the DA. I brought that up and he wasn't terribly encouraging – suggested that if you pled guilty to the charge, he'd settle for five years – you'd probably get out in three with good behavior.

"That's a life sentence. I'm not going to live three years."

"I told the DA about your health – that wasn't news to him – he's been reading the papers and the reports from the psychiatrists. But he thinks he's under the gun. And, I think that he too sees bigger things for himself. Remember, the last San Francisco DA became the Attorney General of California. I asked him what he thought about you getting one year and serving it under house arrest. He didn't bite."

"Do you think he'd take a year in jail?" asked Jason.

"I could ask. I doubt it, but the worst he can do is say no."

"What do you think, Dad?"

"Huh?"

"Would you be willing to accept a year in jail?"

"Hell, no. Remember that I had a heart attack. I've got a pacemaker. That would kill me."

"Can we go for two years, or three years, at home with a bracelet?" inquired Jason of Greenberg.

"Again, it can't hurt. But I'm fairly sure that he wants to see the bars close on your father. Think of the TV commercials from someone running against him. They would show the outside of your house and ask voters if they think that's appropriate punishment for a man who killed a mother of a two-year-old and fled the scene. Fred would be the Willie Horton of the 21st century."

"So, Dad, it sounds like it'll probably come down to at least a year in jail or go to trial."

"Huh?"

"Are you ready to go to court and fight this?"

"Yep. They'll have to pull me by my ears to get me in jail."

Greenberg interrupted the internecine discussion, "If you want to fight this, I'll be glad to be in your corner, but I want you to be very clear that you could end up with a much longer sentence than you would by pleading guilty. You could get ten years – sure, you'd probably be out in five, but there's no guarantee."

"Out in a lot less than five – they'll be taking me out on a stretcher with a sheet over my face. I don't want to go to jail!"

"Enough of that kind of talk. I hear you loud and clear. Another thing you've got to be aware of though is that a trial is going to cost you a ton of money. My hours don't come cheap and we've got to do a lot of legwork to prepare – interviewing witnesses and experts like psychiatrists, looking into the Spencers, researching similar cases.

Fred's expression changed. And then it changed back. "No problem, Counselor. I've got enough money, don't we dear?"

"Yes, honey. We're OK."

"Another thing Fred," said Greenberg, "you thought you were famous before – you haven't seen anything. The papers, the TV stations, and the bloggers – they are all going to be there for the trial. I don't know how Gasparini looks at the issue, but he might allow TV cameras in the court room. If so, you're on national television, and not because of your good looks or good deeds."

"Dad, do you really want to go through with all that?"

"Fred, you make the decision. I'll stick with you whatever you do, but you gotta be sure that you know what going to trial is all about. I love you and I want you at home, but if you do have to go to prison…"

"I am not going to prison!"

"Sure, Dad. Irv, what we'd like you to do is have more discussion with the DA and let him know that we'll take pretty much whatever sentence he wants as long as he gets to spend it in house arrest. Otherwise, we go for a trial."

"OK, Jason. I'll do it but I'm not optimistic."

The three weren't home more than twenty minutes when the phone rang. Greenberg was on the other end. He described the DA's reaction to the offer of lengthy house arrest as one of mirth – DA Gonzales chuckled and said, "See you in court on May 14."

"We've got to figure this out," said Jason.

"The whole family has to be involved in this, Jason," replied Jennifer. "I'll call the twins and see if they can come over tonight."

Phillip, like most radiologists, was free. Robert had a string of colonoscopies scheduled and couldn't get there until after nine. They put the family conference off for one day.

The next evening, the twins walked into the large family room together. "As I live and breathe, look who's here early!" said Robert. "That's a first, Jase. We'll get a plaque made up and put it on the wall as a historical marker."

"I live here, asshole." Jason responded with a grin.

Jason summarized the situation as if he were addressing a jury. Their father was going to be a defendant in a trial ready made for the internet era. The DA had turned down the offer of a guilty plea with a lengthy sentence to be served in a mansion on Pacific Heights. Dad was not willing to accept even a short time behind bars. He had a whiff of being incarcerated on the night of his arrest and didn't like the aroma.

Phillip: "I'm not sure that you are making a good decision, Dad."

Robert: "I agree. You caused the death of Teresa Spencer. And, you didn't stay around to help her. You left and played poker. It's going to be pretty hard to convince 12 of your peers that you aren't guilty and shouldn't be in jail."

Phillip: "What kind of argument can you make that you are innocent?"

Robert: "Yeah, what is Mr. Greenberg going to do to get you out of this?"

Father: "I don't know."

Having finished his summary and engendered initial statements of discomfort from his brothers, Jason called for the assembled family members to strategize. "The facts of the case are all against us. You did it Dad, we can't deny that. So, how do we get a decision that keeps you out of jail?"

Robert: "We've got to convince the jury that there's nothing to be gained by Dad's serving time."

Jennifer: "We have to win their sympathy. They've got to see your father as a nice man, an old man, a man who shouldn't be in San Quentin, where he would be at the mercy of scumbags half his age."

Phillip: "What the hell are we paying Greenberg all this money for if we are trying to come up with our own game plan? He's supposed to be the best. Let him do his job."

Jason: "You're right, Phil, but I think we all agree that we have to make Dad look as sympathetic as possible. How do we do it?"

"Goddam it! Stop talking like I'm not even around! For months I couldn't tell black from white, my ass from my elbow, but I'm better. I may not be back to the way I was twenty years ago, but what 76-year-old is? It isn't any of you that will be going to the slammer. It's me!"

"We're just trying to help you," said Robert. Phillip nodded in agreement.

"Welcome back my love. I'm so sorry that we've treated you like a child," said Jennifer, verging on tears.

"I still don't remember a thing about the accident, but I've heard enough from all of you and from the lawyer and from reading the old articles to know that I am guilty of a terrible crime. That little girl doesn't have a mother. Shit, she won't even remember a thing about her mother as she grows up. And, I did it. I killed her mother."

Jennifer and the three sons were speechless. A full minute later, Fred Klein continued.

"And, I've got to do something about it."

"Does that mean you want to plead guilty?" asked one of the twins.

"If so, you'll have to go to jail," said the other.

"Christ, I know that. I'm not an idiot. No, I don't want to go to jail, so no, I don't want to plead guilty. But I've got to make it up to that child, somehow. I don't even know her name. What is it?"

Nobody else knew her name either.

Glen Fiddich on the Rocks

Life in the Spencer home had fallen into a routine. Mark found that he was a pretty good single father. He continued to turn down all work that involved travel outside the Bay Area. His two partners were none too thrilled about travel to Ivory Coast or Uruguay or even France and Germany. The firm took on two recent MBA grads to do the heavy business class flying and five star lodging. Spencer, Bowman and Clark was doing well.

Meagan was doing well. After exhaustive vetting, she was accepted to one of the top pre-schools in the City, a short distance from home, where she and Carmen would walk every Monday, Wednesday and Friday. She had collected a sizable group of friends with whom she had regular Tuesday and Thursday play days and weekend sleepovers. Ballet classes and other cultural instruction dotted her schedule. She shared with her playmates talk of her mother's heavenly exploits and was, in general, a very happy three-year-old.

Mark was doing well. The Kobe beef caper faded into history. The encounter with Ernesto was not repeated. The office no longer received his calls. The vaquero in Montevideo had found financing elsewhere. Mark golfed, played basketball and ran the hills of the Heights and the flats of Crissy Field in the Presidio – all of which he had put on the shelf after the death of his spouse.

And, Mark had a girlfriend. He had waited a socially acceptable four months before venturing onto the social trails. As a wired early middle-aged man, he knew that his statistically best bet for finding good dates and potential mates was the World Wide Web. He enrolled in two of the more exclusive sites and had dozens of hits, as one might expect for a single rich man in a city in which straight single women outnumbered straight single men by a wide margin. Having the luxury of being able to select from big numbers, he took his time to find women who met his criteria – between four and seven years younger than he, married once or not at all, preferably no kids, non-evangelical (Jewish, Buddhist, Hindu, or agnostic OK), college educated, employed and physically active. In San Francisco, there were plenty that could tick all the right boxes.

He had four dates in the first two weeks. All were acceptably smart and attractive. They were employed as a demographer, an EKG technician, a marine biologist and a hospice nurse. Two were willing, in fact, more than willing, to bed him after dinner. Three, including one of the sexual progressives, insisted on paying their own way for supper; the hospice nurse didn't reach for her purse when the bill came. None warranted, in his selective view, a second date.

Candidate number five was a great date. Mitzi Li was 40, two years divorced from a Highway Patrolman, a graduate of San Jose State, a third grade teacher at a private girls' school, and a lapsed Methodist. Her parents were both from Shanghai, had gone with Chang Kai-Shek to Taiwan in 1949, and moved to California ten years later. Mitzi was a native born San Franciscan. She married Walter Wang, another first generation Taiwanese, divorcing after nine years, during which they never resolved his desire to be a father and her refusal to bear children. She was tiny, vivacious, funny, irreverent, and a treat for Mark's eyes. She insisted on paying for dinner, and declined, or didn't pick up on, his well camouflaged sexual advances on the first date, but accepted the less translucent ones of the second. Within a month, she was a frequent visitor to the Spencer abode, a fetch-buddy of Bob the Beagle, and Meagan's avid playmate. He gave up his memberships of the two dating services. There was talk about her moving in, from her meager apartment in the Haight-Ashbury, but they decided against it, awaiting the end of the legal intricacies. They agreed that it might not look too good for the grieving widower to be shacking up with a pretty school marm.

Mark and Mitzi met for end-of-workday drinks in the St. Francis hotel lobby. Their relationship had progressed from one of great sex to one of true friendship. Mark felt twinges of guilt when he realized that he was more comfortable talking with her than he had been with Teresa. Mitzi was comfortable, aware that she and Mark would never fight about whether or not to produce children.

"You'll never believe what happened to me today," Mark said, on his second Glenfiddich on the rocks.

"Oh, do tell me," Mitzi answered, sipping her first whiskey sour.

"I get a call from an attorney named Schofield. Never heard of him before. I almost hung up on him, figuring he was cold calling for business. But he tells me that he's representing a client who can't be named. The client, he says, has put a quarter million dollars in an account for Meagan to take care of her education for the rest of her life."

"Amazing. Who would do something like that?"

"It can only be Fred Klein."

'Who is Fred Klein?" Mark and Mitzi had never discussed the specifics of his wife's death. He proceeded to tell her about Klein, his reputation as a philanthropist and his medical conditions. "Is a quarter million going to take care of her college, let alone private school and maybe graduate school?" asked Mitzi. "I bet that little girl is going to end up in law school, she's such a good talker."

"The lawyer told me that he will be investing the money so that the quarter million could end up being a million by the time she goes to college. I'll have to send any bills for tuition, books, school bus to the lawyer and he'll send me a check to cover them."

"Why didn't Klein, if that's who it is, just give you the money?"

"I guess because he thinks I'd just go out and spend it. He doesn't know me. Maybe he thinks that I'd buy a Ferrari."

"And why do you think he did it in the first place? Guilt?"

"For sure, there's some guilt. He's Jewish. But I'm thinking that he reckons that I won't sue him."

"Will you?"

"I sure as hell will. If he thinks he can get out of this paying $250,000, he's out of his fuckin' mind."

The Judge

Judges of the Superior Court of California are appointed by the Governor, with approval by the California Commission on Judicial Appointments. The position, unlike that of Federal Judges, is not guaranteed for life. Every six years, each judge must go before the voters of his or her county in a non-partisan election. For most of California's history, the great majority of judicial elections were unchallenged; the twenty-four hour news cycle changed that. Every decision made by a judge was scrutinized by investigative reporters and bloggers and there were few judges who did not occasionally rule controversially. The number of electoral challenges had grown dramatically.

Louis Gasparini had not had any challenges at the conclusion of any of his three six-year terms. He had not done anything controversial. His cases had been of little consequence to anyone but the plaintiffs and defendants, their loved ones, and their litigating attorneys.

He did, indeed, aspire to a higher calling. There was the rumored opening on the First District (San Francisco and other Northern California coastal counties) Court of Appeals. Plus, the US Congress had created two new slots for Federal District Court Justices in the Ninth Circuit, that circuit which included California. Gasparini, who loved criminal cases and, for the most part, found civil ones terribly dull, envied his federal brethren who, by US law, adjudicated all bank robberies, counterfeiters, and interstate kidnappings. The idea of having FBI agents, rather than the often mentally challenged local cops, testify in his court room was titillating.

California was the ultimate Blue State – lots of Democrats and few Republicans. Gasparini was a Republican but he knew he was popular enough to make him a good candidate for either a state appellate or a federal district court slot even with the Democrats in power.

    He knew, however, that he had to make a name for himself. The way he was going to do so was on the back of Frederick Klein. The case had to go to trial. He couldn't overtly influence the plea bargaining. Interference in such matters, even through friends or colleagues of associates of the District Attorney, could get him disrobed. But he had heard from unnamed sources that the Klein family was not going to accept any jail time and that the DA was unwilling to accept house arrest. The Judge was pretty sure that he was going to get his high profile case, even though it appeared to be open and shut. Gasparini, like most attorneys with any knowledge of the case, could not guess what possible defense the great Greenberg was going to invoke during the trial. Gasparini already had it figured out that, in spite of the DA's stance, if the jury rendered a guilty verdict (and how could they do anything but that), he'd probably hand down a sentence to be served in the home of the convicted. After all, if it's OK for Martha Stewart, Lindsay Lohan, and Paris Hilton to get house arrest, why not for Fred Klein, 76 and chronically ill? Even Lt. William Calley of My Lai Massacre fame spent his entire three and a half year term in house arrest as the only military man to serve any time whatever for that tragic episode. Gasparini did not discuss his sentencing ideas with anybody, not even his wife of 32 years, herself a one-time public defender.

Mark Spencer was not the only one sporting a new girlfriend. Jason Klein, now firmly committed to a permanent change of venue to the Bay Area, had been on the prowl for some weeks. Like Spencer, he searched electronically, choosing a service that appealed to Jewish singles, and hooked up with a Marin County divorcee, mother of two, Rebecca Grodzinsky. It appeared a heaven-made match. By the third date, he had met her kids and took more of a liking to the two girls, 8 and 10, than he ever had to his own children. Hers acted like kids, his like obnoxious gifted adultlets. Rebecca was a legal aide for a firm with which his firm did business. Her ex had been a womanizing internist who moved in with his front office secretary after showing no interest in couples' therapy. She had been left with a view house in Sausalito, ideal for grown-up sleepovers. Jason had paid little attention to real estate, happily ensconced as he was in free Pacific Heights lodging. He was not about to invite girls to bed down with him in the same abode as his elderly father and fetching stepmother.

Rebecca knew criminal law. She had spent three years in the Philadelphia District Attorney's office, helping prosecutors in case preparation, communicating with victims and witnesses, and suggesting plea deals. She moved to Marin when her husband finished his residency and took a job with a prestigious group of internists in San Rafael. She was fed up with the public sector and signed on with a big San Francisco firm that performed no criminal work whatever. She missed it, finding civil law nothing more than a way to make rich people richer.

Ms. Grodzinsky was a welcome addition to the Klein family discussions vis á vis the upcoming trial. She, like Jason, Robert, Phillip, and Jennifer couldn't envision a logical legal defense. Greenberg had, in their last meeting, offered that his strategy was to convince the jury that Fred was unaware that he had hit Ms. Spencer. He knew it was a stretch. But even if he couldn't raise enough doubt to win a not guilty decision, he could put his client on the stand and show the jurors, and the judge, that Mr. Klein was not somebody that society would benefit by incarcerating. He had decided on his witnesses: Jennifer, the loving wife, Schofield, the loyal friend, aware of Fred's mental state immediately after the alleged felony, and Jameson, the august physician who could attest to the defendant's exaggerated reaction to the news of his abnormal lipid readings and the need for a change of diet. The star witness would, of course, be the philanthropist himself. Fred truly had no recollection of the event and evidence would show that he did not act like a man who had run down a young woman and left the scene to escape arrest. Enough to exonerate? Probably not, but worth a try.

"I killed that young woman. I know I did...now. But I didn't know then. I swear it. God, I wish that I could go back and undo everything."

"I know you do, Dad," said Jason. He and Rebecca sat with Fred and Jen during predinner libations. The television was on, but muted, during the five o'clock local news. Fred was enamored of Rebecca – a great change from Emily. He hadn't met the daughters yet, but had heard nothing but good reviews from Jason. Fred had never enjoyed the company of the biological grandchildren, now in New York.

"So, what do you think, Rebecca? Am I going to jail? There's no goddam reason for me to go to jail. They'd kill me there."

"I don't know, Mr. Klein."

"Don't call me that. Call me Dad."

"They aren't married, dear," said Jennifer.

"Oh. OK. Call me Fred."

"I'll do that...Fred. You're right that there's no reason for you to go to jail. But that's going to be up to the jury and the judge. I have heard that this judge, Gasparini, can be tough and that he wants to get promoted. So, it's hard to be real optimistic."

"My father doesn't need to hear that," said an obviously perturbed Jason.

"Sorry. That's just what I heard and he asked me the question."

"Lay off, Jason," said Fred. "I can handle it. Don't be nasty to this lovely lady." Fred loved the fact that his son had made contact with a Jew, even though she appeared to be one in name only.

The four dined on knackwurst and beans plus potato salad fresh from Costco. Fred visited his wine collection, returning with a 30 year-old Bordeaux, hoping to impress Jason's new beloved. She drank it as if she was consuming something out of a box. The internist had been a beer drinker and her parents eschewed all forms of alcohol, except Manishewitz at Passover. "Wonderful wine, Dad," Jason said, knowing that the bottle was worth in the neighborhood of $200 and making eyes at Rebecca so that she, too, would toss in a compliment.

"Delicious," she said. She left at least $15 worth in her glass at the end of the meal.

As Jennifer was serving the cheese cake, the phone rang. Jason answered. It was Phillip.

"Did you watch the local news?"

"It was on, but the sound was off. Why?"

"Gasparini was arrested for DUI!"

"Jesus Christ! How did that happen?"

"I don't know. I just saw it come across on the bottom of the screen. They must have reported the story before I turned it on. I looked on the Web but there's nothing there yet. I'll let you know as soon as I learn anything, but watch the eleven o'clock news. They'll have something."

Within seconds of the brothers hanging up, the phone rang again. Jason again answered. It was Art Schofield.

"Did you hear the news?" asked the lawyer.

"Our brother just called and told me that Judge Gasparini was pulled in for a DUI."

"Right. But did you hear how it happened?"

"Huh-uh. What?"

"Irv Greenberg just called me and told me that it happened last night, after midnight. Gasparini was driving his Cadillac and ran into a stop sign. Banged up his car pretty good. But that's not the whole story. He wasn't alone in the car. There was a sweet young thing who hassled the cop when he showed up."

"What sort of sweet young thing?"

"Don't know yet, and we'll probably never know who, but it certainly wasn't Mrs. Gasparini. Gotta believe that it was a pay-for-play girl."

"Anybody hurt?"

"I don't think so. Certainly not the Judge. But he spent a few hours in the jug. I guess he didn't do so well walking the straight line."

"What does that mean for us?" asked Jason.

"One thing it obviously means is that your father doesn't go to trial in two weeks like scheduled. And, it's a pretty safe bet that the presiding judge in San Francisco vs. Klein is not going to be Louis Gasparini."

"Amazing. Any chance they'll just dismiss my father's charges?"

"No way. You father is still a Public Enemy. The DA isn't about to let this case disappear. They'll assign a new judge to the case and, with the backlog in the courts, it's going to take some time getting it on the schedule. I bet it'll be at least six months."

"So, what do we do in the meantime?"

"Can't answer that. You gotta talk to Greenberg. My guess is that you don't do anything different."

"Do you think that the DA would be any more willing to take the offer of house arrest?"

"Interesting thought. Who knows? He obviously wants to get this behind him with a guilty verdict. Again, check with Greenberg."

Jason thanked Schofield and hung up. "Pop, it looks like you won't be going to court any time soon."

"Oh, OK."

Dom Perignon

Fred had improved markedly but was not back to his pre-morbid state. He read more and watched TV less. He talked politics and sports with a degree of expertise, knowing more about Clinton and the 2002 Giants than he did Obama and the '10 and the '12 Champs. He wrote checks; Jennifer approved them. He walked the streets by himself, commenting, on his invariably successful return, that it was time to get another dog.

Fred didn't fret over his legal jeopardy. Unless someone else brought up the matter, he said nothing about it. When it was mentioned, his only contribution was that he absolutely could not go to prison. It would kill him. Strategy, timing, and offers of a deal were the bailiwick of his lawyers and his sons. Just keep me out of jail.

Fred was an old man. Older than other 76-year-old men. He looked older, lots older than he had before the episodes. His aching joints, a mere nuisance earlier, limited his activities. The orthopedist wanted to replace his hip, but the cardiologist refused to sanction the operation. His prostate, the only organ in any human that continues to grow throughout life, had him in the bathroom multiple times every night. Flomax, the medication that was supposed to be so effective, made him dizzy. Twice he almost fainted, scaring the hell out of his wife, who thought the pacemaker had stopped working. His pacer worked just fine but the bulge on his chest was a source of constant displeasure. Something needed to be done with the cataracts but again, the heart doctor refused to sign on. He hated his new hearing aid; he usually left it on the bedside commode. He had a bout of diverticulitis and during the workup for his abdominal pain was found to have a gall bladder full of stones. Fred Klein was both an alleged felon and a walking geriatric textbook. He spent a meaningful percentage of his life in doctors' offices, physical therapy and nutrition facilities, clinical labs and imaging centers. He took fifteen different pills, some twice, one three times daily. Jennifer would take him to most of his appointments, but occasionally he had to go in a taxi, to him a financial setback and cause for complaining.

Mentally he was sharper, but not sharp. He could participate in discussions about politics, movies and TV, sports, and weather. He didn't make his own appointments but remembered that he had them. He rarely said anything terribly astute; he rarely said anything terribly off base. Someone who hadn't known Fred before would find him a fairly normal, but not very interesting, senior citizen. He would not be invited to MC an awards dinner, something he had done several times before, nor would he be invited as a new member of a non-profit board.

Those boards that he had been on did not kick him off. After all, he was innocent until proven not-innocent. His term on the American Heart Association board expired and he was not reappointed, even though he was eligible. His favorite board, that of the SF Symphony, had, naturally, not reelected him as its Chairman. On the other hand, they offered him another term. He attended some meetings when he felt up to it, but said almost nothing, certainly nothing that changed anybody else's mind. He would always try to be the member to move the approval of minutes. When someone beat him to it, he was there with a sprightly second of the motion. He'd vote with the majority or he'd abstain. He didn't want anyone to be mad at him.

Prior to his indictment, Fred tightly controlled his reputation as a philanthropist. He would listen to the pitches of the pitchmen and pitchwomen from the NGO's, the hospitals, the institutions of learning and the cultural centers, watching their Power Points, drinking their 95 point Chardonnays and Cabernets, and meeting their award-winners, their post-operative congenital heart and cleft palate cases, their summa cum laudes, and their visiting virtuosos. He was always good for four figures, often for five and occasionally for six. He had his name on doors, marquees, plaques, and marble floors. There was a Klein Dormitory, a Fred and Barbara Klein Cancer Wing and a Frederick Klein Theater for Emerging Artists.

Even though Fred had improved significantly, his family was not comfortable with him making solo decisions to contribute large sums of money. One of the clan was always present for the pitchpersons' visits. That family member would do everything possible to convince the patriarch that he was the decider while making the decisions him- or herself. The four figure donations grew, the five figure ones diminished in number and the sixes disappeared from the Klein tax forms.

Fred bought a Prius. One of the television news magazines did a feature of hybrids. Fred decided then and there that he wanted to go green. His now well-entrenched guilt over the death of Teresa Spencer made him see his Lexus as an instrument of the devil. It was time for a trade-in.

"Why a Prius, Dad?" asked one of the twins. "I like the idea of a hybrid, but there've got to be 20 hybrids out there. Did you do your due diligence to find the best?"

"I looked at all of 'em. Except for the Prius, they all look like any other car. You see a Prius and you know you are helping to save the planet. If we buy a Chevy or a Nissan, who'll know that we're environmentalists?"

"Do you care whether other people know?"

"Hell, yes. They all think I'm a killer. At least they should be aware that I am not just a killer. You know, boys, I am thinking of putting solar panels on the house. Stupid, huh, that I'd put solar up, here in the Heights where we don't get much sun? I don't care if we don't save a penny. I want the bastards in the neighborhood to see all those panels and know that Fred Klein is green."

"I agree, dear," said Jennifer, a supporter of the elimination of plastic bags and the unplugging of anything electric when not in use. "We'll show 'em."

Counselor Greenberg, not thinking there was any need for a face-to-face, called the Klein house to update his client. He asked Jennifer to put the call on speaker so that both she and her husband could hear.

"First the bad news. The DA is not prepared to take an offer of house arrest, even a long one."

"But I can't go to prison, Irv."

"I know how you feel, Fred, and we're going to do everything humanly possible to make sure that you don't end up behind bars."

"Look Irv, if they sentence me to prison, at my age and my shitty condition, I'll just have to kill myself."

"Oh, my God," was the response Greenberg barely heard from the wife.

"Stop that talk! Unfortunately, or really fortunately, if I suspect that you are about to hurt yourself or somebody else, the lawyer/client confidentiality provision doesn't apply. I'll have to let mental health know what you are up to."

"There you go thinking I'm crazy again. Wouldn't anybody in his right mind think about killing himself rather than go to jail when most of his life is already behind him?"

"No, Fred. Most wouldn't. You know, even if you do get sentenced, it's not likely to be very long. Whatever judge sets the sentence, he or she's got to talk with the probation officers and they take things like age and medical condition into consideration. You aren't going to be serving ten years. That I can guarantee you. And, by the way, I've got to give you the good news."

"How can there be any good news if you sound like you are giving me up. You say I'm not serving ten years. Does that mean I'm getting five or three? It'd kill me."

"No, Fred, I'm not saying that. Now, the good news. Gasparini is, as we were pretty certain, off the case. They don't want to have your closely followed case involving hit and run judged by an admitted drunk driver. I don't think they are going to go after him very hard. First offense, nobody hurt. And, the word on the street is that he'll step down, to spend more time with his family. And the other word out there is that the family, a family of one, the lovely wife, she's probably going to kick him out of the house. The DA will probably get a plea that he did it, and he'll lose his driver's license for a while, have to seek alcohol rehab, and stay on probation for a couple of years. I hear that his blood level was over 2.0, so this was big time drunk driving."

Jen asked, "How's all that good news for us?"

"Actually, the good news is that the case has been reassigned. Woman named Grace Dadekian. Armenian lady, about 65. Appointed by Deukmejian. And, she's been reelected a bunch of times, never with competition. Everybody likes her – low key, pretty easy going on sentencing. And she's not looking for publicity like Gasparini was."

"What does she think about old Jewish guys who kill young Christian mothers?"

"I have no idea. Everybody says she follows the law closely and doesn't let personal opinions get in the way of justice. Frankly, Fred, I think we've got the right judge."

"That is good news, Irv," said Jennifer. "She might look more favorably on house arrest."

"True. And, oh, by the way, she's in a long case right now – some esoteric issue between software companies. Lots of money involved. It's going to be at least a couple of months before she finishes this one up and prepares for ours."

"Reprieve!"

"We're not out of the woods yet, Fred, my friend. In the meantime, stay healthy and keep in touch."

"Actually, Counselor, wouldn't I be better off getting sick…er, sicker?"

"I'll let you answer that question for yourself. Sounds pretty stupid to me."

Later that night, Fred and Jen were home alone. Jason and Rebecca were staying at her place and the televised Golden State Warriors basketball game had ended up with a defeat for the homeys.

Fred pushed himself out of the recliner, stretched, glad that he could still touch the ceiling, and announced that he was going to bed. The 10 – 10:30 period was his usual time to make evening ablutions, read for a very short time and turn off the light. Insomnia had not been a problem for him since the head surgery. In his more active, earlier days, an occasional sedative/hypnotic served him well.

Jennifer, a night-person, usually read or watched movies until the wee hours. But this time, she showed up in the bedroom just as her husband, attired in his usual sleep garb, the day's boxers and a T-shirt, slipped in under the sheets and duvet. He hadn't had a pair of pajamas on since he was eight. "I'm pretty tired too, honey. And there's nothing good on the classic movie channel. I think I'll read in bed, if that's OK with you."

"Sure, why not." Fred could, if necessary, put a night mask on so that the reading lights would not be an issue. Jennifer took her cotton nightgown into the bathroom, washed and brushed, and returned to bed, her mystery novel in hand. Fred didn't look up, his eyes fixed on an old Sports Illustrated. Neither the 76-year-old nor the 44-year-old said anything for a few minutes. Fred didn't notice that his wife hadn't turned any pages even though he knew her to be a speedy reader. Jen did notice that Fred's magazine would briefly drop from his hands only to reassume its upright position as he awoke. Her heart beating stronger and quicker, she folded down a corner and set her book on the bedside table. *If I'm going to do anything, I better do it now.*

"Fred, honey."

"Huh?"

"We haven't made love in a long time – a real long time."

"I know. And, it's all my fault."

"No, no. It's nobody's fault. It's life. But we don't have to give up. Do you want to make love to me…now?"

"Shouldn't we wait 'til the morning? We used to always do it in the morning."

"No, my love, I'd like to do it now."

"I'm not sure that I should or could. You know that I have a bad heart – pacemaker and heart pills. You know that Dr. Jameson wouldn't give me any Viagra – said I wasn't healthy enough for it."

"So, who needs Viagra? You old goat, I bet you'll be able to get it up just fine. Little Freddy has had a good long rest."

"I could have another heart attack and you'd have a dead man lying next to you."

"I'm willing to take that chance, if you are. Your heart has been doing pretty good ever since you got out of the hospital. No chest pain, no skipped beats. You'll do just fine."

"OK, if you really want to. Remember that before the pacer, I always used Viagra, so I'm not sure Fred Junior will be able to grow very tall."

Jennifer laughed aloud. Her husband hadn't referred to his reproductive organ as Junior since early in their marriage. "I'll bet Junior will be ready for quite a growth spurt. If you agree, let me suggest a plan of attack. You lie there and I'll do all the work."

"OK."

"Lights on or lights off? I'd vote for on, sort of like morning."

"Why don't you just leave your bedside lamp on – that's enough light."

"Check." She turned off the overhead light and dimmed the bedside one a notch.

All too aware that she could conceive, Jennifer had been back on birth control pills since the abortion. Fred was, of course, unaware. But she knew well that his years did not make him infertile. Pablo Picasso, Anthony Quinn, and Rupert Murdoch were potential role models as advanced-age fathers, all older than Fred Klein.

"Time to shed the clothes," she said as if she was a physical education teacher for middle-schoolers about to change for their first gym class. Fred started to twist out of his tight gray T. "No, that's my job." She had him sit bolt upright and lift his hands high as if signaling a touchdown. Off it came, exposing the loose chest and abdominal skin and the still ruby-red but well healed incision atop the hockey puck-sized pacemaker.

"Are you cold?" Jen had planned for this by turning the thermostat heat up to 71 from its usual nocturnal 66. Fred shook his head implying that he was fine – not cold and certainly happier with 71 than the usual ambient temperature which he found more than a bit brisk.

"And next…" She grabbed the elastic of the boxers at both hips, asked him to rise up a bit, and slowly, methodically, took off his pants. She purposely looked at Fred Senior's face as she was exposing Junior, but she could not help but get a peek at the latter, finding that the organ she hoped would stand tall lay flaccid like a sea cucumber.

Her strip tease followed. Off went the nightgown in one fell swoop. The silver heart-shaped pendant and earrings, both given to her by him early in their courtship, were the only remaining accoutrements. She had already plugged in the IPod and was playing Mahler's First Symphony, their song. Ideally, she would share a pre-coital joint with him, but in all the years they had together, marijuana was never discussed, let alone used. Instead, she brought a a chilled bottle of Dom Perignon out of the bathroom, popped the cork and nakedly offered her naked husband a fluteful. He gladly accepted and asked for a refill. She had two glasses and became aware that her pulse rate had slowed.

Their sexual encounters in the last few years of his pre-felony life, averaging about once a fortnight, involved little in the way of foreplay - a kiss or two, some foot frolics short of fetish, and mutual hand-on-genital stimulation. The Viagra which Fred would consume half an hour before, in the days before he knew his heart wasn't perfect, made a quite acceptable erection totally predictable. Oral sex had never entered their repertoire. Barbara Klein had an insurmountable aversion to fellatio and figured she couldn't ask her husband to go down, in fact, stopping him the first few times he had tried. Fred had gotten it in his head that his life was going to be void forever of those pleasures and no amount of persuasion by his younger second wife could erase the imprint.

Jennifer lay with Fred on top of the sheets. She held his hand, rubbing his thumb with hers. "I love you, Fred Klein."

Fred smiled, but said nothing.

"I LOVE YOU, FRED KLEIN!"

"I love you too."

She got on her knees, straddled her husband and the still sleeping Junior, and kissed him firmly, forcing her tongue through his first resisting but eventually surrendering mouth. He lifted his arms and stroked her still youthful nulliparous breasts. Beginning to glow inside, Jennifer put both hands between Fred's legs and perceived a little bit of life there. She caressed, she rubbed lightly, she grasped firmly, she squeezed tightly – a little more life, but the shaft didn't rise above the leg upon which it slept. She slid back toward his feet with Junior in both hands and leaned over, mouth agape.

"Please don't do that."

"Why?"

"You know why."

She didn't. "All right, my love. I won't. What would you like me to do?"

"Just lie on top of me."

"I'll do that." She gently settled her body on top of his and he, with the limited strength left to him, wrapped his arms around her. The pacemaker box, pushing out the skin above his left chest wall, forced its way into her right breast. For her it was a unique and not unpleasant experience. They lay face to face, chest to chest, stomach to stomach, groin to groin, thigh to thigh for some ten minutes.

"Jennifer?"

"Yes dear."

"Is there any more of that champagne?"

"There sure is." Jen hid her sadness well. She poured two glasses. It was warm but wonderful.

Chateau D'yquem, 1921

Sixteen months had elapsed since the event on California Street. Much had transpired but most San Franciscans, save, of course, the Kleins, the Spencers, their attorneys, and the Superior Court, had forgotten about the episode. A Google search of Fred Klein or Teresa Spencer would have yielded nothing newer than nine months of age.

Fred was soon to turn 77. He was more youthful than he was as he hit 76, but not close to the young septuagenarian of 75 when no one who met him would have referred to him as old. Jennifer and the boys decided to throw him a birthday party. A year before, nobody but family and maybe his poker buddies would have thought of attending. Who wants to celebrate with the killer of a young mother? The guest list for #77 was not going to be extensive. Fred never was one to accumulate large numbers of friends. He knew many. He confided in few and was the confidant of even fewer. Art Schofield and the five other regular poker players would be there. The CEOs and CFOs of the charitable organizations to which the Kleins had generously contributed and who had reason to hope for more – they'd come and bring significant others, as often as not from the same gender. The stock broker who had helped make Fred and Barbara and Jennifer so wealthy said yes. The only one of his many physicians and surgeons invited was Alison Jameson. She accepted her invitation making Jennifer worried about the menu. Jen did not know of the doctor's marital status, so she addressed the invitation: "& Guest." The guest proved to be a young female Ob/Gyn resident from the General Hospital. Fred and Jen had not become close to their neighbors, but at least the two contiguous ones had treated them well, even after the reporters trod on their lawns, so they got invitations and accepted them. Irv Greenberg was not on the invitation list; Jason advised against it, correctly assuming that he would consider it inappropriate, and decline. The Mayor and Vice-Mayor both sent their regrets. The family dentist, veterinarian (in spite of there being no living Klein pets), optometrist and insurance broker rounded out the list. Only the insurance man sent regrets as he and his 23-year-old fiancée were going to the Galapagos.

Jennifer was thrilled. She hadn't entertained anyone other than a relative or an attorney for almost a year and a half. Their marriage had always included the hosting of cocktail and dinner parties, informal brunches and barbecues. The Democratic Party had frequently asked them to host receptions for visiting politicos. In this most Democratic of cities, that meant greeting the grandees and the celebrities. And, there they would be the next day in the *Chronicle*. All of that stopped when Meagan Spencer lost her mother.

Pouring over cookbooks, Jennifer blurted out, "To hell with Dr. Jameson," to Jason's girlfriend, Rebecca, who had volunteered to help in the preparations.

"Who is that?" she queried.

"Oh, I thought you knew. Dr. Allison Jameson is my primary care person and Fred's too. She's one of those doctors who think that you are what you eat. I doubt she's had a morsel of anything with fat in it since medical school. Fred thinks that she had something to do with his accident – he was so pissed off that she wanted him to change his diet that he couldn't concentrate."

"I thought that he had no memory for that event."

"He doesn't remember hitting her, but does say that he remembers how he felt when he went to his poker game. Here – what do you think of this?" She had picked out a pork tenderloin with a sauce that involved both cream and *fois gras*. "That'll show her."

"It sure will. You'll probably have to arrange an ambulance on stand-by for the heart attacks and strokes."

"That would be funny if Fred hadn't had both at once."

"Oops. Sorry."

Jennifer had declared the fete to be black tie optional. Like most philanthropists, accustomed as they are to attending formal balls, Fred had more than one tuxedo. He chose the 1950s style one over the one from the 80s. The invitees, without exception, came in tuxes and long gowns. Car parkers had been hired, an absolute necessity for large events in San Francisco. Also hired were college students to pass the hors d'oeuvres and beverages. Fred, a wine lover and collector for decades, tapped his collection, figuring that it was time to switch his status from collector to distributor. His cellar contained well over one thousand bottles, many dating back to the fifties and sixties. Why die with them unopened? First growth Bordeaux and Grand cru Burgundies filled the glasses. Jason, who had hoped to be an inheritor of the collection, cringed when he saw obvious oenological ignoramuses downing the five hundred dollar a bottle vintages as if they were chugging Budweiser.

The dinner was a big hit. The pork course with its astronomically high fat ingredients was the *piéce de resistance*. Not heard by the family were mumbles about the appropriateness of pork at a birthday bash for a Jewish man. Sandwiching the main course were a Maine lobster bisque and arugula salad at one end and bananas flambé as the finale. Seven candles in silver sticks were brought out with the dessert and the guests broke into discordant song. The invitees had been asked, in lieu of gifts, to make a contribution to a favorite charity and each person or couple was asked to name aloud the receiving organization, without mentioning a number.

"Speech!" All eyes fixated on the honoree. Fred had a pretty good idea that he was going to be asked to talk. He had jotted notes on the hackneyed back of an envelope. He stood tall but had his hands on the back of an easy chair to brace himself.

"My dear friends, and you too, Jason, thanks for coming. I truly despise having people watch me turn a year older." In fact, except for number 76, during which he was a cognitive wasteland, somebody through love and/or guilt had thrown him a party every year of his life.

"I'm sorry for not having you over last year, but had you come I probably wouldn't have recognized you unless I had just seen you on television. But I'm better thanks to the great care of more doctors and hospitals than I care to remember. But how can I forget? Bills are still coming in from doctors that say they saw me more than a year ago."

A few polite chuckles followed.

"I'm going to tell you some things that I haven't said to anyone, not even my dearest lover, chef, driver, and bill payer...uh...Jennifer. A year and a half ago, I was involved in a terrible traffic accident. A young lady named Teresa was killed."

Art Schofield, with the help of the cane that he had been using since his knee replacement six months earlier, forced himself out of his chair and approached his client.

"Please sit down, Art. I know what I'm doing here." Art slinked back into his seat.

"Yes, Teresa Spencer died and they say that I caused it. A two-year-old, now almost four, named Meagan, has no mother and Mr. Mark Spencer, from what I hear a fine gentleman, does not have his wife at his side. I say to you in all honesty that I do not remember the accident and from what I can put together, I did not know when it happened that I had done anything but brush somebody who had gotten out of her car in the middle of the street as I was going to a store to buy chips and dip. Am I legally guilty? I really don't know. I'll leave that up to a jury and to my criminal attorney, Irving Greenberg. The trial will start in about two months and I'm prepared to deal with any outcome.

"But let me say to you, my closest friends on earth, that I am truly sorry for what I have done. I'm 77 today and who knows how many more years I have left. I am proud of what my life has been so far, at least until that horrible moment a year and a half ago. I want to be remembered as so much more than the man who took Meagan's mother away from her.

"And now, please get back to the party. Anyone here like desert wines?" About four of the thirty-some guests raised their hands. "Glad to see there aren't more than that. I'm going to open my greatest bottle of wine, a '21 Chateau d'Yquem and I'd hate to have to split it thirty ways." He sat down as another dozen hands went up.

Thirty seconds later, Art Schofield sat on the arm of Fred's easy chair. "Can I have a minute of the birthday boy's time in private?"

"Come on Art. The party's just warming up."

"It'll only take a couple of minutes."

"OK. But just a couple of minutes. I don't want that Yquem finished before I get to try some."

"Maybe you ought to get a bit before we talk. And, pour me some too."

Phillip had accidentally bisected the 90-year-old cork in his attempt to open the valued vintage. As his father approached, he was in the process of forcing the sticking half into the bottle. "Stop!" said Fred, too late, as the bottom portion of the stopper, now made up of dozens of cork bits, fell into the cherished liquid.

"Phil! Phil! What have you done? That bottle is worth four thousand bucks!" Phillip was speechless. His expression was like that of a nine-year-old who had been caught by his mother with shoplifted baseball cards.

"Don't worry Fred," said one of the early hand raisers, who obviously knew wine. "All you've got to do is filter it through a little bit of cheese cloth."

"Jennifer, bring me some cheese cloth!" he yelled across the room, above the heads of most of the guests.

"What is cheese cloth?" she responded.

"Goddamned if I know. What is cheese cloth?" he asked, directing the question to the guy who told him not to worry.

"It's a loosely woven cotton cloth - all kitchens have it."

"It's a loosely woven cotton cloth. You gotta have it in the kitchen. Everybody does," he yelled again.

"You don't need to holler, honey," Jen said calmly having slalomed her way through the crowd. "I don't have cheese cloth, as far as I know. When is the last time I made cheese? Never."

Philanthropist

The wine guy spoke up again. "No problem if you don't have cheese cloth. You can use a coffee filter."

"I know damn well that you make coffee. Please get me a filter...now! And some kind of big bottle to decant it into."

"Simmer down, dear. It'll be all right." She brought the filter and the filter holder and a large thermos, the closet thing she could find to a big bottle. The viscous nectar flowed slowly through the paper filter into the thermos, from which it was served in very small dollops. Phil breathed a large sigh of relief. He wasn't going to be disowned.

"That's magnificent!" said one of the guests, not immediately recognized by the honoree.

"It's awesome!" exclaimed Dr. Jameson's youthful date. Even with that recommendation, Jameson didn't taste.

"You know, Fred, I don't usually like sweet wines, but this is pretty nice. Any idea where I can pick up a couple of bottles?" asked a rich man.

"This is truly heavenly. Legendary. I've had the '57 and the '72, but nothing comes close to this. I am honored to be at the site of the opening," said the man who recommended cheese cloth. A doyenne of something took a larger than average portion of the sauterne, tasted it, grimaced as if she had been force-fed a spoonful of Splenda and put it down on the coffee table, walking away from the glass, now containing some eighty dollars' worth of the most costly wine anyone at the party had ever tasted or smelled. Fred pointed it out to Phillip the pourer who in turn ordered the shapely coed hired for the event to pick up the glass and put it in the refrigerator. Whatever she did in her policing gig, she was not to throw any white wine in dessert glasses down the sink.

Schofield finally was fed up waiting in the easy chair with no one to talk to and hobbled over to the wine tasting venue. He asked Phillip for "Just a little bit. I'm driving."

"Sorry Art, it's all gone. I didn't get any either. Neither did Jennifer. I don't think she cared. Thank God that Dad got to taste it."

"Did he like it?"

"You know, if you blindfolded him, I doubt he could tell the difference between d'Yquem and Cherry Coke, at least since the accident. I hate to say it, but our father has always been the ultimate wine snob. I don't think he knows the first thing about what's good and what's dreck. If you put Gallo into a Mouton Rothschild bottle and served him out of that bottle, he'd have an orgasm on the spot and if you did it the other way around, he'd vomit. The man's got tens of thousands of dollars' worth of wine from all over the world. I hate to think what we will do with it when he dies. None of us cares much about wine - maybe Jason does - who knows what that's about - but I don't think either Robert or I drinks more than a glass or two a week, and that's usually cheap stuff."

"How do you think his thing with wine is now compared to before his surgery?"

"Not any different. Nothing sophisticated then, nothing now. Better than it was when he was really out of it. He didn't seem to remember that he had a stash of great bottles."

"Thanks for the information, Phil. I've got to talk to your Dad about that speech of his.

"I bet you do."

Art found Fred surrounded by guests waxing eloquently about the wonders of fine wine. He slipped his arm through the bend in Fred's and told him that he needed a minute of his time. They went upstairs into Jennifer's study.

"How about that wine, Artie Boy?"

"I didn't get any. All gone when I got there. No big deal. You know me and fancy wine. Give me a cognac any day. But let's talk Fred, what the hell was that all about?"

"I'm really sorry Art. I expected that there would still be some for you to try. I would have come over to get you if I thought it would run out."

"I'm not talking about wine. I'm talking about your little speech."

"What do you mean 'little'?" Was it too short? Should I have thanked more people for coming?"

"No, Fred. It wasn't too short. It was too long. As soon as you opened your mouth it was too long. How about 'Thanks for coming.' and sitting down. You had to go and destroy everything that your lawyers have done for you. Greenberg…and me. That line, 'I am truly sorry for what I have done.' That apology has blown your case out of the water."

"But I am sorry."

"I'm really moved by that fact, Fred, but for God sake, keep that information to yourself and maybe to your wife and kids and lawyers. Don't go blabbing to the world."

"Everybody here is a friend of mine. Nobody is going to tell anyone else. The word isn't going to get out."

"Are you nuts? Is your brain damage coming back? There are forty people out there and you don't think that they are going to talk to their friends about your admission to the most publicized crime in San Francisco since Dan White shot the mayor and Harvey Milk? Just read the papers next week - you are going to be playing a major role in the society section once again."

"I'm sorry, Art. I didn't mean to blow up your case."

"Don't be a jerk. I'm not worried about myself. I don't want to see my good buddy go to prison. I want him here for poker games."

"I am not going to go to jail. It would kill me."

"Yes, you've told me that before - a million times."

"And don't tell me that my brain damage is coming back. My brain is just fine, thank you."

"It's me that's sorry this time. I shouldn't have said that."

"So should I go downstairs and tell everybody that I didn't mean what I said?"

"No, God no. It's bad enough as it is. Don't compound it."

"You know something Schofield? You are a real schmuck."

"And why am I a schmuck, my dear friend?"

"I don't know. You just are. But I love you anyway." For the first time in the more than sixty years that they'd known each other, they hugged.

Larry Hill

Schofield rejoined the party and Klein went down to the wine cellar, where he extracted another bottle of d'Yquem from the refrigerator - not a 1921 but a 1955 - after the 21, one of the great vintages of the 20th century.

A Funeral

Jacob Ross of Russian Hill died. Father of two and grandfather of four, he passed away after a prolonged bout with chronic leukemia at the age of 81. His funeral was to take place at Temple Emanuel the following day. For decades, Ross had been the Klein family CPA.

Ross was the first in Fred's poker game to depart from his earthly existence. It was a resilient group. Of the original seven that had started dealing more than thirty years earlier, prior to Ross, only two stopped coming to the low stakes, high energy, and gastronomically plebeian game. Ed, 77, a retired shoe-monger, went to Arizona to be with his son after his wife succumbed to a stroke, and Ernie, 85, whose true profession was never clear, became so demented that his colleagues were no longer willing to take his money.

Fred learned of Accountant Ross's passing from Art Schofield. No chance that he'd not go to the funeral. The only time he had set foot in a synagogue since Barbara's death and funeral was for the funerals of others. In one's 70s, funerals become a standard and not entirely depressing social occasion. Their frequency goes up in the 80s, declining the following decade as the number of friends and associates eligible for such an event rapidly diminishes.

"You willing to go with me, dear?" he asked of his young wife.

"Of course," she responded. She was not about to let him go alone.

"How about you, Jason?"

The son, fervently agnostic with little contact with Judaism since his Bar Mitzvah, was surprised to hear the request. But recognizing that the improvement of his relationship with his father, seemingly strong for the first time in years, was fragile, he responded, "I'd be glad to, Dad. And,

I bet that Rebecca would come with us. She knows her way around a shul."

The following day, half an hour before the service was scheduled to begin, they showed up at the Temple, a massive red domed structure that would have seemed more appropriate in Istanbul than in San Francisco. Fred insisted that they use the Prius even though the back seat was not as commodious as that of his wife's car. He wanted to be sure that his high-flying co-mourners saw his green side.

CPAs tend to have smaller turn outs at their funerals than do doctors, lawyers, politicians, and Indian chiefs. Though Ross was well known in the trade and by a group of friends, most of whom played cards, his event was not likely to put a dent in the massive sanctuary, so those who figured out such things scheduled his in a side room with a capacity well under one hundred.

The Klein party of four was among the first to arrive and took seats in the third row on the aisle. Fred, as was his wont, insisted on an aisle seat. He blamed his need on arthritic knees but his actual motivation was the chance of seeing, being seen by, and pressing the flesh with important people attending the same event. The two women sat to his immediate right and Jason occupied the fourth seat in.

Reform funerals are not very long -- a few prayers, centering on the Mourner's Kaddish, some singing of hymns, a rabbinical statement summarizing the positive accomplishments of the deceased while ignoring the negatives, and, occasionally, words from family and friends, usually engendering laughter rather than tears. During the service itself, Fred looked right and was thrilled to see Rebecca reciting the prayers and singing the hymns not only in English but in Hebrew, without looking at her prayer book. "Please God, make him marry her." He reckoned that a prayer in this particular holy place couldn't hurt. Neither he nor his son was in any way religious, but it would be a whole lot better than Emily and her nasty parents.

The event was finished in less than an hour and the mourners filed out, back to front. As Fred stood from the plain wooden pew, his knees buckled and his head filled with clouds. He attempted to resume his seated position but failed, falling to the carpeted aisle in slow motion. Jennifer had the presence of mind to cushion the back of his head to prevent another Eddy Street bar scene. "Help me!" she yelled.

It is a rare Jewish transitional event in which there is not a near-minion from the medical profession. Ross's funeral was no exception. Within seconds of Jennifer's plea, three doctors, average age 77, were at the fallen man's side. Not one of them had an active medical license. One, a dermatologist, started CPR, including mouth to mouth, before collecting data as to the nature of the episode. "Wait, Nate," yelled the youngest of the three, an internist. He put two fingers on the patient's neck. "He's got a pulse! Slow - about sixty - but strong. And, he's breathing. Stop the CPR." Nate ceased the compressions and the breaths.

The third doctor, an octogenarian psychiatrist, recognized that he didn't know much about such matters, but did remember that when somebody faints, his legs should be elevated above the heart. He correctly assumed that a faint was the diagnosis of the man lying on the ground. He had learned of Fred's identify before the service when he came into the room and was told by his daughter that the man shaking everybody's hand was the infamous mother-killer of California Street. "Get some pillows!" he ordered to no one in particular, not having any idea where one finds pillows in a synagogue.

"I don't think we're going to need any pillows. He's waking up," said the internist. Fred had been supine for less than two minutes.

"What happened to me?" He looked around at the gathered seniors, his trophy wife, his son and Rebecca and immediately remembered where he was and why he was there. "Shit, I fainted. I knew it was going to happen."

"Watch your language Dad. You're in a house of the Lord."

"God dammit! It's those shitty piss pills. Every time I stand up, I get dizzy." Rebecca, embarrassed, stepped away from the group.

"Can I get up?" he asked the internist who seemed to be in charge of the medical attendees.

"Yeah, you can. But do it slowly and let us help you." Fred followed instructions and took a few hesitant steps in the direction of the lobby before regaining his usual brisk, elderly stride. As he was walking, the sound of an ambulance was increasingly audible.

"He's over there!" somebody yelled at the two EMTs, both females in their early twenties dressed all in blue, who cantered into Emanuel's lobby. The 911 people had received four calls from cell phones describing, in four wildly divergent ways, the man down in the synagogue.

Caller A - There's blood all over
Caller B - He's awake but his wife is hysterical
Caller C - I think he's dead
Caller D - He doesn't look Jewish

"Who's the patient?" They saw nobody in obvious distress, let alone someone on the floor.

"That guy without the yarmulke. The one with the two young women," offered an old man.

"Sir, how are you doing?" the thin one of the two asked of Klein.

"Just fine. Why don't you just go on back to where you came from? I don't need an ambulance."

"Let's just check you over. We heard that you fell and were unconscious. Please sit down. Go get that chair!" the thin one said to the stouter, younger one.

"Get his vitals!"

"BP 100 over 60. Pulse 60 and regular."

"Sir, those are pretty low numbers for a man of your age."

"How do you know how old I am?"

"Just guessing, Sir. Figure you to be about 80?" In the first class of any health-related school, be it school for doctors, nurses, dentists, chiropractors, acupuncturists or reflexologists, the student is warned never to guess too high for an adult, too low for a child. You think the lady is 65, say 55. And a child looking 4 should be told you think he's 6. The flip-over point is about 22.

"You got that wrong, Miss. I'm 77."

"Still, Sir, those readings are pretty low. I think we'd better take you to the hospital and let them check you out. Who knows, you may have had a heart attack. You may need a pacemaker."

"I already have a pacemaker, goddam it. And, I already had a heart attack. I know what a heart attack feels like and, this, young lady, is no heart attack." He didn't point out that he had no pain at the time of his myocardial infarction in the bar, at least no pain that he could remember.

"Again, Mr. Klein, we better take you over to General Hospital just to be safe. You could die." Her partner had learned his identify from one of the 911 callers and passed it on.

"Look around you, my dear, at all these old bastards. Any of them could die in the next ten minutes, too. The only difference between them and me is that I just fainted and they didn't and that I have a pacemaker and they don't, or at least some of them don't. Forget about putting me in your fucking ambulance." Jennifer and Jason were incredulous at the clarity of his words. Rebecca continued to stand well away from the action.

The two EMTs simultaneously shrugged their shoulders, picked up their paraphernalia and left, the elder one explaining to the Kleins on her way out that they weren't responsible for anything that happened to him. The comment was ignored as Fred and his entourage sauntered toward the Prius parked in the handicapped spot across from the temple.

"Looking good, Fred." "Atta boy!" "Go for it Klein!" Departing members of the congregation saluted him as if he were in the final stages of a marathon.

A Venezuelan

The sun shone dazzlingly, unusual for Pacific Heights. Jennifer basked in the rays atop the rarely used chaise lounge, protected from view by high hedge rows. She was attired only in Ray Bans, a floppy Digger hat and the lower portion of her purple bikini, the top half tossed randomly aside. She was reading something risqué. She had inhaled a few tokes of marijuana and was feeling just right. She heard the sliding glass door open, looked over and saw her stepson, Jason, wearing his business suit with a bright floral tie. More handsome than she remembered. He walked slowly and silently toward her, looking, as best she could tell, only at her eyes. She did nothing to find and replace the top half of her outfit. He reached the chaise and spoke. "Bend your knees, Jen."

She did.

He deftly slipped off the bottom of her bathing suit and tossed it in the general direction of its mate.

The mild breeze felt good between her legs.

He took off his navy blue suit jacket, let it drop to the grass, and began removing his tie.

"Jennifer!" The voice was from inside the house, clearly that of her husband.

She awakened in her bed, covered in sweat. She looked at the LED of the alarm clock - 2:46. Fred was asleep three feet away. He was snoring as was his custom, but the grunts were barely audible over the white noise machine that Jen always had turned on high.

She very much wished that she could have a man inside of her right then. Fred was not a candidate as evidenced by their attempt a couple of months before. She hadn't owned a vibrator since she married him and wished that she found masturbation more satisfactory. Better than nothing, but not much. Oh, how she wished she could get back into the dream and follow it to its logical conclusion. But the partner in the fantasy was her husband's first-born son. And, he's with someone else. Jesus, what am I thinking about?

The following morning that dream, unlike so many others she had, was remembered in every detail, including the color and pattern of the tie and the specific location of the bikini top. She had just sat down for breakfast with her usual bowl of Cheerios with blueberries and coffee when Jason walked into the kitchen, poured himself grapefruit juice and toasted half a bagel. He had given up coffee when his family and he had split.

"I didn't know you were here last night. Problems?" she asked.

"No problems. Becca's in Denver investigating something and I'd just as soon stay with you guys, if that's not a burden. Not only do I get to see you, it's a lot closer to the office so I can sleep a little more."

"No burden at all. We love to have you. It's really good for your Dad to have you around. By the way, in case you couldn't tell, we really like Rebecca. You gonna marry her?"

"Not so fast! I've only known her for about three months. I like her too, but I'm, shall we say, gun-shy after my first attempt at marital bliss. Stay tuned."

"Sorry for the forwardness. You know, you were in my dream last night."

"No, didn't know that. I hope I wasn't a serial killer or a mad rapist."

"Oh, no, nothing like that."

"So, was it a good dream? Tell me more."

"Actually, I don't remember much about it," she lied. "But I don't think you committed any capital offenses. Jase, I gotta go. Big day of shopping ahead."

"See ya. Let me know if you remember anything more about the dream. It's not too often that a good looking woman tells me that she dreamed about me." His eyes remained connected to hers just a bit longer than she would have expected.

Jennifer's love life was nothing worth writing a novel about. She could count on two hands the number of men with whom she'd gone to bed.

The younger of two daughters of Graham Kesselheim, a non-tenured professor of statistics at Princeton, she'd done OK in school and was universally agreed to be one of the two or three best looking girls at the public high school in the town that may have more PhDs per capita than any other in the world. During her junior year, she scored a prom invitation from the power forward on the basketball team, a tall white guy who had already committed to some midwestern college – she couldn't remember which. He, as did she, bore academic genes, being the off-spring of a biology professor mother and classicist father, both Princeton professors. He excelled in the art of persuasion, convincing the young Jennifer that full-bore sex at sixteen was a pretty good idea, as a way to understand her own psychology and physiology. "And, oh, by the way, my team will be playing here in Princeton next year so we can hook up again soon." She didn't have the sports savvy to ask whether it was fairly certain that he would be on the traveling squad of the team. After a pair of couplings that night, she did learn quite a bit about psychology and physiology.

Jennifer had neither the interest nor the GPA to attend Princeton U or any other big- ticket institution of higher learning. She at least surpassed the educational exploits of her older sister who married right out of Princeton High. Jennifer got a bachelor's degree, majoring in psychology with a minor in physiology, from a combination of a junior college, a southern party place, and San Francisco State University. At each stop, there were men in her life with whom she shared sexual experiences, but she reacted to most of the encounters as she did to the lectures in her courses, as educational episodes. The pain from her initial experience did not regularly reappear, but the pleasure that she expected, and was a given in several of her psych lectures, was slow in developing. It was not until she had graduated and entered into a lengthy affair with a married policeman did she accept that there really were joys of sex. There were two or three other satisfactory, albeit brief, matches after the dispiriting breakup with the cop, with good mating playing the central role in each. Then she met and married Mr. Taylor, the franchisee, and found sex with him to be abhorrent. She knew it going into the marriage but figured the security of marrying a rich man was more important than physical fulfillment and that she, now not only a fan of intercourse but well educated in its psychological and physiological underpinnings, would be able to change him. She had too high an opinion of her skill set. The sex act was as unpleasant and unfulfilling during the middle of the marriage as at its beginning and end. During the latter half of the Taylor era, Ernesto Contreras made his entry into her life, and sex became for the first time a really big deal. Frequency was not essential. They generally bedded monthly, occasionally more, almost never less. Quality was more important than quantity and the quality was top grade. During the gap between Taylor and Klein, she stepped out with a handful of other men, mainly those with whom she felt there was at least a slight chance that she'd want to enter into matrimony. With some, sex was good, others, not so good. None was as breathtaking as Contreras or as atrocious as Taylor. None passed the marriage eligibility requirements until she met Fred Klein walking his dog. Copulation with him was OK – orgasms were rare but she was not entirely dissatisfied, especially knowing that the nuptials did not signal the end of the dalliances with Ernesto. All was acceptable until the fall and resultant brain injury. She had had sex only once since, that in the disorder of Ernesto's house in the Excelsior. It looked like there was little if any chance of a change on the home front and there were no likely candidates amongst those men that she had enough contact with to logically make a move. It had been many months since she sat with Ernesto in the Botanical Garden. She picked up the phone.

Ernesto answered after the second ring. *"Hola, mi amor."*

"How did you know it was me?" asked Jennifer, assuming correctly that he had not figured out how to identify a caller on his cell phone.

"Oh. Is that you, Jen? I'm so sorry. I thought it was somebody else. It's great hearing from you. How are you?"

"I'm OK. What do you mean somebody else?"

"Come on Jen. We've been apart a long time. You don't think I was just sitting around waiting for you to call, do you?"

"No, of course not. But '*mi amor.*' That's me, isn't it?"

"Yes, sure. But there is someone else. Jennifer, I'm getting married. Next month."

She said nothing. He said nothing. After an exceedingly long pause, he said, "Are you still there?"

"Yes, I'm here. I don't know what to say. Who is she?"

"Nobody you know. Her name is Margarita. She's Venezuelan."

"Oh. Venezuelan, that's nice."

"Yes, she's very nice. She is much younger than me – just 28. Her father left Caracas when Chavez took over. He had been a minister in the previous government. He was frightened that he'd lose everything that he had made."

"I see. How long have you known her?"

"Just a few months. I didn't know her when I saw you last."

"That's nice to hear, I guess. What else?"

"I met her at the restaurant. She came in with her mother and brother and we just started talking. She's smart, like you. Went to college and has a job as an interpreter with the Gap. And Jennifer, I am going to be a father."

Another pause in the conversation. "That's great news, Ernesto. Congratulations. But aren't you more careful than that? You know, since you knocked me up?"

"Come on, don't talk like that. Yeah, I should have been more careful, but she doesn't seem to be too upset. Her parents aren't happy, but I guess they like me OK and are going to throw a big wedding for us. And they are buying us a house – nothing big, but in San Francisco, anything is great."

"Yeah, right."

"Do you want to be invited to the wedding? Her father said we can invite anyone we know."

"Jesus Christ! What an incredibly stupid idea! No, I don't want to be invited."

"I guess that was stupid. Sorry. By the way, why did you call?"

"Oh, no reason. I just wanted to see how you were doing. Our last time together wasn't the best. I hated to see what we had end like that."

"True. But I don't think it would be a good idea for us to see each other again."

"You're a genius. Ernesto. Incidentally, does she know about me?"

"No, she doesn't. She knows that there have been a few women in my life, but she doesn't ask questions."

"A few women in your life."

"Oh, guess where we are going on our honeymoon."

"I don't know. Uruguay?"

"Close. We're going to South America - Chile and Argentina. I always wanted to go to South America."

"Yeah, I know. Have a great life."

A Can of 7 Up

Two weeks to go before the trial was to begin, Greenberg had decided that his only rational defense was to try to convince the jury that his client didn't know that he had hit anybody. Pretty far-fetched he knew, what with the aborted attempts to cover up things like the dented car. But on the witness stand, the proper presentations of the poker players, Dr. Jameson and maybe Jennifer, he might be able to sow the seed of doubt. Furthermore, it was an easy call to put Fred himself on the stand, more as a sympathy-seeking move than a source of meaningful and exonerating evidence. The odds were that there'd be a guilty verdict, putting the sentencing in the lap of Judge Dadekian. Greenberg did not remember a case he had taken to trial in which a guilty verdict could be considered a victory -- a victory because the sentence, turned down in negotiations by the prosecutor, was acceptable to the convicted. House arrest – good for the convict as he didn't go to prison and, at his age and state of health, he wasn't likely to be doing much out of the house anyway except going to doctors. Good for the taxpayers as he wouldn't cost anything to house and feed, and he'd be financially responsible for his own medical care, not the case were he to be incarcerated. Not good for the DA as it would offer grist for TV spots to any competition he might have in future political races. Soft on Crime! Rich Guy Who Killed Young Mother Serves Sentence in Luxury!

The civil case had received little attention, except in the Spencer home, the office of Spencer's personal injury attorney and, more recently in the office of Klein's new lawyer, PI defense attorney Garth Gladstone, USC Law School '97. The case had been filed a few months after the crime but was back-burnered in anticipation of the criminal case and the information that would surface in the interim. Gladstone had heard from

Philanthropist

unknown sources about Klein's admission of guilt at his birthday bash. He knew that there would have to be a settlement; Art Schofield couldn't take the case to trial. The lawyers had run some numbers. Gladstone/Spencer wanted thirty-million, Schofield/Klein/Insurers offered ten. Counter offers were put on hold pending criminal developments.

One week before the trial was to begin, the Kleins were called into Greenberg's office for coaching. Jennifer's testimony initially seemed pretty straight forward. The lawyer had pointed out to her that she had the right to refuse to testify as she was the wife. But if she testified at all, she'd have to answer all questions that the judge deemed appropriate.

"No problem. There was nothing he told me that made me worried that he had done something wrong."

"So what happened that night?"

"He came home from the poker game and told me that he lost fifty dollars. Nothing more."

"How about the next morning?"

"He was in the kitchen when I got up, reading the paper."

"Anything unusual about that?"

"Nope. He always read the paper in the morning."

"Then what?"

"That was my volunteer day. I volunteered at the airport – Traveler's Aid. So I left. I think he said something about taking his car in."

"Why was he going to do that?"

"I don't remember. Some mechanical thing, I think."

"Do you remember why you were going to take the car to the shop, Fred?" asked Greenberg.

"I don't remember anything."

"So, what else, Jennifer?"

"Nothing. Next time I saw him was when he told me that he might have hit the woman. And then the police came and took him away."

"He told you that he hit the woman the same day that you saw him at breakfast and everything was OK?"

"Right."

"You know, that doesn't look too good for our side if we are going to try and sell the idea to the jury that he didn't remember anything. Maybe we better invoke the spousal privilege and keep you off the stand."

"Whatever you say."

"You OK with that Fred?"

"Sure, why not."

"So," said Greenberg, "it looks like you'll be our only witness, except for Dr. Jameson and one or two of the poker players who will say that you seemed normal when you played that night."

"Yeah, right, I was normal 'cause I didn't think I hurt anyone."

"Let's go over some of that, Fred. What do you remember about that night?"

"Nothing. What I know now is what they've told me since."

"They?"

"Jennifer, Jason, Artie, and some others, I guess."

"You don't remember driving to the poker game?"

"No."

"You don't remember hitting anyone?"

"Huh-uh."

"You don't remember that you had a big tray of vegetables in the car but did a U turn to buy Doritos and dip at the 7-Eleven?"

"No, I don't. I do remember doing that before – I always brought the dip and chips."

"You didn't buy any chips or dip that night?"

"So they tell me."

"Do you remember coming home and telling your wife that you lost fifty dollars?"

"Nope, and I would normally remember that. I don't think I ever lost that much at one of our games. I usually won."

"And, do you remember getting arrested and spending a night in jail?"

"Sort of. Sort of like a dream. I couldn't tell you anything specific about it. I just remember that I hated it."

"You know what the prosecution is going to say, don't you?"

"How would I know that?"

"They are going to say that you hit the lady and left the scene because you were afraid that you'd be arrested and accused of drunk driving. That you tried to hide your dented car, knowing that somebody had probably seen you hit her. That you knew full well that you had hit somebody, maybe causing a serious injury and that you committed a felony by leaving the scene of the accident."

"But I didn't know that I hit her, at least not enough to hurt her."

"How do you know that if you don't remember anything?"

"I just know. I know what kind of man I am."

"Fred. That's going to be really hard to sell to a jury."

"I guess it is. But you're the best. You can do it."

"Thanks for your confidence. You're more confident that I am. I got to tell you that you may well be convicted."

"So you think I'll go to prison?"

"Remember, we talked about that. Our best bet is to convince the judge that society is better off with you under house arrest than in the penitentiary."

"Oh yeah. You did tell me that. Make sure it happens."

"Not my call. It'll be up to the judge. Let's hope she sees it the same way. In the meantime, I'm going to make one more attempt to get the DA to see it our way and accept the plea bargain for house arrest."

Greenberg talked directly to the DA. He said they'd accept as many as five year's house arrest. The DA did not see it their way. Jury selection was set for three weeks hence.

A week later, Jennifer and Fred lay together in bed, both finding it impossible to fall asleep. Sex, previously a precedent and instigator of sleep, was, after the failed attempt of three months earlier, not an alternative. They rarely had talked about the possibility of their not being together, either because of his death or his incarceration. They almost never talked about anything after the lights were out. With the trial getting close, that changed.

"Jennifer."

"Yes, darling."

Fred sat straight up. "I'm guilty. I killed Teresa Spencer. I took away the mother of a child, as surely as had I shot her with a gun. How can I not go to jail?"

"I don't want you to go to jail. I need you with me. I love you, old man."

"How can I have you in my bed when I am responsible for Mark Spencer having to sleep alone?"

"Come on, my love. What good will come to Mark Spencer if you are in prison? You've paid a big price already. Your life has been shattered, beyond repair."

"But I'm alive. Teresa is dead. The price I have paid is tiny compared to hers."

"Isn't that why you are going to have a trial – to let others who don't know you and didn't know her decide what price is right?"

"Jen, I think I should call Greenberg and tell him to accept a prison term."

"I don't want to talk about it now. Let's just go to sleep and talk about it tomorrow."

Neither mentioned the issue the following day or the days thereafter. Greenberg did not receive a call.

It was Optometrist Lenny Gettleman's turn to host the Friday night poker game the weekend before the trial. Klein had not attended, or been invited to attend, since the aborted four-man match many months earlier. The late Jake Ross's spot had been filled by JJ Munther, a transplant from Ft. Worth, but Munther was away at a high-end Texas Bat Mitzvah. The idea of inviting Fred was floated; Schofield was of the mind that his friend was up to the task. Jennifer agreed, with minimal hesitation. She bought the big bag of Doritos and two tubs of hummus. At Schofield's recommendation, she purchased the groceries to obviate any publicity that might result from the alleged felon making a return visit to the now famous convenience store on California St. The case and impending trial had been resurrected as a feature story in print and electronic media.

"You up to this, Fred?" asked the attorney as they circled Gettleman's block in the Sunset District, looking for the ever elusive parking space.

"Yep. Good to go." Klein was dressed, once again, in his poker outfit, just back from the dry cleaner.

"You weren't so good to go six months ago. You acted like you had never played. Tell me. Does a flush beat a full house?"

"Cut the shit, Artie. You think I'm an idiot?"

"Does it?"

"Yes, goddamit. No, I mean, no."

"I'm worried about you, Fred Baby."

"Don't worry. How much could I lose – another fifty bucks? I'm a rich son-of-a-bitch. I can afford it." They found a parking space four blocks from the Gettleman place.

"OK. Let's give it a try."

As Art opened the door to get out, Fred said, "Just a second."

"Change your mind? Want to wait 'til after the trial?"

"No, that's not it. I want to play. It's about the trial. I want to plead guilty and serve time."

"What the hell do you mean by that?"

"Just what I said. I should go to jail."

"Why?"

"Because I'm guilty. I killed Teresa Spencer, then I ran away."

"Jesus, Fred, that's quite a change of pace. Let's talk about it after the game. We've got plenty of time. There are seven guys tonight, not four like our last go-round. We can't keep 'em waiting." Fred, whose gait was considerably friskier than that of his friend, slowed his pace to allow Art and his cane to keep up.

The two entered Gettleman's modest home. The other five players were already at their fold-up metal chairs. The host had covered the pool table in the middle of the family room with plywood and draped it with a mauve blanket. Seven stacks of red, white and blue chips were already positioned around in anticipation of the game about to begin. Fred and Art each added four ten dollar notes into the traveling rosewood bowl and set the chips and hummus, plus Schofield's coconut cream pie, on the snack table. All of the five early-comers had open beers in front of them. Art followed suit while Fred popped a 7 Up. The distribution of the first seven cards selected the man to the left of Klein as the initial dealer. He was a young Indian-American guy, maybe 35, whose name Fred couldn't remember after having been introduced three minutes before. He dealt out a quick hand of five card draw, jacks or better to open, which was won by one of the old boy network, Smith, who wore a 49ers cap and a neck brace. Fred, having nothing higher than a ten in his hand, dropped out before the draw. The deal rotated to Klein.

"Gentlemen, how about a hand of seven card stud, high-low?"

"Sounds good to me." "Go for it."

Art became anxious. The game was more complex than draw. No way that his good friend would have dealt a hand of stud last time they got together.

His shuffling technique was clumsy but there was no doubt that he had done a workmanlike job of rendering the cards in random order. Seven stud involves giving each player two cards face down, then one face up, followed by four more up cards, one at a time. Bets take place after each round of up cards. The high-low addition requires that each of the remaining players decides after the last card is dealt if he is going to go after the half of the pot that goes to the best hand at the table or the half for the worst. Dementia, even mild dementia, would make the task of dealing and controlling a hand of this game essentially impossible. Fred succeeded. He dealt flawlessly. His hand showed no promise after the second up card, so he folded. The pot was shared, half to the Indian man who had a straight and half to Bill Kreutzer who had 7,5,4,3, ace, known in the trade as a seventy five, an excellent low. The old banter for which Klein was famous (pair of whores and a bullet = two queens and an ace), was absent, but his motor and cognitive skills were fully intact. Each player got the right number of cards in the right sequence – up when they should be up, down for down. Fred was back!

The deal passed around the table clockwise. Every seventh deal fell to Fred Klein and every time he chose a different game, never failing to get the cards to the right player at the correct time. It was like he had never been gone. He won a few, lost a few more and folded early in the majority of hands. By snack break, he was about five dollars in the hole.

"What's this dip, Fred? Where's the clam and sour cream? This one's got beans in it," asked Gettleman.

"Talk to my wife. She bought it. Said that it was healthier than clam dip."

"Screw healthy! At least you brought Doritos and not some lo-cal thing."

Scattered on the snack table, in addition to Klein's contribution and Schofield's pie, were gourmet popcorn, herring in wine, garlic nan and, from the host, a big plate of cold cuts including turkey, pastrami, and lox. All went well with coconut cream pie. By the end of the break, most of the players were complaining about gut aches and/or the desire to vomit.

They reassembled at the pool table at eleven. "Ninety minutes to go, gentlemen," announced the host. Decades earlier, the games would go into the wee hours, often ending not long before sunup. That changed as the players aged. For most, a windup time of 12:30 was well beyond their bedtimes.

Fred won two of the first three hands after the restart. His status changed from low level loser to fairly significant winner, as not only did he hold good hands, but so did some of his competition, just not quite as good as his. The pots that he raked in were, as a result, sizable. He folded the next three hands and the deal rotated to him.

"Let's play Omaha, high-low." Schofield was impressed that his friend was prepared to take on the most challenging game that the group had in its repertoire. Omaha involves each player getting four of his own cards and five common cards for all to use. The final hand requires each player to use two from his own hand and three from the shared group. It's a complex poker game, a bigger logistical challenge than the usual draw and stud.

He successfully doled out the four cards to each player. A round of betting eliminated only one of the seven. Of the five shared cards, three are uncovered at once. Four, ace, ace. Very, very good group for those going either high or low. Nobody folded when Smith bet two dollars. Next, one card. A six of hearts. No obvious help for the highs, good for the lows. Smith bet two dollars again, the Indian guy raised and Gettleman raised him. Two dropped out. Schofield and Klein called by throwing in six dollars each. "Last card, my friends," said Klein as he reached for the deck.

He picked up the cards with his left hand. His right hand grasped for the top card to turn over, revealing the last up card of the deal. The card was in his hand and then it wasn't. It fell out, face down in front of the dealer, not face up to the side of the previous four up cards. Klein's right hand dropped to the table top. "Ugghh."

"What's up Fred?" asked Schofield, seated to his right.

"Ugghh." The deck dropped out of his left hand. He moved his left hand to retrieve them but missed them by three inches.

"Hey, Fred. Talk to me."

"Uh. Ugghh." The left side of his mouth moved normally. The right side was fixed in a half open position.

"Let's go over to the couch Fred." Art put his hand in his lifelong friend's armpit and raised him up from the metal chair. His left leg supported some weight. The right leg was motionless as Klein, unbalanced, fell to the floor. He did not hit his head on the hardwood flooring. Four players lifted him, one on each extremity, and carried him to the sofa.

"Can you hear me, Fred?" asked Schofield.

Klein looked at him, fear in his eyes. "Ugghh." He shook his head, as if to say, NO, NO, NO.

"Call 911. I think he's having a stroke." Smith pulled out his smart phone, punched the buttons and asked for help.

"My wife has a blood pressure cuff upstairs. Shall I get it?" asked Gettleman.

"I don't know what we'd do with the information. Forget it. What's his pulse?" Art asked the question and got the answer by holding his left wrist. "Feels pretty normal to me. Fred, you're going to be fine. None of that slow pulse problem like you had before. We'll get you in an ambulance and get you taken care of."

NO, NO, NO. He shook his left hand and his head. He attempted to sit up. No luck. A tear appeared in his motionless left-facing-right eye.

Sirens heralded the arrival of the City Ambulance which pulled up into Gettleman's driveway. The two EMTs darted into the family room and cut off Klein's shirt. They put an oxygen mask on and turned it to high flow. They slapped a monitor on his chest then wrapped their blood pressure cuff on his good arm. 180/80. Pulse 60. EKG monitor showing that his heart was entirely under the electronic control of the pacemaker, but it was working just fine.

"How are you doing, Sir?

"Ugghh." He flapped his left hand as if waving goodbye.

"Can you shake hands with me?" He offered his boxer-like right hand. There was no response from Klein. "How about those feet?" No movement from the right, moderate movement on the left.

"Who knows anything about this man?"

"I do, he's my best friend," answered a distraught Art Schofield.

"Tell me what you know. What's his name? How old is he?"

"Fred Klein and he's 77."

"THE Fred Klein? The one whose trial is next week?"

"Yes. That's him."

"I'll be damned," said the lead EMT to his sidekick who was busy putting an IV in the patient's right arm. "I pulled this guy out of some bar in the Tenderloin a couple years back. As I recall, he had a stroke then too and something wrong with his heart. It wasn't 'til the next day that I found out he was the guy who ran into and killed the Spencer woman."

"Please talk with more respect if you will. I think that Fred can understand everything you are saying."

"Sorry. You're probably right about that. What can you tell me about what's happened?"

"You were correct about the heart. He had a heart attack and his pulse got very slow. So he fell. No stroke. He bled into his skull and suffered brain damage, but he was pretty much back to normal after surgery and a pacemaker. Tonight, we were playing poker."

"Yeah, I can tell."

"He was dealing and suddenly a card fell out of his right hand and he couldn't do anything but grunt. We tried to get him to walk to the couch, but he fell. We caught him on the way down. Looks like he can move the left side but not the right. I think he knows when I'm talking to him but he can't talk back to me."

"Was he drinking?" The EMT saw the scattering of beer cans on the table.

"No, he drank 7 Up. Except for a few drops of wine at a party, I don't think he's had anything since the last time you saw him."

"Smoke?"

"He hasn't had a cigarette since college. He might smoke one cigar every five years."

"Marijuana? Cocaine? Does he shoot up?"

"Jesus, what a stupid question! No."

"Gotta ask. This is San Francisco." The EMT radioed into San Francisco General. "We've got a 77-year-old male who appears to have had a left middle cerebral stroke. Dense right hemiparesis and severe aphasia. Has a pacemaker, working OK. Vitals are normal. We're out in the Sunset. Maybe 15 minutes. We'll use the sirens." Rapid response is everything in the emergency treatment of a stroke.

"Jennifer, this is Art. Bad news, I'm afraid. I think that Fred's had a stroke."

"Oh, God. What happened?"

"He was doing fine and suddenly he couldn't move his right side and he couldn't talk – just grunt. The ambulance is just leaving, going to General."

"Oh, no, not there again. Can't he go to UC or CPMC?"

"The EMT said he was going to General. We didn't complain and Fred couldn't if he wanted to. They did a pretty good job with him last time. And, it doesn't hurt that they know his case already."

"But that's a hell hole. He hated it."

"You know, Jen, he probably wouldn't be alive if it weren't for the care he got there when his heart and brain both needed treatment. We can always move him after he gets stabilized. I can't imagine that he'll need surgery this time."

"Jason's here. We'll go over right now. You going?"

"Of course, I'm going. He's my friend. And Jen, guess what?"

"What?"

"He was the big winner tonight. And he was the Fred of old."

The General Hospital Emergency Room was its usual chaotic self for a Friday night/Saturday morning. Gun shots, stabbings, falls, auto wrecks, psychoses, chest pains, breathing difficulties, bloody noses, ear wax blockages, pink eyes, acute abdomens, delirium tremens, cocaine and heroin ODs, broken hips, arms, and collar bones, and itchy rashes that had been there for ten days but just got itchier that night. The ambulance had made it, sirens blaring, into its bay from the Sunset in less than fifteen minutes. Being a weekend night, the same silver-haired nurse that had triaged Klein after the fall in the Tenderloin was again on duty. She had heard from the EMT that a VIP was on the way; she had made sure that the three fat volumes of medical data, accumulated during his extended stay, were available for the ER docs to peruse. The nurses were vets, the docs and students, for the most part, rookies.

"Mohammed, we've got Fred Klein coming in with a possible CVA!" yelled the triage nurse.

"Who is Fred Klein, please?" asked the first year ER resident. This was his second night on call in the Mission.

"Don't you read the papers, man? He's the guy who is supposed to go on trial Monday for a hit and run. We had him here for a subdural and an MI right after his crime…'scuse me, alleged crime."

Time to teach. Two third year med students were starting their ER rotation, one hefty black guy who had been a linebacker on the hapless Dartmouth varsity, one ultrathin blond for whom some half of her spoken words were either 'awesome' or 'like.' "The ambulance people say he's had a stroke. What's the differential?" asked the resident.

"Hypoglycemia?" volunteered the linebacker.

"Good. What do we do to rule that out?"

"Find out, like, if he's a diabetic?"

"He can't talk. Maybe he wears a wrist band, but most don't. What else?"

"Give him glucose. Like 50 cc of 50%."

"Right – he'd wake up right away. What else in the differential?"

"Drugs?"

"What drugs?"

"Narcotics. Sedatives."

"He's 77. Any chance he'd do drugs?"

Probably not, but maybe. Suicide attempt?"

"Sure. Don't forget trauma. His chart showed that he came in last time with a subdural. Could happen again."

"You're an awesome teacher, Dr. Choudhury."

Fred was gurneyed in. It became clear from the history offered by his friend, the lawyer, that he wasn't diabetic and that the patient who had just come from a poker game surrounded by six upstanding low stakes gamblers, had not been shooting narcotics or swallowing sedatives or involving himself in activities that could lead to head trauma. He couldn't talk any better than he had earlier – unintelligible grunting only. His left hand and leg moved, even on command, but not a twitch on the right. He was awake and appeared to be aware of his surroundings, but clearly, he'd stroked. The question that had to be answered was whether the stroke was caused by an obstruction in the artery or a bleed from something like an aneurysm. The treatment and the prognosis were very different. He was whisked off to X-ray for a CT scan. Ten minutes later, he was out of the machine. There was no bleeding. The left middle cerebral artery, the vessel that supplies blood and oxygen to the part of the brain that controls movement on the right side of the body and allows for communication was obstructed, probably by a clot. No reason for even considering surgery. He was wheeled back to Emergency.

Dr. Choudhury, shadowed by the two students, was with Fred as Jennifer, Jason, and Art came into the holding room.

"Freddy, it's me, Jen. Are you OK?" She leaned over to kiss him on the cheeks.

"Ugghh. As she was on his right side, he could not move his eyes to look at her.

"I'm Dr. Mohammed Choudhury, one of the residents on the trauma service." He offered his hand, grasping hers sympathetically. "You are Mrs. Klein?"

"Yes. Tell me what's wrong."

Your husband can understand everything we say, I believe," he said, looking directly at the patient. "He's had a stroke, in fact, a very large stroke. The CT showed that he hasn't had a bleeding aneurysm, so there's nothing that can be done surgically. Obviously, he will have to be admitted to the hospital, to the neurology unit where they take care of stroke patients."

"Can't we take him over to Cal Pacific, or even to UCSF?" asked Jennifer. "They are so much closer to home and, honestly Doctor, he hated this place."

"The magic number in stroke care is three hours. Anything longer than that, the newer treatments aren't nearly as effective. If we send him to another place, and both of those are good, it'll be well beyond the three hours since his symptoms started."

"All right, but let them know that we want Fred out of here as soon as possible."

"I will."

Larry Hill

The next doctor that entered the area, almost sprinting, was no more than five foot three, black- bearded, wearing a wrinkled white coat with stethoscope, reflex hammer and other tools of his trade threatening to fall out of the pockets. A diamond stud pierced his right ear lobe. His rolled-up sleeves of his white jacket revealed a pair of tattoos of wild animals. He looked young enough to be Jen's son, Fred's grandson. "I'm Doctor Behrens from Neurology." He acted as if the only person standing in the room was the ER Resident. Two students and three friends and family of the patient did not register. "What do we have here?"

Choudhury gave a concise, logical two minute presentation of the case, including the past history of his subdural hematoma. Behrens approached the patient. "What brings you to the hospital?"

"Ugghh."

He raised his voice. "WHAT BRINGS YOU TO THE HOSPITAL TONIGHT, SIR?"

"Ugghh."

"Does this patient speak English?"

"Yes, Doctor, my husband speaks English, very well."

The neurologist flashed a light in Klein's eyes, pried open his mouth to look at his tongue, bent his neck back and forth, tested his limbs for spasticity, poked his feet and hands with a sharp rolling device, and banged on reflexes in his arms and legs. Knowing full well that there would be no decipherable answer, he asked questions of his patient, including the day of the week and the name of the governor of the state.

"You know, I think I recognize this guy. Was he in here, like two years ago?"

"Yes, that was when he was in for the subdural," said Choudhury.

"Yeah, I was a student on my neurosurgery rotation. I think I scrubbed in. And, isn't he, like famous?"

"Please, Doctor. We can talk about that another time," said Schofield.

"I saw the CT on my way over. Big ischemic stroke. No blood. No tumor. Usually, we'd try to break up the clot with tPA, but he's had a bleed, that subdural last time, so he can't get it. Nothing we can do but put him in and hope for the best – maybe some physical therapy. I'll dictate a consult note when I have time." He sped out of the room, returning a few seconds later to pick up the reflex hammer that he left on the bed. An attempt by Jason to get him to talk with him in the hall produced the same response as the attempt to get a second cup of coffee in a busy eatery.

Jason returned and asked Choudhury to speak to him, in a spot where his father couldn't hear. The linebacker and the blond followed silently.

"What a jerk! Is that guy always that awful?" Jason asked.

"I don't know. I'd never seen him with a patient before. They say he's a good neurologist."

"If that's how a good neurologist works, I'd hate to see one that wasn't any good. So, tell me what we learned, please."

"What Dr. Behrens said was that your father had a major stroke caused by an obstruction of one of the major arteries in the brain, the right middle cerebral artery. The artery was blocked, probably by a clot from the heart or from the carotid artery in the neck – you know, the one you feel when you check for somebody's pulse."

"What did he say about treatment – that there is none?"

"Sometimes, neurologists use a drug called tPA – they use it for heart attacks too – a chemical that dissolves clots rapidly. It helps sometimes, although it's not a magic cure. At least half of the patients don't see any improvement and many of the ones that do would probably get better on their own. But still, it's used. Problem is that a person who has had any kind of bleeding in his head, at any time in his life is not a candidate for it."

"Why?"

"There's a chance, in fact a fairly large chance, that he'd bleed again, in the same area as the last time. Even people who haven't had previous bleeding in their brains get it in the area of the stroke. The arteries in the area of the stroke are already weakened by the event and can rupture making the problem all that much worse."

"So, what do we do if he can't get that stuff?"

"There's not much. We have to treat him with physical therapy, blood pressure control and other things to prevent yet another stroke, and hope for the best."

"Do you think he'll get back to normal?"

"I'm no neurologist, but I'd have to guess that the chance of that is pretty small. His weakness is profound and, as you can obviously see, his ability to communicate is terribly limited. He's not a young man and he's had previous problems with his brain. The next week or two will be an important time – if he's not showing at least some improvement by then, the prognosis is not good."

"Is he going to die? I mean, is he likely to die soon?"

"I don't know. When I was a child, the answer to that question would be Inshallah. God willing, he will be alive and be well."

"I know what that means. Thanks. Now, is there any good reason to keep my father here? I know he'd prefer to be at CPMC; it's a whole lot closer and, just between you and me, it's a lot nicer environment."

"I really see no reason that he needs to stay here. Let me talk to the Chief Resident and see if we can't make the transfer."

The ultrathin blond med student approached Chowdhury after Jason had returned to his father's bedside. "Not only are you a very good teacher, you are an awesome doctor. I hope I can be half as good."

It took four hours to transfer Fred from General to California Pacific Medical Center, near to his Pacific Heights home. His condition on transfer was no better, no worse. Monitored on the way and in the intensive care unit when he arrived, his pacemaker worked liked a Timex and his blood pressure returned to a more acceptable 140/85. The neuro team responded like a firefighting squad, efficient and speedy. They agreed with Dr. Behrens in immediately ruling out a surgical approach. One aggressive neurologist opined that he would have taken the chance with tPA as it had been many months since his subdural hematoma. It had, however, been much more than the magic three hours between symptom onset and his second evaluation; tPA treatment was no longer an option.

The following day produced no demonstrable improvement. Nor the day after that or the following one or the next. Physical therapy and speech therapy were initiated in the ICU, and intensified when, after ten days, he was moved to a regular room in the Neurology Unit. His range of motion on the right was full, as long as somebody else did the moving. His index finger twitched a millimeter or two on command. The rest of the hand, arm, leg, and foot were paralyzed. Nothing. The left side moved well. He comprehended commands and squeezed, bent, straightened and wiggled as the therapist ordered. Fred showed no signs of improvement in his speech. "Ugghh." On day three, he strung two grunts together: "Ugghh, eehh, "he said while pointing with his left hand at a glass of water on his bedside table. Jen put the straw in his mouth, held the right side of his mouth shut and he took a swallow. All meals involved spoon feeding by family or staff. His appetite was good.

The *San Francisco Chronicle* reported the stroke on the first page of the Bay Area section on Sunday, the day before potential jurors were to assemble at the court house for selection.

FRED KLEIN HAS MAJOR STROKE
TRIAL ON HOLD

Jennifer Klein spent at least four hours at her stricken husband's bedside every day. Jason, the twins, and Art Schofield visited daily, sometimes alone, sometimes with wives and children. Rebecca Grodzinsky was heroic in her willingness to help. His room, at least for the first two weeks of his six week stay, was festooned with flowers, stuffed animals, and get well cards for the man who surely would not get well.

After a month and a half of barely discernible improvement, the hospital decided, against the desires of family and with reluctant consent of the treating doctors, to transfer Mr. Klein to a skilled nursing facility noted for rehabilitation. There he stayed for three months. By the end of the rehab, he could help in his transfer from hospital bed to reclining chair. His left arm became strong enough that he could pull himself up in bed, one handedly, using a steel bar suspended from a longer steel bar by a steel chain. Initially, he could not play a role in his getting on a bedpan. Later he could help in stationing himself on a bedside portable toilet. His ability to swallow improved. There was little fear that he'd choke on his pureed breakfasts, lunches and dinners. Staff did not trust him to chew the foods he loved. His daily diet was high in protein, low in fat and cholesterol; Dr. Jameson approved. He watched a lot of TV.

Four months after the stroke, Klein was home. One of the bedrooms had been converted into an upscale rehabilitation space. Aside from rare wheelchair-aided trips to doctors' offices (Jameson made twice monthly home visits) and a weekly ride around the area in the minivan purchased from a dealer who was thrilled to get the Prius in trade, he was to spend the rest of his life in his home, as if he was under house arrest.

The criminal case of The City and County of San Francisco vs Frederick Klein was dropped after Dr. Roger Stern reported to Judge Dadekian that Klein would never regain the ability to aid in his own defense.

At the advice of Personal Injury Defense Lawyer Gladstone, the civil case of Mark Spencer vs. Frederick Klein was settled for twenty-five million dollars. The insurance company paid about half of the settlement. Jennifer sold a chunk of their equity holdings to cover the remainder. The chunk was not large enough to make a major dent in their net worth. With the acceptance of her stepsons, plans for the Frederick and Jennifer Klein Institute for Aging Research were drawn up, to be established at the University of San Francisco.

Judge Louis Gasparini resigned from the bench and joined a local law firm specializing in criminal defense. Charges against him in his driving and drinking case led to a three month suspended sentence and loss of his driver's license. His wife, no longer stressed by the presence of a female passenger in his car at the time of his arrest, drove when they went out.

The DA never ran for higher office.

Six months after his divorce was finalized, Jason Klein married Rebecca Grodzinski in a small ceremony at Temple Emanuel, coincidentally, in the same room where his father had fainted. Jason's eldest child with Emily would end up a highly regarded Foreign Service Officer, fluent in Mandarin and Korean. The younger one spent much of his teens and early twenties in rehab.

The same week that Jason remarried, Mark Spencer and Mitzi Li said vows in a lavish event at the Mark Hopkins Hotel. Meagan, a top performer in her highly regarded preschool, was the flower girl. Carmen Contreras continued her employment in the Spencer home, with no evidence of a significant other.

Margarita and Ernesto Contreras had a baby boy, Hector. Hector was born at California Pacific Medical Center. He was entitled to two passports, American and Venezuelan. Carmen attended the baptism and first communion. Jennifer did not.

For all intents and purposes, Art Schofield lost his best friend. He visited often, at least early on, knowing that Fred knew that he was there. It took him a longer time than it should have to tell the poker buddies that it was time to find another regular. The chair was eventually taken by Sheldon Epstein, a local electronics importer and philanthropist. Epstein was 81.

Jennifer Klein was abstemious as long as her husband lived.

Fred Klein, beneficiary of the best of American medical care, lived for a long time. He observed and understood great changes in his world, his city, his family and himself. He was never again able to utter an intelligible word, phrase, or sentence. He was not able to say, "I'm sorry."

About the Author

Larry Hill, MD, is a graduate of the University of California, San Francisco, School of Medicine. He spent eighteen years in private practice of internal medicine and oncology in Eureka, CA. He then joined the US State Department where he served sixteen years as a Regional Medical Officer in Mali, Bangladesh, the Philippines, Washington, DC, South Africa, and China. He presently lives with his wife, Terry, in San Francisco, where he is a volunteer teacher of medical students at his alma mater.

Philanthropist is his first published novel.

THANKS to all of the fellow doctors, nurses, administrators, lab and X-ray techs, professors, instructors, and especially patients, who have allowed me to understand the human body and the massive infrastructure that is required to reassure lots, cure some, alleviate the pains of others and all too often allow me to lend meager support at the end of life.

Thanks to Dr. Roger Lauer who gave me a much greater understanding of mental health, including the fundamentals of forensic psychiatry.

To the several readers, including Hedi Saraf, Sheila Gordon, Edith Bennett, Steve Spellman, George Gmelch, Sharon Gmelch, Michael McNulty, Lee Gordon (one of the world's great nonagenarian poker mavens) and others, who enabled me to turn a hodgepodge into something that enabled me to get over the fear of pushing the "Publish" button on Amazon Kindle.

Undying thanks to my writing teacher, Joan Mininger. She took a retired doctor who, in the past, had attempted to write fiction with amazing lack of skill, and turned him into a scribe with at least a modicum of self-confidence. Many times along the way I had reached the "chuck it – nobody would want to read this stuff" stage and each time she brought me back from the abyss.

And, to my wife Terry, editor par excellence, who has accompanied me around the world, invariably finding something of consequence to occupy her time as I learned a trade, improved my skills in residency, practiced in two rural California communities and rubbed elbows with world leaders and diplomats in Africa and Asia. Were I to get assigned to be the resident physician on the Moon, she'd be there with me reveling in the lunar wonders.

Larry Hill, San Francisco, September 2014
chinadochill@yahoo.com

CPSIA information can be obtained at www.ICGtesting.com
Printed in the USA
LVOW07s1737050315

429406LV00015B/1049/P